10 seconds that changed everything...

9...8...7...6...5...4...

3 Babies each finding

2 Parents making

1 Happy Family!

Millennium
Baby

Kristine Rolofson is the author of over two dozen bestselling romances for Harlequin Books. While she comes from ten generations of seafaring New Englanders, anyone who has read her stories knows that her heroes have always been cowboys. Kristine admits that the sight of a man in denim and boots leaves her weak in the knees. She has been married for over twenty-eight years and is the mother of six.

Bobby Hutchinson is the author of over twenty romance novels and is a resident of British Columbia, Canada. To her, writing a story about a baby is a really good time. When she was a little girl, she used to tell anyone who asked that she wanted to get married and have twelve babies. Well, she grew up and had three fine sons, and of course reality set in. Luckily her daughters-in-law have been generous, giving her four grandbabies, but she's still an incurable baby junkie!

Judith Arnold is the bestselling author of more than sixty-five romance novels, and has fans worldwide. The winner of numerous awards, including *Romantic Times Magazine*'s Best Series Romance Novel of the Year, Judith makes her home in Massachusetts with her husband and two sons. Juggling a full-time writing career with motherhood is challenging but rewarding. Judith's husband has always been an active father. While the three men of the family are at the theater watching alien invasions, she's at her computer, working on love and happy endings in her latest book.

Kristine Rolofson
Bobby Hutchinson
Judith Arnold

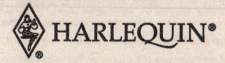

TORONTO • NEW YORK • LONDON
AMSTERDAM • PARIS • SYDNEY • HAMBURG
STOCKHOLM • ATHENS • TOKYO • MILAN • MADRID
PRAGUE • WARSAW • BUDAPEST • AUCKLAND

ISBN 0-373-83418-7

MILLENNIUM BABY

Copyright © 2000 by Harlequin Books S.A.

The publisher acknowledges the copyright holders
of the individual works as follows:

BABY, IT'S COLD OUTSIDE
Copyright © 2000 by Kristine Rolofson

ONE-NIGHT-STAND BABY
Copyright © 2000 by Bobby Hutchinson

BABY JANE DOE
Copyright © 2000 by Barbara Keiler

Visit us at www.romance.net

Printed in U.S.A.

CONTENTS

BABY,
IT'S COLD OUTSIDE

Kristine Rolofson

For Glen, for always

CHAPTER ONE

No one paid much attention to the cowboy.
Not since he'd stowed his gear in the luggage
compartment in the belly of the bus and climbed
aboard five hours ago, in Albuquerque. He'd
stretched out across two empty seats, made a pillow out of a thick leather jacket, lowered his hat
and gone to sleep. He slept through four stops,
each one lasting less time than the one before.

"Quite a storm," the bus driver worried,
peering through the snow. "I'd like to hurry up
and get to Denver before this gets any worse."

None of the passengers argued with that. All
nine of them—the elderly couple who settled in
the front seats so the old man could discuss the
weather and the route with the driver, the exhausted mother of two in the middle, the three
teenagers who giggled in the back seats as if it
was summer vacation and the cowboy who slept
slouched down in his seat—wanted to get to
Denver. So they climbed down from the bus and

hurried across parking lots to restaurants with stale coffee and hot chocolate and bathrooms. They bought cold sandwiches and candy bars, they hunched against the wind, and they said things to each other like "What an awful night" and "The waitress said it's supposed to be a bad one."

And as the night wore on, none of the passengers slept, except for the cowboy. The old man remembered his brief days on the circuit and silently figured the young man was exhausted from having sex with lively, high-breasted women, while his wife remembered the son who had died and thought the cowboy looked like he could use a good home-cooked meal. The harried mother paid no attention to the sleeping man except to keep the kids away from his boots that stuck out a few inches into the aisle, because anyone who could sleep like that didn't need to be awakened by her girls. The teenagers paid no attention to anything except to gloat that they were having the adventure they wanted. How could anyone sleep on New Year's Eve, especially the one that turned into the year 2000?

So the bus churned through the snow, wound through the Rockies, heading north toward Colorado Springs and the straight, flat highway to Denver.

But when it skidded at a stoplight in a small town, tipped gently into a snowdrift and settled in Colorado City for the rest of the night, the laughter of the teenagers woke the bus's one sleeping occupant.

"What the hell—excuse me, ma'am," he said to the wide-eyed mother across the aisle. He tipped back his hat and yawned as if he was accustomed to lying tipped at a thirty-degree angle. "I guess we're in Denver?"

THE BALL WAS GOING to drop soon. And Phoebe Winslow was so happy to be home. It had been a good idea to refuse the invitation to Kim's dinner party. And the dance at the Legion Hall. She didn't feel much like dancing. Or socializing. Or standing in the middle of a crowded room watching other people kiss at the stroke of midnight. Besides, the weatherman had said to expect a real old-fashioned blizzard and Phoebe wondered if the town partygoers would head home early before the snow got any deeper on the main road through town. She couldn't tell if anyone had plowed yet or not, but it didn't matter. There was no reason to go anywhere. And no place else she'd rather be.

It was a quiet little life. And exactly what she wanted. And if sometimes in the middle of the night, long after Ian had fallen asleep and she'd watched the latest controversy discussed on *Nightline* or read the new issue of *Bon Appetit* from cover to cover, she admitted she was, well, lonely.

Thank goodness it didn't last.

Phoebe held her sleeping toddler, sipped some overpriced French wine and hummed along with her new Andrea Bocelli CD. The television was on, the sound turned off. She'd had no desire to hear Dick Clark scream over the sounds of a zillion people reveling in New York City, but she wanted to see the entrance of the new millennium. She wondered if she'd feel any different in four and a half minutes.

She didn't think so.

She was wrong.

THE BUS DRIVER POINTED to a large Victorian house across the street and told them to try to get a room. "It's a bed-and-breakfast in the tourist season," he said. "And there's a light on in the living room, so you're in luck."

Will wasn't sure this could be called "luck." He'd intended to be in Denver, at a party to kick off the annual Stockman's Show, with Garth Brooks and that tall country-and-western singer, what's-her-name Twain, the one with the long legs. He'd have given a lot to see those legs in person. But his truck had broken down and the rest of the guys had left early, so he'd had no choice but to buy a bus ticket. No way was he going to fly on New Year's Eve, not with all the newspapers full of Y2K warnings.

Which was a lot of crap, but sometimes even Will knew when not to press his luck.

"I'm heading over to that pay phone," the driver said, nodding toward a nearby gas station. He pulled a knit cap over his bald head and raised his collar. "We're not going anywhere else tonight, folks. It's just too dangerous."

"Well," the old man sighed, "I guess we'd better get a leg on, Mother, and see if we can get us a bed."

"What about the suitcases?" the mother asked the driver, who promised to open the luggage compartment for those who wanted their stuff.

The teenage girls worried aloud over how

much a room would cost and maybe was there another way to get to Denver?

No one bothered answering. Leave it to kids to ignore a blizzard. And besides, as they piled out of the bus, the wind blew their breath back into their mouths.

Will stood, glad to stretch. His knee ached like a bastard, which meant the pain pills Doc had given him had worn off. He let the woman, the youngsters and the adolescents leave first, so by the time he got outside his duffel bag was the only thing left in the luggage compartment. The little band of travelers struck out across the empty street in the direction the driver had sent them.

"Wait," Will said, hurrying ahead despite the pain in his leg. "Follow me," he suggested, cutting through the ten inches of snow first so the old couple wouldn't have to struggle.

He took the old man's massive suitcase in one hand and took the old lady's elbow with the other, his duffel slung over his shoulder, then he helped her navigate the unshoveled steps that led to the inn's massive front door.

"You okay?"

"Thank you, young man," she said, blinking against the snow. "You're a real gentleman."

The old man winked at Will. "She's an old flirt. Don't mind her."

"Let's hope this place is open." He heard some guy singing real loud in a foreign language, so Will set down the luggage and knocked as hard as he could on the door. It didn't take long to see someone approaching through the frosted glass oval above the doorknob. Will hoped like hell there were some empty beds.

The door swung open, revealing one of the most beautiful women that Will had ever seen. Dark, almost black, hair hung past her shoulders, shoulders that were covered by a pale green robe. "Yes?" Her eyes were green, he noticed immediately. A rich emerald shade. And she was frightened, her fingers gripping the drowsy baby she held against her hip.

"We were on the bus," Will began, trying to remember why he stood there. "There was an accident."

"Was anyone hurt? I can call the police—"

"No one's hurt," the old lady said, "but the driver said that this is a bed-and-breakfast. We hope you're not full."

The elderly man spoke up. "We were supposed to be in Denver hours ago."

The woman looked past her to the straggling band of people crowded on her ample porch. "How many are here?"

"Nine," the old man said. "Ten if you count the driver."

She opened the door wider and the baby lifted its head and stared at the strangers. "Come on in. We'll figure out something."

"Thanks," Will said, stepping aside to let the rest of the travelers pass before him. Which was why, after picking up his bag once again, he was the last one to step inside.

"Is it midnight yet?" someone asked.

"Almost," the woman said. "You can put your wet boots by the fireplace and hang your coats on the rack here in the corner."

The group huddled together, suddenly shy in the elegant hallway as they removed their wet clothing. Off to the right was a large room, the promised fireplace in the middle of one long wall; a television in the corner, bookcases, lace curtains, overstuffed chairs and a flowered rug completed the comfortable picture.

"I'm Phoebe Winslow," the green-eyed woman said. "And this is my son, Ian."

"You're very kind," the old man said.

"We're Jack and Sarah Knight, from San Antonio."

"Ellen Barnes," the woman with the silent, exhausted children said. "Heather, eight, and Holly, ten."

"Welcome," Phoebe said. "It's going to take me a while to get your beds ready. Why don't you all warm up in front of the fire?" She smiled down at the young children. "The ball is going to drop soon. Do you want to see it?"

"The girls and I will help you with the beds," Ellen Barnes declared, looking as if she would cry from relief.

"That's not—"

"No," Ellen said, a hand on each girl's shoulder. "It's the least we can do."

Jack took his wife's arm and headed toward the living room. "Mother and I will rest a bit."

Will glanced toward the teenage girls huddled by the door. "You want to help, too?"

The middle one with the long braid looked worried. "How much is this going to cost?"

Phoebe smiled. "We'll work it out in the morning," she said. "There's a phone in the kitchen and also upstairs in the hall if you want to call your parents and let them know where you are."

"Uh, sure," another one said. "Thanks."

Which meant that their parents didn't have a clue where they were in the first place, Will realized.

"We'll help you," one of the other girls offered. "And we can wash dishes and stuff tomorrow."

The third one chimed in, "I baby-sit."

"In a few minutes we'll go upstairs and figure out where you're all going to sleep, but first you'd better put your things by the fire," the beautiful landlady suggested. Her gaze lingered on Will, and the baby stuck his thumb in his mouth and stared at him, too. "And your name is...?"

"Will Briggs, ma'am." And here he'd thought his body was too tired to respond. Where in hell was the woman's husband?

The baby struggled to leave its mother's side.

There was another knock on the door; it was the bus driver covered in fresh snow. "I just wanted to see if everyone was all set," he said.

Phoebe opened the door wider. "Come on in. I'm sure I can find a bed for you somewhere."

"I'm okay, thanks," the man said. "I've got a friend here who'll let me sleep on his couch. But I'll be in touch in the morning." He lowered his voice and leaned toward Will. "I'm not sure we're gonna get out of here tomorrow, either."

So much for Garth Brooks and long-legged girl singers. So much for the college bowl-game parties and the chili and the beer and hot bean dip. "No?"

"You won't leave without us?" one of the teenagers asked worriedly.

"I won't leave anyone behind," he promised. "Don't worry about that." He said good-night and trudged down the stairs to the street. Will turned back to his new landlady. Her little boy stared at him and stuck one hand out to touch his hat.

"Cow," the boy said, and took his other arm from around his mother's neck to stretch both arms to Will. "Cow, cow, cow."

His mother attempted to shift her weight, but the pudgy baby tilted alarmingly and threw himself at Will, who automatically opened his arms to catch the kid.

"Happy New Year," Mr. Knight shouted from the living room. "The ball just dropped! It's the new millennium!"

Will looked down at the child in his arms, a child who frantically tried to claw the Stetson off his head. This was not exactly the kind of celebration he had planned.

CHAPTER TWO

THE WORLD SHIFTED.

She really had to get some clothes on was Phoebe's first thought. In the past few seconds the century had ended, and here she stood in front of a group of strangers—including a man who looked like he'd just been kicked off a horse—wearing her fancy new Christmas robe. She was suddenly very aware of the fact that she wore no underwear.

She really needed to do something. Anything. Her son was wrapped around a scruffy cowboy and the man's battered and wet hat was being pounded and poked by Ian's pudgy fingers as the rest of her houseguests hurried into the living room to watch New York City go crazy with excitement. She and the cowboy paused just inside the room.

"I'm sorry," she said, attempting to retrieve her son. Ian burst into tears and clung to the stranger as she tried to take him into her arms. "I've never seen him act this way before."

"I guess he likes the hat," the man said.

"Yes, I'm sure that's it," Phoebe agreed, gazing at her adored son, the same child who wouldn't return to her and acted as if he didn't know his own mother. "He doesn't usually like strangers."

The cowboy looked like he didn't believe a word she said. Those piercing gray eyes of his seemed to take in everything—her silk robe, bare feet and embarrassment.

"I guess your husband doesn't wear a Stetson," he said, that clear gaze returning to her face.

"No." Once again, she tried to take her son, and the cowboy—Will Briggs—tried to give him to her. Then they both gave up because Ian's piercing wail was louder than the crowd in Times Square. Mr. Knight had found the remote control.

"Happy New Year," the teens said, looking as if they were beginning to cheer up and enjoy this new adventure on their way to Denver.

"Happy New Year," Phoebe answered, her gaze taking in everyone except the man holding her son. This was all very strange, but she was grateful for the company.

"What do I do with him?" the cowboy asked. He didn't look as if he held babies very much, and Phoebe suddenly wanted to laugh even though she was certain the man wouldn't appreciate it.

"Would you mind hanging on to him for a minute while I get the beds ready?"

"There's no hurry," Mrs. Knight said, beckoning everyone into the living room. "Why don't you come in here and watch the celebration? I swear, I've never seen anything like this in all my years."

"I'm sure you want to go to bed," Phoebe began, but eight of the nine guests paid no attention. It was New Year's Eve, it was the beginning of a new century and a new millennium and everyone wanted to watch it happen.

"I sure wouldn't mind," the cowboy said, "but there's no hurry." He nodded toward the crowd filling the television screen. "I can't picture being in the middle of that. Can you?"

"No."

"Mr. Briggs," the old man said, "you and that boy come over here beside Mother. I'll bet she can get that baby to sit on her lap."

"Call me Will." He did as the man said, settling himself awkwardly between the elderly couple. "I'd take off my hat but the kid here seems to like it."

He was nice enough, Phoebe thought, for a stranger. Ian seemed safe and Mrs. Knight looked as if she was going to keep an eye on him. The cowboy didn't seem at all used to babies. "I'm going to fix something for you to eat," she said. "You must be starving after all those hours on the bus."

"We stopped a few times," the redheaded teen said. "We got candy bars and potato chips because there wasn't time for anything else."

Mrs. Knight shook her head. "The driver, poor man, was afraid we would get stuck somewhere if he didn't hurry us along, but you shouldn't go to any trouble, my dear. We're very grateful that you let us in out of the cold."

Phoebe smiled. "I guess we're having a New Year's Eve party, even though I'm sure you'd all rather be somewhere else tonight."

"We were heading to Denver to visit some friends. Jack doesn't like to fly and it was too long a drive for him, so here we are."

"I could have driven," he grumbled. "I can still see just fine in the daylight."

His wife made a face.

"We're going to get my father in Pikes Peak," Ellen said. "I'm driving him back to El Paso since he won't part with his old Cadillac."

"Grandpa's sick," the taller of the two girls volunteered.

"I'm sorry to hear that," Phoebe said. "Let's hope the snow stops so you can see him very soon." She went over to the corner and opened a cupboard to reveal a modest selection of alcohol, along with glasses and soda water. "Anyone who's old enough to drink, please help yourself. I'll bring some ice out in a minute."

"Well now," Mr. Knight said, his eyes lighting up, "this is what I call a party."

The teenage girls volunteered nothing except to politely ask if they could help her with anything. The girls followed her to the kitchen, so within minutes she'd sent them back to the living room with a platter of cheese and crackers, cans of soda pop and glasses for wine. She filled a kettle with water for hot chocolate and tea, then set a pot of turkey soup on the stove to heat. She'd made gallons this morning, planning to freeze it in small portions.

As soon as that was done, she hurried up the back staircase to change into jeans and a sweater. She opened the doors to the guest bedrooms and turned up the thermostat. She would put everyone upstairs but the cowboy. He could sleep in the pullout sofa in the den downstairs.

Handsome cowboys were not her typical houseguests. And handsome cowboys who made her aware that she shouldn't be wearing a silk robe in front of strangers needed to sleep as far away as possible. She wasn't ready for flirting or awareness or any of those things that seemed so delicious before she was married. And widowed. Now she just wanted to be left alone.

Most of the time.

HERE LIVED A WOMAN who liked to clean, Will decided. Every inch was either polished or dusted or vacuumed or wiped off. It was downright scary. He wondered where her husband was. He couldn't be asleep upstairs, not with the television blasting loud enough to wake the dead. There was one half-filled wineglass beside a magazine on the coffee table. Will assumed Mrs. Winslow had been celebrating New Year's Eve all by herself.

Maybe the husband ran a snowplow and the poor bastard was out in the storm trying to keep the roads clear. Or he was a doctor out saving someone's life. Will couldn't think of any other reasons to leave a beautiful woman like Phoebe Winslow by herself at midnight.

"My goodness," Jack said, looking around the room. "This sure is a pretty house. Solid, too, the way they built them in the old days."

Will winced as the baby poked a finger in his eye. Here lived a woman with a baby who'd never seen a cowboy before. He'd helped kids ride ponies and he'd given kids rides on his horse, but he'd never had to hold one on New Year's Eve. He'd planned on holding a warm and willing woman, planned on spending at least part of this night naked.

Which was a hell of a good way to start any new year. Damn transmission. He should have had it checked earlier.

The kid finally succeeded in removing Will's hat and, clutching it to him, fell asleep with his head against Will's shoulder.

"What a sweet boy," the old lady said. "Do you have children, Will?"

"No. I've never been married."

"Nowadays that doesn't seem to matter much," the old man said, shaking his head. "This younger generation have their kids first. I don't get it, do you?"

"No kids, no wife," Will declared. "But I do have a horse."

Mrs. Knight clucked. "A nice boy like you isn't married?"

"No, ma'am." He grinned. "I've never stayed in one place long enough."

Ellen gave them a tired smile. Her girls were curled up on the floor at her feet. "Marriage isn't all it's cracked up to be, Will, so don't be in too much of a hurry."

"What brings you to Colorado, son?"

"The Stockman's Show in Denver. It starts next week. I'm a bronc rider."

Jack's face lit up. "Well now, that's something. I did bull riding one season."

"Bulls? That's very dangerous, isn't it?"

Will turned to see Phoebe in the doorway. Unfortunately, she was dressed.

"Yes. I'm not saying it's safe," Jack said, winking at the teenagers. "But it's one way to make a living."

"He's asleep. Thank goodness," Phoebe said, looking at her baby and not at Will. She came over and lifted the child easily out of Will's lap. "Thanks."

"No problem," he said, grabbing his Stetson before it went tumbling to the carpet.

"There's turkey soup," she said to everyone. "And the makings for hot drinks, too, out in the kitchen. You can help yourselves while I put Ian to bed."

"You're an angel," Mrs. Knight declared as her husband helped her to her feet.

Will reached out and steadied both of them before they toppled back onto the couch. He figured they must be at least eighty years old, maybe more. But they had a lot of spunk to go traipsing into Colorado in the middle of the winter. Lucky for the old folks that Phoebe had taken them all in.

He watched the landlady tiptoe carefully out of the room, her son nestled against a very shapely pair of breasts covered by a dark green sweater.

"She's lovely," Mrs. Knight said, watching him watch the woman.

"Yes."

"And kind, too." She leaned on Will's arm as he led her through a dining room toward the smell of turkey soup.

"And married," Will added, having seen the gold band on Phoebe's finger when she'd lifted her son from him.

"Widowed," the old lady whispered.

"How do you know that?"

"There's a look in her eyes."

"They're green," he heard himself say. And he winked at Mrs. Knight, who chuckled and patted his arm.

"I thought you'd notice that, seeing how you were so close to her a couple of times," she said. "Now where did my husband go?"

Will looked back and saw Jack serving himself from the makeshift bar. He hesitated, unwilling to get the old man in trouble. "He's fixing himself a, uh, tiny drink, ma'am."

"Good," she said, moving carefully around the fancy dining-room table. "He always sleeps better when he's had a little booze or a little sex."

"Yes, ma'am," Will said, fighting back his laughter. "I guess we all do."

CHAPTER THREE

PHOEBE KISSED her sleeping son gently before putting him in his crib. She half expected the child to wake up and say "cow, cow" again, a word he'd gotten from one of his favorite picture books. The cowboy, wearing a hat and riding a white horse, was one of Ian's favorite pictures, but she'd never seen him react like that to a real person before. And there were more than a few men who wore cowboy hats in Colorado City.

None as handsome as the tall Mr. Briggs, though.

And none that had held her son.

Downstairs she found her odd band of guests gathered around the kitchen table eating soup and crackers and becoming better acquainted. Mr. Knight was asking the children about their Christmas gifts and Ellen Barnes distributed hot chocolate to the teenagers. Sarah Knight was deep in conversation with the cowboy, but they both looked up when Phoebe entered the room.

"Your soup is delicious," the elderly woman said. "You have been so kind to your unexpected guests."

Phoebe smiled at the chorus of thank-yous that followed. "You're very welcome. I hate to think what could have happened to you out in this storm. Can I get you anything else?"

"No," Sarah said. "Come sit and visit with us." She patted the empty chair next to her, directly across the table from the cowboy. "Will and I were talking about our New Year's resolutions. Do you have one?"

"I haven't given it much thought," she fibbed, taking a seat and trying to ignore Will Briggs's curious stare. "What's yours?"

"I'm going to eat more pie," Sarah declared. "I'm tired of vegetables, and a person my age should be able to eat what she wants."

"You're a woman after my own heart," Will said. He looked at Phoebe. "I haven't made any resolutions, either. I guess I'm just used to taking things one day at a time."

"And one rodeo at a time?"

"Yeah. I don't think it pays to look too far ahead."

"No," she said, thinking of the accident. Seventeen months ago, she thought she had her whole life planned and now look.

"Life does have a way of turning us upside down," Sarah agreed, lifting her teacup with a trembling hand. "My eighty-three years have been full of surprises. Why, look at all of us here tonight! Who'd have thought we would end up in such a lovely house in Colorado City?"

"It's a far cry from a motel in Denver," Will agreed, pushing back his chair. "Mrs. Winslow, I'm going to join Jack by having a drink. Can I get you anything?"

"I left my wineglass—"

"By the chair," he finished. "I'll get it for you. Would anyone else like something?" When the others declined, Will headed toward the living room.

"He's so handsome," Mrs. Knight whispered to Phoebe after the cowboy left.

"Yes, in a Western sort of way." His eyes were a light gray and he had those crinkly laugh lines in the corners. He looked like a man who spent a lot of time outdoors and who didn't let anything bother him. She wondered what it would be like to be free and alone and able to take one day at a time.

"In any way," Ellen Barnes added. "If I were fifteen years younger—"

"Mom!" her older daughter cried.

"Oh, that's right," Ellen said. "I forget I'm at the age where I embarrass my children."

"It lasts a long time," Mr. Knight said. "But our kids get used to us eventually."

Ellen smiled at Phoebe. "How old is your son?"

"Eight months."

"That's a good age," Ellen said, turning to the teenagers across the table. "And what about you? Where are you girls from?"

They exchanged looks before the middle girl answered. "Socorro."

"New Mexico? You're a long way from home," Phoebe said. "Feel free to use the phone and call your parents. I'm sure they're worried about you."

"Uh, we did," the redhead said. "Back at the last stop."

Phoebe wasn't convinced. They seemed like nice enough girls, but what kind of parents would let three teenage girls go to Denver in December on a bus? Will came from behind and set Phoebe's refilled wineglass in front of her, brushing her shoulder briefly. An unaccustomed shiver ran down her arm. Which was a ridiculous reaction, she told herself.

"Thank you," she told Will Briggs. She couldn't understand why she was so tongue-tied in front of him. She really had to get a grip on herself.

"You're welcome." He looked around the table. "Can I get anything else before I sit down?"

Sarah yawned, then apologized. "No, young man. I think we're all going to be ready for bed soon. Do you know it's almost one o'clock already?"

"I'll show you your rooms," Phoebe said. "Ellen, you and the girls will have connecting rooms and share a bathroom. Sarah, you and Jack will have the room just to the right at the top of the stairs, with a bathroom right across the hall." She turned to the teenagers. "The three of you can share the third-floor loft. It might be a little dusty, but it's warm and cozy up there." She took another sip of wine before talking to the cowboy. "Uh, Will, would you mind the pullout sofa down here in the den? There's a small bathroom nearby and you can shower upstairs."

"That's fine," he began, but Jack Knight interrupted.

"Mrs. Winslow, Phoebe, can Mother and I take the den? She doesn't do stairs too well anymore."

"Of course, but it's such a tiny room—"

"We won't mind," Sarah assured her. "I'm sure it's as lovely as the rest of the house."

"We're helping make up the beds, remember?" Ellen Barnes and her daughters stood up and started clearing the table.

"We'll do that," one of the teenagers said, looking at Phoebe. "We'll put everything in the dishwasher, okay?"

"Sure. Thanks."

Jack leaned back and sipped his whiskey. "Will and I will wait for you to give us something to do."

"Isn't that just like a man," Sarah exclaimed. "Come on, Jack. You can find our suitcases and bring them into the den."

"Isn't that just like a woman," Jack moaned, winking across the table at Will. "Can't stand to see a man sitting still enjoying himself."

Phoebe couldn't help laughing at the old man. "Don't you dare move," she said. "The two of you would only be in the way."

"What would they do without us?" Jack countered, grinning.

Will lifted his glass in a mock toast to Phoebe before taking a sip. "I don't know what your secret is, Jack, but women seem to do without me just fine."

Phoebe didn't believe that for a minute. A good-looking man like Will Briggs would have left a trail of hearts as long as the rodeo circuit.

Sarah patted his shoulder as she struggled out of her chair. "You haven't met the right woman yet."

"No one wants to put up with a rodeo man, ma'am. We spend too much time on the road."

Jack nodded. "It's quite a life for a young man. You qualified for Denver, then?"

"Yep."

"You must be real good."

The cowboy shrugged. "It hasn't been a bad year except for a broken-down transmission, a sick horse and a bum knee." He grinned, so Phoebe assumed that cowboys were used to all three things going wrong. "Seems like lately I've been in the wrong place at the wrong time."

"Except for tonight," Sarah teased.

"Yes, ma'am," he agreed, his gaze lighting on Phoebe. "Except for tonight."

"WELL, MOTHER, WHAT do you think?"

Sarah eased herself into bed and made sure her nightgown covered her legs. She hated to be cold at night, and luckily Jack put out enough heat for ten men. "What do I think about what?"

He turned off the light and took her into his arms. "Our landlady. We'll have to send her something real nice after we get home."

"She's very sweet."

"The rodeo man fancies her."

"Of course he does. He's not blind." Sarah inched her toes over to put them on her husband's legs. He would fuss, but he never said no.

"Dammit, woman, your feet are cold!"

"And yours aren't," she said, keeping her feet wedged firmly against him. "Oh, that feels better. It's a shame Phoebe is sleeping alone."

"Maybe there's a husband somewhere."

"No. This is a woman's house," Sarah declared. "A lonely woman's house."

He chuckled. "And you want to change that in one night?"

She leaned over and kissed his scratchy cheek. "Our rodeo man needs to settle down. Did you see how good he was with that baby?"

"I saw a man who was being polite."

"He's too old to be on the rodeo circuit. Did you see the way he was limping when he got off the bus? He's hurt."

"Every bronc rider has some aches and pains. That doesn't mean he's too old for the life."

"He likes her."

"Who wouldn't? She's easy to look at."

"There's more—" she began, but Jack stopped her.

"Better to leave it alone, Mother. The young people today have a way of figuring things out for themselves."

He rolled over and began to snore, so Sarah knew the conversation was over. Once Jack fell asleep, that was it. She pulled the comforter up to her chin and snuggled deep into violet-scented pillows. Tomorrow before they left, she'd find out what happened to Phoebe's husband.

That dear baby needed a father, and no one made a better father than a cowboy. Or, for that matter, a better lover.

WILL COULDN'T SLEEP. Oh, the beautiful landlady had bustled around the bedroom showing him his pillows and his extra blankets, but she'd stayed far away from him as if she thought he would jump her. She was an excellent hostess. And she served excellent Scotch. He'd wondered if he and Jack were sampling the husband's private stock, but Phoebe had urged them to help themselves.

Not that he was a drinker, but after the past few days of traveling hell, Will sure hadn't minded being out of the weather and sipping a little of something expensive. He still had the glass and there was still a swallow or two left.

Down the hall he heard the teenagers scurrying in and out of the bathroom. He wanted to take a shower, but he decided to wait until the female population of the house had settled down for the night. It was late, almost two. And yet he wasn't at all tired. He'd slept on the bus, but that was because the pain pills had made him drowsy.

He'd had some pretty strange evenings, but this one rivaled anything he could remember. Maybe that's the way the year 2000 would be, one strange event after another coming after him, raining down on him like hail.

Will sipped the last of his Scotch and sat in an overstuffed chair in the corner of the yellow-striped room. Phoebe Winslow knew how to make a place feel comfortable. Oh, he'd had his share of broken trucks and blizzards, of course. And there'd been that time when he and Ben had trouble with rattlesnakes when they'd been trying to fix a flat tire. There'd been plane trouble when he was flying to Salt Lake to compete last July. He shook his head at his own foolishness. This Y2K hoopla had gotten to him, that was all it was. That and having a baby throw himself into his arms.

And tiptoeing around a green-eyed woman wearing a wedding ring and a silk robe.

CHAPTER FOUR

PHOEBE TIPTOED OVER to her bedroom window and pulled back the curtain. In the second hour of the new year, there wasn't much to see outside except snow. What with getting the rooms ready for guests, she'd forgotten the reason they were there. And here she'd thought she wouldn't open for guests until May, not realizing she'd been lonesome ever since she'd put up the No Vacancy sign on the first of November.

She'd been right to stay home tonight. Otherwise she would have missed out on her own New Year's Eve party. Tomorrow when Kim called, Phoebe could tell her all about her surprise guests and they would laugh about Ian's reaction to the cowboy hat the rodeo man wore. She wouldn't tell her best friend that this rodeo man made her skin feel hot and too tight, that somehow she knew he was entranced with her flowered silky-satin robe, the one her mother had sent her for Christmas. She wouldn't describe the color of his eyes or the way he'd glanced at her breasts when he thought she wasn't looking. She wouldn't admit that despite her original plans, he'd ended up sleeping in the bedroom that lay on the other side of Ian's room, with only a locked door between them.

She really needed to get a grip on her imagination. She padded into the connecting nursery to check on Ian, who was sound asleep and probably dreaming of cowboys. And just to be sure, she glanced at the lock that kept the rooms securely separated. And then she went back to her own room, to her own bed, and slept better than she had in almost eighteen months.

WILL TOOK A SIP OF COFFEE and knew right away that Phoebe Winslow was the most dangerous woman he'd ever met. He ignored the display of yogurt and fruit salad and eyed the basket of oversize blueberry muffins that sat less than a foot away from his coffee mug.

He loved blueberry muffins almost as much as he loved a good steak. And these had crackly sugar tops, which made them better than steak.

"Help yourself," the witch said, refilling his coffee mug. "I'm cooking bacon and eggs. How do you like yours?"

"Any way at all," he managed to say. She smelled faintly of vanilla and cinnamon, which made him feel a little dizzy. Yes, the woman was dangerous. These domestic and cheery homemaker types always were, and he'd seen friends of his meet women who could cook and pretty soon they were married. *Married.*

And all because of a good meal.

He looked nervously out the window but could only see snow. In fact, he could still hear the wind blowing outside.

She noticed the direction of his gaze. "We're lucky we still have electricity."

"I don't think we'll be going anywhere today."

"No."

He helped himself to a blueberry muffin and tried not to look like he'd never seen one before. Where in hell was her husband? And why wasn't he here at the breakfast table? Will never went near married women. It was a good way to get your face bashed in, depending on the temper of an affronted husband. Will had seen more than his share of barroom brawls, and married women were at the center of them at least sixty percent of the time. He picked up his coffee and inhaled.

The woman wasn't shy about making a good, strong cup of coffee.

He wondered what else she wasn't shy about and dared a glance at her back. She wore jeans again today, and those jeans fitted nicely over a shapely set of hips. She wore a white blouse tucked into her jeans, and little green beads dangled from her earlobes when she turned to refill his coffee cup.

"Thanks" was all he could manage. Between the blueberry muffins and Phoebe's smile, his brain couldn't function properly. Like the time he'd gone headfirst off Old Dan and couldn't remember what to do after he hit the ground.

Hell, he hadn't known what state he was in for at least thirty minutes.

"Will?"

"What?"

"Is the muffin okay?"

He realized he'd been staring at it instead of eating it. "Blueberry's my favorite."

She gave him an odd look before she went back to the stove. Her cheeks were flushed and that long hair was tied back into a knot at her neck. Phoebe Winslow was one hell of a good-looking woman.

"Where's the boy?" he asked after making

short work of the muffin. He wondered if he dared have another. He wondered if he dared ask, *Where's your husband?*

"Still asleep," she said, breaking eggs into a skillet. "Go ahead and have another muffin if you want. I have another batch in the oven."

"You're a mind reader," he told her, and she laughed, a tinkling sound that made him want to laugh with her, but instead, he helped himself to another muffin and was glad he was the first one up this morning.

"I like to cook," she admitted, glancing over at him. "Which is terribly old-fashioned, I know. Last summer I gave my guests the option of having dinner here on weekends just so I could make a big meal."

"How long have you been running this place?"

"Since before my husband died," she said, answering his question. "We bought the house with the idea of running a small business like this in the summer when the tourists are everywhere." He watched her flip his eggs and give the frying pan a little shake. "After Ted died, I thought this was the best way to stay home, earn money and raise Ian."

"I'm sorry about your husband."

"Thank you," she said, arranging his eggs, bacon and toast on a delicate china plate and delivering it to him.

"I'm not used to this kind of service," he said. "But thanks."

"Don't you eat in restaurants a lot?"

"Well, yes," he said, picking up a sterling-silver fork monogrammed with a *W*. "Trust me, Phoebe, none of them were like this."

She poured herself a cup of coffee and sat down across the table from him. "Can I ask your advice about something?"

He swallowed. "Sure."

"I think the girls are runaways."

Will nodded. "Could be. I noticed they didn't give their names."

"They're nice girls, though. They offered to help with the dishes and automatically cleared the table. They don't look like runaways."

He shrugged. "I took off when I was fourteen."

"Fourteen? Why?"

"I didn't like rules," he said. "And there were a lot of rules where I lived."

"And your parents weren't worried about you?"

"There were no parents," he said. "So I

struck out on my own and learned how to compete in rodeo. That was all I wanted to do anyway."

"Nothing else?"

"No." He took another sip of his drink. "I'm thirty-six years old and I've got a bum knee and I've had more broken bones than I can count, but I still don't know what else I'd do if I couldn't ride."

"But when you ran away, wasn't anyone worried about you? Didn't anyone try to find you?"

"Not that I know of." He shrugged. "I was pretty much on my own by fourteen."

"Somewhere out there are three sets of frantic parents."

"Maybe yes, maybe no." She'd fried the eggs in real butter. And the bacon was cooked just right, not soggy but not turned into charcoal.

She sighed. "I think I should call the police."

He savored the last bite. "Why don't you talk to the girls first?"

"I will," she said, but she still looked worried, so Will figured she wasn't through asking for advice, though why she was asking *him* for advice he couldn't figure.

"What else is bothering you?"

"The Knights."

He smiled. "You think they ran away from a nursing home?"

"Maybe yes, maybe no," she said, giving him a quick smile as she imitated him. "Don't they seem a little, well, old to be traveling around the country on a bus? What would have happened to them if I hadn't been home? Or if the bus had been stranded somewhere along the highway?"

"Yeah," he answered. "I wondered about that, too. Especially Sarah being so shaky on her feet and all. They barely made it across the road to this house." He wiped his mouth with his napkin—a blue linen square that matched the tablecloth, he noticed—and picked up his coffee. "Well, we can't call the police and we can't call their parents."

"I'm serious."

"So am I. Have they mentioned having any family?"

"No, they just said they were going to Denver to visit some friends. I'm worried that they don't have enough money to get where they're going."

"I'll talk to Jack today and see what I can find out," Will offered. He'd do anything to erase that worried look in her eyes. "And make sure you give me the bill for their room," he said. "Tell them there's no charge and then no-body has to know any different."

"I'm not going to charge anyone for staying here," she said, "but that's really sweet of you to offer."

"Phoebe, you can't do this for free," he insisted, at the same time wondering if she thought he was some kind of broke rodeo drifter. Which, now that he thought about it, he was. Except for the "broke" part. But he made a decent living and he had a savings account. And she was a widow with a child to raise.

She reached for the basket and set it down in front of him. "Have another muffin and don't argue with me anymore."

"Sweetheart," he drawled, unconsciously using an endearment that came naturally, "give me the whole basket and I'll do anything you ask."

Phoebe laughed again and Will could have sworn the sun came out right there in the middle of a Colorado blizzard.

IAN WANTED NO ONE but the cowboy. To Phoebe's embarrassment, her son was in the process of creating a scene in front of her guests. If Ian continued to behave this way, she didn't know what she would do. Obviously, Will

Briggs wasn't used to having kids try to smear him with a spoon filled with oatmeal at the same time as he was trying to get into the cowboy's lap.

"I'm sorry," she called for about the tenth time, starting for the high chair, but Sarah put a bony hand on her arm before she could cross the kitchen.

"The boy's fine," she said. "And so is the man."

Strangely enough, Will didn't seem to mind that the baby was performing for him. And Ellen Barnes and her giggling daughters, lingering over breakfast at the table, seemed to be enjoying the baby's antics and teasing Will. "But he's making such a mess."

The elderly woman shrugged. "A man like that doesn't mind a child's mess. Jack's the same way."

"A man like what?" A man who looked so handsome, clean shaven and with his dark hair still wavy and damp from the shower that Phoebe could barely put two sentences together from the moment he'd walked into her kitchen this morning? A man who had called her sweetheart and made her ridiculous heart pound faster? A man who looked at the breakfast she'd served him as if it were a platter full of gold nuggets?

"Men like that are used to dirt and mess and blood and bruises," Sarah whispered. "Men like that like babies and children and newborn calves. And they like women," she said, giving Phoebe a knowing look. "Men like that take care of what's theirs, you understand?"

Phoebe was afraid she did. "But he's always on the road."

Her newfound friend chuckled. "Phoebe dear, that's because he has nowhere else to go. And nothing of his own to care for."

"I'll bet he has a horse."

"And I imagine he drives a broken-down truck, too," Sarah added. "But if he's a good man, what else does a woman need?"

"I'm not looking for another husband," Phoebe assured her, hoping that no one would hear their whispers.

"You're a young woman. And a pretty one, too." Sarah chuckled and helped herself to another cup of coffee. "You don't have to do the looking. The men must mill around you in droves."

"Not exactly."

"Well, whatever you do, Phoebe, I'll tell you

this," Sarah said, her eyes twinkling with delight. "You can't go wrong hooking up with a cowboy. Especially not a kind man like that one."

Phoebe turned to look at Will, who was in the process of lifting her son from the high chair.

"Help!" He laughed, holding up her son from under his arms. "Phoebe? What do you want me to do with him?"

"See?" Sarah asked under her breath. "A man like that's hard to find."

And hard to keep, Phoebe wanted to add. But instead, she smiled at her sticky-faced son and picked up a washcloth. There was no sense daydreaming any longer.

CHAPTER FIVE

PHOEBE TOOK the portable phone from the night-stand. She reached over and handed it to one of the girls. "Call your parents and let them know you're okay."

The three girls swallowed hard and then looked at each other.

"Or," Phoebe asked, "should I call the police in Socorro to see if you're wanted for something?"

"Don't do that," the blonde said. "Please? I'm Becky Taylor."

"Kara Bickford," the redhead said.

"Martha—Marty—Jones," the one with the long braid announced. Then, "No, Phoebe, my name's really Jones. Honest."

"We're all from Socorro," Becky said. "We wanted to go to Boulder for the New Year's Eve weekend because Kara's cousin goes to school there and said it was going to be really wild."

"Wild," Phoebe repeated, not knowing what

"wild" meant to teenagers in the year 2000. "How wild?"

The three girls looked at each other and back to Phoebe.

"We're high school seniors. Honor students," Kara said as if that explained everything.

"We never do anything wrong," Marty added. "Not even jaywalk. Or get detention. Or stay out past curfew."

"Or date the kind of boys our parents wouldn't like," Becky said. "We don't even *like* those kinds of boys."

"So what was in Boulder?" Will asked, leaning in the bedroom doorway. Phoebe hadn't known he was there, but he must have been listening to the conversation for a few minutes instead of checking out the college bowl games downstairs with Jack. "If you don't mind my asking."

"We didn't know," Kara replied, looking up at him. "We just wanted to have an adventure."

"Just do one bad thing. To see what it was like," Becky added.

Will crossed his arms in front of his chest. "Sex, drugs and rock and roll?"

"Well," Becky said, starting to smile, "rock and roll would be okay."

Phoebe let out a sigh of relief. At least the girls weren't deliberately looking for real danger, though there was a big chance they'd find it if they went to a strange town on New Year's weekend. "Call your parents. They must be frantic."

"We told them we were sleeping over at each other's house for the weekend."

Phoebe pointed to the phone. "Call. Tell them where you are."

Becky gulped. "And then what?"

"That's between you and your parents," Will answered. "But we'll help you out any way we can."

Phoebe left the girls alone to decide who would make the first call. Will followed her down the stairs to the second-floor hall.

"Sorry to barge in like that," Will said. "But Sarah sent me to find you. Ian's asleep in her lap."

"Oh, poor Sarah. She must be so tired of holding him." Phoebe turned to hurry toward the stairs, but Will touched her shoulder and stopped her.

"No," he said, laughing a little. "Sarah's doing fine, but she thought you might have him on some kind of schedule or something. Don't panic.''

Sarah was matchmaking, of course, but Phoebe couldn't tell Will that. "I'll get him and put him down for a nap. I hope everyone is finding something to do.''

"Ellen Barnes was on the phone for a while and now she and her kids are putting together the jigsaw puzzle you started and the Knights are watching the Rose Bowl parade and two football games." He smiled. "Jack has the remote control, so we never know what we're going to see from one minute to the next.''

"We could hide it in the couch cushions," she suggested.

He shrugged. "Let him have his fun. There are going to be football games on television all weekend. If I have to, I'll wrestle him for it when the Texas A&M game starts this afternoon.''

She opened her mouth to say that there was another television in her bedroom he could use, then realized how it would sound. *Come into my bedroom and I'll let you have my clicker?*

"What?" He looked down at her and waited.

"Nothing.''

She really had to be more careful.

SHOVELING SNOW WORKED better than taking a cold shower. Will had found Phoebe's snow shovel leaning against the wall on the front porch and for the past hour he'd set out to battle piles of snow while keeping his mind off making love to the landlady.

It wasn't easy work. Not with the icy wind stinging his face or the trickles of melting snow that leaked past his collar and along his neck. Or the muffled sounds of laughter heard from inside, where everyone else gathered in the large living room to stay warm and celebrate the first day of a very new century.

No, it wasn't easy to remain outside clearing a sidewalk and a driveway that were snow covered soon after he cleared them. A snowplow went by a few times and the driver waved. Only two cars drove past, slipping and sliding despite their slow speed; one skidded across the intersection but managed to stay on the road. Their bus had somehow been removed from the snowdrift and was probably safe in a parking lot nearby. It was no day to be on a bus, he decided, leaning on the shovel while he looked back at Phoebe's front porch. As if by magic, she opened the door and smiled at him.

"Come in," she said. "Your game's about to start."

Come in. He could picture her saying that as she led him into her bedroom. He'd bet she'd have a soft bed with lots of quilts and enormous pillows and flowered sheets. He wasn't a big fan of flowered sheets, but for one afternoon...

"I'll be there in a minute," he called, willing his body under control. He had the damnedest reaction to this woman, as if she was already his. Had been his for a long, long time. She smiled and shut the door, leaving him to the cold and the snow and the wind, which was fine with him. He was safer in the middle of a blizzard than he was next to that woman.

But an hour later, he was sitting in front of the television with Phoebe less than three feet away. On the table between his chair and the TV set was an amazing array of crackers and cheese, plus peanuts and popcorn, potato chips and cold cuts.

"I was supposed to bring appetizers to a party today," Phoebe explained, shrugging off the compliments of her awed guests. "I'm glad you're here so it won't go to waste."

Everyone gathered around, filling small plates with various snacks. Will noticed that the three teenagers looked a lot happier than they had this morning. They were gathered around the dining-room table playing cards with Ellen Barnes's daughters. "Did you get in touch with your parents?" he called over to them.

Becky grimaced. "They weren't exactly thrilled."

"My dad said he expects us to turn around and come home as soon as the snow stops," Kara added. "But we have to go to Denver to get the bus that takes us home, so at least we can say we went there."

Jack chuckled. "And here I thought Mother and I were the only ones who wanted to get to Denver so bad we'd risk a snowstorm in winter."

Will caught Phoebe's look. "Do you have any family in Denver, Jack?"

"No," the man replied, helping himself to another piece of jalapeño-dotted cheese. "We were just going to see some friends, watch a little football, that kind of thing."

Which didn't tell him much. "I've always liked Denver," Will said. "Have you ever been to the Stockman's Show?"

"A few times," Jack replied.

"When we were younger," Sarah added.

"We sure didn't plan this trip very well, did we, Jack? And here we end up with Phoebe and all these nice young people." She turned to Phoebe. "Now you're going to let us help with supper tonight, aren't you?"

"Actually, I have some frozen lasagna and garlic bread I took out of the freezer, so there isn't much else to do." She gave Will a look that said, *Ask him some more questions.*

He took a swallow of root beer and tried to think of how to ask the Knights if they were broke and on the run from a retirement village. Nothing came to mind right away. "If you get to the show next week, I hope you'll come see me ride."

"Well, son," Jack drawled, his eyes lighting up. "We'll try to get us some tickets so we can sit in the front row and cheer you on."

"I'd like that." Front-row seats would have been sold out months ago, but Will didn't see any sense in disappointing them. He looked back at Phoebe, who gave a little shrug. "Phoebe, have you ever been to a rodeo?"

"Not since I was twelve."

"It's very exciting," Sarah offered. "Why don't you come with us and watch Will here ride?"

"Oh," she said, looking flustered, "I couldn't. Ian—"

"Bring him with you," Jack suggested. "It's indoors."

Will pretended to watch the football game. For some reason he had no trouble picturing Phoebe in the rodeo stands, but he couldn't picture trying to concentrate on bronc riding if he knew she was in the same county. "Texas A&M is about to score," he said. "They're on the nine-yard line, third down."

Jack leaned closer. "Well now, how about that? Those boys get better every year."

"Was your husband a big football fan?" Sarah asked.

"Yes," Phoebe said, smiling a little. "Do you watch a lot of football…where you live?"

"Not too much," Sarah said. "It seems like there's too much to do all the time."

"It sounds like you keep busy. Didn't you say you were from Texas?"

Sarah frowned. "I think I hear the baby, dear. My hearing is the one thing that has worsened with age."

Phoebe cocked her head. "I think you're right. Thanks, Sarah."

"Mother has the ears of a good hunting dog," Jack said, patting his wife's knee.

"I'm not sure that's a compliment," Phoebe told him, making Sarah laugh as she hurried out of the room.

Will watched her leave and hoped she'd hurry back with the little boy. He got a kick out of Ian's antics. He'd never been around babies much, but something told him this boy was something special.

"What a lovely young woman," Sarah said, giving Will her attention. "And what a shame she's all alone. What is wrong with the men here in town?"

"Maybe she's not interested," Will offered, hoping Sarah would change the subject. Jack winked at him and turned back to the television. The crowd roared and Will realized he'd missed seeing the touchdown.

"She must be waiting for someone special," Sarah said. "Where do you live when you're not on the road?"

"East of Albuquerque, ma'am."

"Do you have a ranch?" she asked.

"Not exactly. Just a few acres, enough for one horse. I'm not there much."

"Of course you're not," Sarah said, seeming very pleased with herself.

"Leave the boy alone, Mother," Jack warned, motioning toward the television. "He wants to see the replay of this. That quarterback made it look easy."

Will turned obediently toward the TV screen, but he might as well have been watching a golf tournament. He sure hoped the bus would leave first thing in the morning, before he got much too accustomed to this domestic life. And before Sarah Knight's matchmaking resulted in anything he couldn't resist.

CHAPTER SIX

"IT'S STILL SNOWING," Kara said, standing in front of the living-room windows. "Does anyone want to go out and build a snowman?"

Quite a few people did, including Ellen and her daughters and Phoebe and her little boy. Will watched as she bundled him up in a thick blue snowsuit, mittens and hat until he looked like the Pillsbury Dough Boy. Then she took a camera from a desk drawer and announced she would record the event.

The first day of the new millennium had seemed endless, no matter how much television he watched or how many times he looked out the window at the snow. Will was restless, so he retrieved his drying boots and gloves from in front of the fireplace and went outside once again. He would shovel again while the rest of them played.

Jack had fallen asleep during halftime, and Sarah, curled up in a bright blue afghan, waved a cheerful goodbye as the rest of the group hurried outside to play in the last hour or so of daylight. Phoebe held Ian so he could watch the making of the snowman, but Will stayed far away from both of them. Instead, he grabbed the shovel and cleaned the walk. And the front steps. And the driveway, too, until there was nothing left for him to do but help lift the heavy balls of snow in place. And then, of course, they talked him into putting his Stetson on the snowman so Phoebe could take a picture. He held the laughing baby and stood by the Western snowman with the rest of its enthusiastic creators while Phoebe took more pictures.

"For Ian's baby book," she said. "That was his first snowman. And his first cowboy," she added, laughing as she returned Will's hat to him.

He brushed off the snow and put the hat back on his head. "I guess we're not your usual kind of tourists, Phoebe."

"Runaway honor students and bronc riders are definitely a new experience," she said, reaching to take Ian. The baby sat, tall and content, tucked in Will's left arm. His bottom lip jutted out at his mother.

"He can stay with me for a while," Will said,

wondering at the same time what he would do with the kid. Walk him around? Pretend to count snowflakes? Talk about the weather?

"It's pretty cold out here," she said.

"He's got plenty of clothes on. He's not shaking or anything."

"Well…"

"Come here, kid, let's look at the snowplow." Will took the boy over to the sidewalk to look at the plow coming down the road. The little boy's eyes grew wild and his little body stiffened as the noisy machine came closer.

"It's okay," he assured him, and Ian darted a glance at Will's face as if to make sure the man was telling the truth. "It's just a plow. Watch." He pointed to the snow piled alongside the road. The plow was widening the road this time around, sending streams of snow high into the air.

Ian laughed, a huge laugh that bubbled up from deep in his belly. His mittened hands clapped in joy. Will laughed, too, surprised at the kid's reaction. He turned to see if Phoebe saw them, but she and Ellen had gone back into the house, leaving the five girls with nothing to do but throw snowballs at each other.

He'd never thought much about having kids

of his own. He hadn't had much experience with kids except for the older boys who hung around the horses. Sometimes he'd take them for burgers or something to drink, especially if he'd had a bad ride. The enthusiasm of the would-be rodeo riders never failed to cheer him up when he was feeling lower than a snake's belly.

He shifted the boy in his arms so he was higher. The snowplow went noisily down the street, blowing up snow, and the baby watched until it was gone.

"Hey, Will, watch out!"

A snowball whizzed about two feet from his shoulder.

"Sorry!" Becky called. "I meant to hit Kara. She's behind you."

He turned to see another laughing teenager. He felt about a hundred years old. "I'm getting out of the way," he said, heading toward the front porch. He'd better give this boy back to his mother. Holding a baby was giving him strange ideas. He had a lot of prize money to win before he could even think about settling down.

If he ever thought about settling down.

"THAT WAS YOUR BUS DRIVER. He says he'll pick you up across the street in the morning at seven o'clock,'' Phoebe announced, setting the phone down on the kitchen counter. ''The bus is fine and the weather reports are saying the storm will end tonight. The roads should be clear enough tomorrow.''

''Well,'' Jack said, ''I sure hope he's right. The Broncos have their play-off game at four o'clock.'' He turned to Sarah. ''You think we'll make it?''

''We might miss the first quarter,'' she said. ''But we'll see most of it.''

Phoebe figured this was her chance. ''Do you have hotel reservations in Denver, Jack? I have some brochures if you want.''

''No need, Phoebe.'' He winked. ''We've got friends expecting us, said they'd roll out the red carpet. I called this morning and told them we were stuck in the storm.''

''So someone is expecting you,'' she said, relieved to know that the elderly couple would be taken care of.

''Oh, yes, honey.'' Sarah took another sip of hot chocolate. ''This is so good. I can't believe it's instant.''

''I couldn't believe how cold it was outside.''

''Looks like your boy enjoyed it.''

"Yes, he did." Phoebe watched as Will reached across the kitchen table and gave Ian another marshmallow. The baby's face was a sticky mess of marshmallow and chocolate milk, but he looked pleased with himself. And he was laughing and showing off for the Barnes girls, who egged him on.

"So I guess you're stuck with us for one more night," Will said, looking at Phoebe with an expression she couldn't read.

"We won't be any trouble," Jack promised. "There's football on till at least midnight."

"You won't be any trouble, believe me," Phoebe told them. "I already have the lasagna in the oven. And I'm glad to have the company. I don't like being alone in the house during storms."

She didn't like being alone in the house at all, really, but she'd gotten used to it. She just didn't tell anyone that sometimes the house was so big that she heard her footsteps echo in the hallways. A house like this was made for people, not echoes. Maybe she should sell the place and move to Florida near her mother.

"I'm going to miss the company," she told her guests. "And Ian will, too." Her son was now banging the tray of the high chair to make the chocolate milk spray on Heather Barnes, who sat closest to him. "Ian! Stop that!"

While the others laughed, Phoebe grabbed a warm cloth and headed toward her son.

"Toss it here," Will said, holding up one hand. "I'm closer. I'll do it."

She did, surprising herself by flinging the cloth across the table. She was even more surprised that the cowboy managed to clean up her son.

"Nice catch," Jack said, chuckling. He turned to his wife. "Remember when Johnny used to do things like that? I always said he'd end up playing ball somewhere."

Sarah nodded. "That boy was always throwing something."

Phoebe began to clear the table. "Johnny is your son?"

Jack nodded. "Yes, and what a fine boy he—"

"Phoebe," Sarah interrupted, leaning on the table in order to stand, "don't you wait on us anymore."

"All right." Phoebe sat back down again. She didn't want to hurt Sarah's feelings.

"We'll do it," Becky said, and in the next few minutes the table was cleared and the kitchen cleaned. Will plucked Ian from his high chair and carried him over to his mother.

"I think he wants you."

The baby held his arms open to his mother and Will handed him to her, but when he gave her the child, Phoebe was bumped by one of the girls moving behind her to the sink. And Will's hands grazed the sides of her breasts. She pretended it didn't happen as she took Ian in her arms. She fussed with the child's shirt and didn't look at Will, didn't acknowledge the low "Excuse me" he uttered before leaving the room.

I think he wants you were the words that repeated in her head. And she wasn't thinking of her son. No, she knew, the problem was that she wanted *him*. The rodeo man. Which was embarrassing and—considering the fact that she hardly knew him—even a little bit promiscuous, though she had only slept with two men in her entire life.

"Phoebe?"

She looked up to see Jack standing by the table, his gaze on the baby. She realized they were alone. "Yes?"

"Your husband's been gone a while now?"

She swallowed the lump in her throat. "Yes."

"You must miss him very much." Phoebe

nodded, unable to answer for fear of crying. Jack shoved his hands into his pockets and looked sad. "I know it's not easy, honey," he said. "But it does get better."

"I wish I could believe that."

"You think an old man like me would lie to you?" He winked, then smiled at her in his sweet, grandfatherly way. "It's a whole new year, you know. Time for new beginnings."

Ian wrapped his arms around her neck and gave her a hug as Jack left the kitchen. She loved the feel of that sturdy little body in her arms, but he was getting heavier every day. He was growing up.

And, yes, it was a time for new beginnings. But how was she supposed to decide what her new beginnings would be?

"HE SURE REMINDS ME of Johnny."

Sarah stopped rearranging the clothes in her suitcase and looked at her husband. "I know." Her husband sat on the bed, his shoulders slumped as if he was very tired. Sarah went over to him and, pushing her clothes aside, sat down beside him. "What's the matter?"

"You were right, Mother. They'd make a nice couple."

He didn't have to explain who "they" were. "Of course they would. Didn't I tell you that last night?"

He patted her knee with one large, gnarled hand. "Yes, you did."

"Tired?"

"A little, but stop looking so worried. I might just take a little nap."

Sarah stood and started taking things off the bed. "You lie down, then. Have a little rest before dinner."

To her surprise, Jack didn't argue. Instead, he stretched out on the bed and tucked his hands behind his head, which Sarah knew was his "thinking" position. "I wonder how much longer Will can rodeo."

"Not much, I suppose." She didn't think it was the right time to remind him that she had stated that concern aloud last night.

"We could use some help on the ranch right about now."

"That's true." She turned off the lamp next to the bed.

"We should go see him next week, watch him ride."

"That would be real nice," Sarah agreed.

"Maybe we should see if Phoebe would like to join us."

"Leave that part of it alone, Mother. A man can choose his own wife and Will Briggs is no fool." He closed his eyes. "You'll wake me for dinner?"

"Of course," Sarah said, hiding a smile as she left the room. What man had ever gotten married without a little help from those who knew best? She hadn't gotten this old without learning that much.

CHAPTER SEVEN

THE POWER WENT OUT around seven, in the middle of dinner. Suddenly, they were plunged into darkness. Phoebe shouldn't have been surprised since that usually happened whenever there was a big storm, but she thought she'd made it through the worst of the weather this time.

"Just stay where you are," she told everyone. "I'll get the candles."

When she returned with matches, a flashlight and candles, she lit the unused tapers that formed the holiday centerpiece her mother had sent for the table. Will gently took the matches from her hand and followed her around the dining room and then the living room, helping her light the rooms with a gentle, flickering glow. An intimate glow, Phoebe realized, though Will kept his distance as he helped her.

Ian was safely in bed, tucked in his crib until morning, so Phoebe didn't have to worry about his grasping at the flames. The fat cranberry candles on the mantel above the fireplace looked and smelled especially nice, she decided.

"Would you like me to build a fire?"

"I think we're going to need the heat," she said, kneeling in front of the hearth. She'd had a fire last night but had been too busy today to think of fixing another. She handed him her flashlight. "There's plenty of dry wood in the garage. There's a door in the kitchen—"

"No problem," Will said almost as if he was glad to get away from her. She must seem very needy, she reflected. A lonely widow who looked ready to cling to any man who walked in the door? Phoebe stood, stiffened her spine and resolved never to ask him for help again. She didn't want him to feel sorry for her.

For some reason, she had to blink back tears before joining the others at the dining-room table. She should be helping Will with the wood, but she was a coward. A pathetic, lonely coward.

"This is so festive," Ellen said. "But I wonder if this means there are wires down and we won't be able to leave tomorrow."

"I guess we'll just have to wait and see," Jack said, looking as if he didn't care if he ever left Phoebe's house or not. "I'm sure we have lots of blankets and lots of candles, so there's nothing else to do but relax and tell ghost stories.''

"Oh, no, you don't, Mr. Knight," Ellen said, laughing. "Unless you want to be awakened by two girls having nightmares."

"He's such an old tease," Sarah said. "He can't even watch a scary movie without closing his eyes."

"Gives me an excuse to hold on to you, Mother." He stood and peered out the windows. "Looks pretty dark out there. I'll bet the whole town lost their power. At home we have a generator, which sure comes in handy." He turned when Will entered the room, his arms full of firewood. "Here, Will, let me help you with that."

Any woman would be attracted to Will Briggs, Phoebe told herself. Anyone with a few hormones and decent eyesight. She gathered a stack of newspapers and brought it to the hearth, then all she had to do was stand back and watch. Jack and Will were clearly used to building fires.

Jack brushed the dirt off his hands. "Do you have any other fireplaces in this house?"

"My bedroom, but—"

"We might as well get one going upstairs,"

he said, turning to Will. "Just in case the heat is off for the night. Or longer."

"Phoebe?" Will waited for her permission.

"Okay," she said, thinking of Ian. The other times they'd lost their electricity, she'd been surprised at how the house had cooled down after a few hours. "The girls will be warm enough in the loft because the heat stays trapped up there. But Ellen, you and your girls might want to sleep downstairs by the fire. Will, you might, too."

"I'll be fine," he said, filling his arms with a load of firewood. Jack took the flashlight and Will followed him up the stairs.

"Heather and Holly can sleep upstairs with us," Becky offered. "It'll be like a pajama party."

"Cool," the Barnes girls said in unison.

"We'll help you clean up, Phoebe," Ellen offered. "And at the risk of sounding too much like a mother, I think everyone should get to bed early tonight since the bus is leaving at seven."

"Leave everything where it is," Phoebe said. "I'll put the rest of the food in the fridge, but the rest of it can wait until we have hot water."

"Are you sure?"

"Positive. Come sit by the fire for a few

minutes. Maybe we'll luck out and the lights will come back on.'' She helped Sarah across the room and guided her to the couch. The kids sat on the floor in a semicircle around the hearth and whispered to each other. ''Are you sure you're all right to travel tomorrow, Sarah?''

''I'm fine, dear. At my age, just waking up in the morning takes a lot of energy.'' She turned to Phoebe. ''You'd better go upstairs, dear, and check on the men. There's nothing Jack loves more than fussing with a fire, but I do feel better knowing that Will is in charge.''

So she'd been sent upstairs to her room. She stood and shook her head. ''Are you matchmaking again, Sarah?''

''Who, me?''

Ellen laughed. ''You'd better do as you're told. Just think, tomorrow you'll be rid of us.''

Phoebe found she didn't like that at all. ''You all have to promise to come back and see me.''

''You'll see us again,'' Sarah promised, tucking the afghan around her shoulders. ''And if I were you, I wouldn't let Will Briggs get away.''

Phoebe blushed. ''You're a terrible old woman.''

Sarah and Ellen both laughed.

''Men like that don't come along every day,''

Sarah declared. "You've got to grab 'em when you see 'em."

"I am not grabbing *anything*," she told the women. "Except a few extra blankets."

"If I were sixty years younger," Sarah said, "that man could build a fire in my bedroom any time he wanted."

THIS WAS DEFINITELY a woman's room. From the pastel quilts folded neatly on the wide bed to the polished oak furniture to the lace curtains and the bottles of perfume on the dresser, it was all woman. Even the mantel over the fireplace was painted white and lined with old photographs in silver frames, dried roses and thick ivory candles in silver holders. Will lit all of them while Jack fussed with the kindling he'd found in a basket on the hearth.

"Ever done any ranching?" Jack asked.

"Some."

"It's a good life. You want to give me those matches?" Will handed them to the old man and watched as he lit the kindling and the fire began, a small blaze that with any luck would turn into something that would warm Phoebe tonight.

"I've thought about raising cattle. Or horses for the rodeo."

"Yeah?" Jack stood and crossed his arms in front of his chest. Both men stood there and watched the fire take hold. "Might be a good idea. When you quit bronc riding, that is."

"I'm saving up," Will said. "I try to keep my expenses low and I put as much as I can in the bank."

"Good idea. My father gave me some good advice years ago." He grinned. "He said that the fastest way to double your money was to fold it up and put it back in your pocket."

"Did he give you any advice about women?"

Jack chuckled and replaced the screen in front of the fire. "Nothing that worked. I just got lucky when I met Sarah, that's all."

"I guess I've never been that fortunate."

The old man clapped him on the back as they headed for the hall. "You're still young, son."

"Sometimes I feel about a hundred." Especially at night, when his knee got to aching. And then there were the other times, when he felt like an awkward teenager any time Phoebe was in the same room. He would be glad to get out of here tomorrow and miles away from the pretty widow and her inviting bed.

So when she appeared in the door of her bedroom and asked if there was anything she could do to help, Will had nothing to say. Once again, he was tongue-tied with lust.

DESPITE EVERYONE'S best intentions, it was several hours before they went to bed and the dark house became quiet. Ellen was happily settled on the couch in the living room, the Knights had sworn they'd be fine with extra blankets, and Will had stacked more firewood by the hearth.

Phoebe fiddled with the fire until the blaze shot up, orange and gold in the darkness. The candles on the mantel provided enough light for her to find her nightgown and get ready for bed. She left the door open to Ian's room after covering him with extra blankets and assuring herself that he was warm enough.

She would have brought him into bed with her if she wasn't afraid he'd fall out and hurt himself. He was at the wiggly stage now, old enough to crawl and explore. She wouldn't want him exploring the fire. So Phoebe went back to her quiet room and listened as her house stilled.

It would be like this tomorrow night, she thought, as she crawled under the covers and tried to get her pillows and blankets arranged just so. But tomorrow she would have the television for voices to listen to and she would be able to read in those long hours before dawn when it was easier to find a book than to find peace. But tonight it was heaven to know the house was filled with people and she closed her eyes and fell asleep in seconds.

Ian's cries woke her sometime in the middle of the night. She hurried into his room to find him standing in his crib, holding on to the side and whimpering.

"Ian, sweetheart," she crooned, lifting him into her arms, "are you having a bad dream?" He put his head on her shoulder and sagged with relief as she spoke to him. Phoebe patted his back and rocked him gently until he quieted, until his breathing was soft and regular again. Long moments later, after her arms began to ache, she put him back into his crib and covered him with the blankets.

There was a soft knock on the connecting door, and Will's low voice. "Phoebe? Is anything wrong?"

She unlocked the door before he could knock again and wake the baby, forgetting for a moment that she wore nothing but a nightgown. Phoebe opened it a few inches and could barely see Will in the darkness of the room. "It's fine. Ian had a nightmare, that's all."

"I didn't know babies had bad dreams," he whispered, running a hand through his unruly hair. "I thought he might be sick or something."

"He's fine." She hid a yawn behind her hand and opened the door a little wider so she wouldn't seem rude.

"How's the fire?"

"I think it's pretty much out by now."

"No power?"

"No."

"Give me a minute to find a shirt and I'll come work on it."

"You don't have..." she started to say, but he had turned away and she heard him rustling through his clothes, heard him muffle a curse as he stubbed his toe on something. She went into her room to see if she could poke the logs a little and get a flame going so she didn't look like such a helpless female.

"Let me do that," he said, stepping softly across the room. He wore jeans; his feet were bare and his shirt was buttoned in two places. He took the metal poker out of her hand and squatted in front of the fireplace to rearrange the coals. Then he added kindling and some narrow pieces of split logs until the small glow became a flame and began to catch.

"You're very good at that."

He stood and absently wiped his hands on his jeans. "I have a fireplace at home."

"Home?"

He turned and looked down at her. Then he reached over and tucked a strand of hair behind her ear. "It's a small place, just four rooms and a few acres. Not fancy like this."

"But you like it."

He shrugged and seemed to study her face as his fingers trailed from her ear along her jaw and then to her chin. "It'll do. I've never wanted anything else. Until now."

"Now?" she whispered, wondering how he got so close. She swore she could feel the heat radiating from his skin.

"Now there are lots of things I want." He lowered his mouth to hers and, keeping her chin gently tipped up, kissed her.

Phoebe didn't react. She let the kiss happen, felt his lips on hers for a brief second, and then they were gone. She hadn't even had time to close her eyes.

"That was one of them," he said. "And this is another."

But this time when he kissed her, it wasn't brief. She had more than enough time to close her eyes and lift her hands to his shoulders. It was a gentle exploration, a teasing, let-me-taste-you kiss. She matched him kiss for kiss and tongue to tongue and breath to breath as they stood embracing in the firelit room. Seconds or minutes or moments or hours didn't register because kissing Will Briggs wasn't something Phoebe wanted to stop doing.

It was later, when they stood there, breathless and looking at each other, that he took her hands from his shoulders and brought them to his lips.

"I'm leaving in a few hours," he said. "I'd better try to get some sleep."

"Yes" was all she could manage to say. She wasn't prepared to take him into her bed. Or her body. "Good night."

He smiled, just a little. And kissed her forehead before releasing her hands. "Good night."

She crawled back into bed after he'd shut the door behind him. This wasn't the way she'd envisioned starting off the new year.

CHAPTER EIGHT

WILL CURSED HIMSELF for going in that room in the first place. He cursed himself for leaving it, too, but Phoebe deserved more than a one-nighter with a man who wouldn't be returning this way again. She'd end up feeling used and he'd feel real bad thinking he'd taken advantage.

He didn't sleep much the rest of the night. He heard the heat go on at dawn, saw the bedside clock start blinking 12:00 and figured there'd be no reason the bus would wait another day. When he climbed out of bed and looked out the window, he saw that the streets were in better shape than yesterday. The snow had stopped and even the wind had died down. His watch said 5:07. It didn't take him long to shower and dress, didn't take more than a few minutes to pack up his stuff and place it downstairs by the front door. He even took time to make the bed and reset the electric clock.

When he couldn't stall any longer, he followed the aroma of freshly brewed coffee into the kitchen, but he still hadn't thought about what he would say to Phoebe. Should he apologize?

Hell, no.

Just the thought of having her in his arms like that made him hard. She'd knocked him over by kissing him like that. Two seconds more and he'd have had her flat on her back on the floor in front of the fireplace. To hell with the bed and to hell with the flannel nightgown.

And to hell with his freedom, he reminded himself as he paused in the doorway of the kitchen. Phoebe had her back to him as she stood at the counter mixing something in a bowl. She wore black slacks and another one of those green sweaters that he liked, and her hair was loose on her shoulders. He wanted to lift it up and kiss her neck, wanted to wrap his arms around her waist and lean into all that female softness. She would smell like cinnamon and she would be his.

She turned as if sensing his gaze. And then the color on her cheeks deepened. "Good morning."

"Morning." He took his time getting to the coffeepot, where she'd set out mugs, sugar and cream. He poured his coffee and watched her spoon batter into cake pans. "What are you fixing?"

"German pancakes. I thought you—everyone—might like something a little different." She didn't look at him, just kept spooning the batter. "I'll put yours in the oven now."

"There's no hurry."

She glanced at the clock above the stove. "Is anyone else up yet?"

"I heard the girls moving around upstairs, but the rest of the house is quiet." He watched as she bent over to put the pans in the oven, then set the timer and turned to face him.

"I'm sorry about last night," she said, and he noticed her eyes had shadows underneath them. So she hadn't slept much, either.

"Why?"

That confused her. She returned to stirring pancake batter. "Well, for one thing, I don't go around kissing my guests. Not ever."

Which was an invitation to fluster her some more, Will decided. He set his coffee down and stepped closer, to within touching distance. And then he touched her. He took her wrist very gently and lifted her hand from the wooden spoon and put it on his waist. It was easy to

gather her into his arms, easier still to touch her
lips with his. He tasted sugar; he smelled vanilla.
And he wanted Phoebe, especially when her
other hand crept up to his shoulder and held on
to him as if she were drowning. Her lips parted
when he urged her to open them for him. His
hands found the curve of her back and held her
body to him, touching in places he wished
weren't covered in denim. He wanted to carry
her upstairs to bed.

He wanted to lift her onto the kitchen counter
and press into all that sweet softness. He wanted
to drop to the floor and make love to her on the
rug. He cupped her bottom and fitted her to him
and prayed that no one would walk in and in-
terrupt.

She relaxed against him for one heart-
stopping second and then pulled away. "I
can't," she said. Or at least that's what he
thought she said. There was a buzzing in his
ears. Phoebe gave him a pleading look. "They'll
burn."

The buzzing stopped when she turned off the
timer on the stove. He watched in a state of un-
resolved passion as she pulled on mitts and
checked the baking pancakes. Why go to so

much trouble to bake a pancake when you could fry them up in a skillet in a few minutes?

I am getting on a bus, he told himself. He was not coming back here because domestic women wanted husbands, and he wasn't ready to give it all up and start chopping firewood and greeting overnight guests and playing Daddy to a toddler who would just as soon chew on his Stetson as wear it.

"Go sit down and I'll fix your plate."

"You don't have to wait on me."

"I know, but I think it would help if you were on the other side of the room," Phoebe said, giving him a shy smile. "Or I'll never get breakfast finished in time for everyone before the bus leaves."

He could offer to stay, Will thought, watching her pile sausages and canned peaches on his plate. But she wasn't the kind of woman a man took advantage of. Phoebe was different; Phoebe's heart, he suspected, was not easily given. "Thanks" was all he said when she put the plate in front of him.

"I don't do things like this," Phoebe said, giving a little shrug. They both knew she wasn't talking about breakfast.

SARAH PUT HER FINGER to her lips and refused to let Jack and Ellen move past her toward the kitchen. "Shhh."

Her husband gave her a blank look. "Why?"

"They're kissing."

"Ahhh," he said, turning to Ellen. "I bet we don't have to ask who she's talking about, do we?"

Ellen smiled. "No. It's pretty obvious that he can't take his eyes off her."

"And she looks at him the same way," Sarah whispered. "I thought I'd give them a chance to—"

"To what?" Heather asked, coming up to her mother. "Holly won't wear her red sweater. She says it's itchy."

Ellen guided her daughter toward the hall. "I'll come up and talk to her. Come on, let's make sure that we're all packed."

"You already checked."

"Let's check again," Sarah heard Ellen say before they went up the stairs.

She turned to her husband. "Now what?"

"We should eat before we get on the bus." He looked at his watch. "We're gonna run out of time, Mother. And that coffee smells real good."

Sarah sighed. "Oh, all right, go on. Maybe they're finished by now."

"Let's hope they were only kissing." He winked at her.

"Don't wink at me, old man," she told him. "You're no help at all."

"I've got a few ideas of my own," Jack said, taking her arm and leading her toward the kitchen door. He raised his voice. "Well, Mother," he said, shouting as if Phoebe and Will were deaf, for heaven's sake. "Something in the kitchen smells real good!"

"You wouldn't win any of those acting awards," Sarah fussed, laughing in spite of herself.

"But you always tell me I'm as handsome as Paul Newman when I get dressed up."

Sarah ignored his teasing as she peeked into the kitchen. Phoebe was back to baking and Will was eating breakfast like he didn't have a care in the world.

They couldn't fool an old woman.

"ABSOLUTELY NOT." Phoebe refilled Jack's coffee and then her own. "I'm not going to argue about it for another minute, so there."

"Phoebe, please," Ellen said, her checkbook in her hand. "You have to let us pay."

"My mom gave me her credit card number," Becky said. "We're all going to pay her back when we get home." The two other teens nodded. "Honest."

"No one is paying for anything," Phoebe declared, reaching over to take Ian's spoon away from him before the banging gave anyone a headache. "You were wonderful guests and you made this New Year's Eve very special." She didn't dare look in Will's direction. "Besides, you spent most of last night without heat or hot water. You were good sports."

"No, my dear," Sarah said, struggling to stand. Will hurried to help her get on her feet and Sarah went over to Phoebe and patted her hand. "You were kind to take us in. We all could have frozen to death."

Phoebe didn't want to tear up, so she blinked hard and tried to smile. "I didn't tell you there were two motels on the other side of town because I was happy for the company."

Will glanced at his watch and looked at everyone but Phoebe. "I think we'd better get our stuff together. The bus will be coming in about ten minutes."

Seven o'clock came too soon. Up until the last minute, Phoebe was busy collecting addresses and promises to keep in touch. She and Ian were hugged numerous times and the teenagers ran up and down the stairs retrieving last-minute forgotten items.

"I'll see that they get on the bus heading home," Ellen promised Phoebe as the teenage girls took turns kissing Ian. "And I'll watch them like a hawk all the way to Denver."

"Thanks for all the help." And then the teens surrounded her for hugs and giggles, Jack gave her a kiss on the cheek and promised to return while Sarah sniffed back tears and clung to her husband's arm.

"We'll be back," she promised. "Now that we know where you are."

"I'll look forward to it," Phoebe told her. She watched as Will slung his bag over his shoulder, then picked up the battered suitcases that belonged to the Knights. He paused, the last one out the door.

"I don't suppose you'd want to come to Denver to see the rodeo," he said, letting Ian grab at his hat one more time.

"Cow," the boy babbled. "Cow, cow, cow."

"You need to get Ian his own Stetson," Will said, his hand on the doorknob.

"Maybe when he's older," Phoebe replied, wishing she was the kind of woman who could jump on a bus and have an adventure. Wishing she was the kind of woman who wouldn't give her heart when she gave her body. And wishing she didn't know how life could grab you by the throat and tear your heart out when you least expected it.

He didn't kiss her though he looked at her lips like he was considering it. Phoebe pasted an idiotic smile on her face.

"Good luck in Denver. I hope you win."

"Thanks."

She shut the door behind him, heard his boots crunch on the step.

The rodeo man was gone.

CHAPTER NINE

"MY PILLS," SARAH CRIED, rifling through her purse. "I must have left them in the bathroom."

Jack stopped before getting on the bus and frowned. "I thought I saw—"

"No," she said, snapping the bag shut. "I'm sure of it. I'll be right back."

"You can't cross the street by yourself," her husband fussed. The driver was on the bus, the engine warming up, and everything was ready to go. "You'll break a hip."

Will finished storing their bags in the luggage compartment and walked over. "What's the matter, Sarah?"

"I left my medication at Phoebe's. I feel like such a fool, but I really need them."

"Okay," the dear man said, pulling his collar up against the wind. "I'll be right back. You get on the bus and stay warm."

"Thank you so much," Sarah said, giving him her best grateful-old-lady smile. She watched as he crossed the street and stepped up onto Phoebe's porch before she turned to her husband. "Quick, get his duffel bag."

"Mother—"

"It's for his own good," she said, pointing to the faded khaki bag. "Drag it onto the sidewalk."

Jack did, but Sarah could see his heart wasn't in it. "The boy's going to be mad at us."

"He won't suspect a thing." Sarah took Jack's elbow and, with the help of the bus driver, managed to get up the steps to her seat. "Now," she told the driver, "step on it."

"But what about the cowboy?"

"He changed his mind," she fibbed, watching as Phoebe opened her front door and let Will inside. "He's staying for a while."

Ellen tapped her on the shoulder. "Are you serious? He's staying with her?"

Sarah smiled as the bus jerked into gear and started down the street. "Yes. Isn't it romantic?"

"SARAH LEFT HER MEDICINE in the bathroom," Will explained as soon as Phoebe, Ian still attached to her side, opened the door. The little boy grinned up at him and Will stepped inside, shutting the door behind him so the cold air wouldn't enter the house.

"Oh, okay," she said. "I'll go get it." She returned moments later, empty-handed. "I checked the bathroom and the den, but I couldn't find it. I even looked under the couch."

"She said she—" That's when he heard it, the unmistakable sound of a bus shifting gears as it picked up speed. Will opened the door and watched the bus disappearing down the street.

Phoebe stepped up beside him to look outside. "Was that the bus?"

"Yes."

"It left? Without *you?*"

"Obviously."

"But your bag—"

"Is sitting right there on the sidewalk." He pointed across the street. "Where someone took it off the bus and left it."

"But who would do that?"

"The Knights."

"But why...oh," she said. "Sarah was matchmaking again." Her cheeks reddened. "I'm really sorry. I didn't have anything to do with this."

"I know. Let me get my gear and then I'll

come back and make a few phone calls. There has to be another way to get to Denver.''

A sudden gust of wind hit him in the face as he crossed the street. The town was just beginning to stir and he had to wait for two cars to pass before he could retrieve his bag. He knew he should be angry, but when he thought about that old woman pulling off such a simple stunt, he wanted to laugh. Did she think he wouldn't rent a car or get on the next bus or hitch a ride out of town with the next Denver-bound salesman anxious for someone to talk to?

He didn't bother to knock when he returned to the house. He left his bag in the hall and went to the kitchen, where he heard the rattling of dishes and running water. When he walked in, he was still smiling, which seemed to catch Phoebe by surprise when she looked up from unloading the dishwasher.

''You have to love her,'' he said, pausing in the doorway. ''I fell for every word she said.''

''Cow, cow,'' Ian called, pounding a spoon on his high-chair tray.

Will waved at him and the boy waved back.

''What are you going to do now?''

''Call the bus company,'' he said, thinking of the way she'd kissed him this morning, the last time they were alone together in this room. It was hard to forget how she felt in his arms. "I'll figure out something."

"I could drive you," she offered.

"No." He shook his head. "That leaves you driving back alone with Ian. And on these roads? No way."

"This is awkward, isn't it?"

"You notice I'm staying on the other side of this island."

Phoebe smiled. "If you want to come over here and get a cup of coffee, I'm sure it would be okay."

"I could help you clean up first."

"I wouldn't refuse." She tossed him a damp sponge. "You could wipe off the counters and the table."

He hesitated. "You don't think I did this deliberately?"

She seemed to have to think about it. After a long moment, she replied, "No, I don't. You'd be more direct than this. And besides, I'm not exactly your type."

"And that type would be…?" Will walked over to the table and started wiping off crumbs. Ian giggled and screeched when he came closer, so Will took off his hat and hooked it over the back of a chair where Ian could see it but not beat it to death.

Phoebe set a cup of coffee in front of him. "You know. Someone young. Someone...free. Who likes rodeos."

He ignored the coffee and waited for her to look at him. "A buckle bunny."

"What?"

"That's what they're called," he said. "The girls who hang around the chutes and the locker rooms."

"Oh."

He took a sip of coffee and then went back to wiping the table. He'd make sure it was the cleanest damn table in Colorado because he was not going to kiss Phoebe. He was going to dial an 800 number and find out when the next bus came through town and he was going to stand at the bus stop twenty minutes ahead of time and not do any favors for elderly ladies until he was on the bus and the bus was heading north. He could go sit in a café somewhere and read the paper until he saw that bus and he wouldn't let the damn thing out of his sight.

"I'm sorry you're stuck here."

"Yeah," he drawled. "I know."

"That's not what I meant. I mean I'm sorry

for *you*. That you're stuck here. I know you'd rather be in Denver doing whatever it is you do before a rodeo."

"I would have stayed longer if you asked me," he told her, forgetting that he wasn't going to kiss her.

Phoebe actually looked surprised. "Why?"

Will didn't think he could do anything else but take her hand and tug her into his arms. And then he kissed her, just a tiny kiss to show that he wasn't really serious. That he was only flirting.

And then another kiss, to tell her he liked the first one. He liked the way she tasted. He liked the way her breasts touched his shirt. And when she started kissing him back as if she was melting into him like butter on a muffin, well, there wasn't a lot he could do except show how much he appreciated that soft little body of hers.

Will ended up showing his appreciation so much that after a second or a minute or a week, he was sitting on a kitchen chair and Phoebe was on his lap. He'd managed—he thought with her help—to remove her sweater and she'd somehow figured out how to unbutton his shirt because whenever her lacy peach bra touched his bare chest, he thought he'd expire from the heat.

But he never stopped kissing her because it would have been impossible to stop unless they both stopped breathing and fell to the floor.

And then something hit him on the head and clinked on the floor.

"Cow," Ian hollered. "Mama, cow!"

Will lifted his mouth and whispered into Phoebe's ear, "Your son is protecting you."

"I've probably warped him for life," she said, climbing off Will's lap and picking her sweater off the floor. "When he's fourteen, he'll be telling some therapist about this."

"He only knows a couple of words," Will teased, watching those beautiful breasts being covered by cotton. "How much can he say?"

"I shouldn't be doing this in front of him," she muttered, going back to the sink full of dirty dishes. "I can't believe I was going to have sex in the kitchen at eight o'clock in the morning."

"We were going to have sex?" Will stood and buttoned his shirt.

She gave him a withering look and started scrubbing the lasagna pan, so Will took Ian out of his high chair and carried him over to his mother.

"We're going into the living room and play."

"You are?"

He leaned over and kissed her, which made Ian laugh. "Yeah."

"What about the bus? And the phone calls?"

"There's plenty of time," he said as Ian patted his head and pointed to the cowboy hat still hanging on the chair. "I'll be out of your way soon enough, I promise."

"Cow," Ian ordered, and Will took him across the room to retrieve the hat, which he held in his chubby fingers.

"You're going to have to buy this boy a Stetson, Phoebe. He wants to be a cowboy."

Her gaze went to Will. "I guess there are worse things to be."

"I'll take that as a compliment," he said, and decided to leave the kitchen before he started taking her clothes off again. Ian had turned out to be a damned good chaperon, which, Will told himself, was for the best. He'd no business getting tangled up with a woman who obviously needed a husband. In fact, the sooner he got out of town, the better.

After he played horse with the boy.

IT WAS THE SEXIEST THING he could have done, taking her son off to play like that. Phoebe scrubbed the pans, loaded the dishwasher, sprayed the countertops with disinfectant, tossed the damp dish towels into a laundry basket and swept the kitchen floor. And the entire time she cleaned and polished and fussed, she tried to talk herself out of making love with Will Briggs.

It wasn't as if the world was going to end if she had sex. The local newspaper wouldn't use Hot Bed-And-Breakfast! for a headline in next week's paper, she wouldn't be stoned in the village square, and if her mother ever found out, even *she* would approve.

And so would Ian's father, who had loved her so dearly and died without knowing he was going to be a father. He would want her to be happy. He'd never wanted anything else. And she was so very tired of pretending she wasn't lonely.

CHAPTER TEN

"I'VE COME TO RESCUE YOU."

Will scooped Ian off the floor and pretended to toss him in the air, which made the child shriek with delight, before he turned toward Phoebe. "Who are you talking to? Him or me?"

She smiled. "I'm not sure. Which one of you is ready for a nap?"

"You sure you want me to answer that?" He handed her the boy, who made a show of refusing to go to his mother. "Never mind. I'm doing my best to behave myself till the next bus comes."

Phoebe settled the boy on her hip. "And when is that?"

"I'm going to call and find out right now." He picked up his hat and started poking the dents out of the crown.

Phoebe swallowed hard. "There's no hurry."

Will forgot all about dents. He forgot he

owned a hat. He might have even forgotten his name. "What did you say?"

"You said you'd stay longer if I asked," she said. "Are you going to make me ask?"

"You've changed your mind about the kitchen floor?" Visions of Phoebe naked on polished oak flashed before his eyes.

"I think a bed would be better."

"I've always thought that myself." He smiled, remembering the minutes spent in her bedroom last night, and tossed the hat onto the couch.

"I need to, uh, take care of Ian." She backed up a step. "I'll see you in a while."

"A while," he repeated as she turned toward the hall. "Phoebe?"

"Yes?" She looked over her shoulder.

"Want me to build a fire?"

Her laughter surprised him. "I thought you already had."

AFTER THAT, IT WAS EASY. Even Ian cooperated by yawning after she read him a story and then he'd gone uncomplainingly into his crib. When she was satisfied that he was asleep, she tiptoed into her bedroom and carefully closed the door behind her. Will sat cross-legged in front of the fireplace, rearranging logs so they would burn evenly over the flames.

"That was fast," he said, turning toward her. Phoebe walked past him to pull down the window shades against the light.

"He was up early. I think all the excitement of the past couple of days has caught up with him."

Will looked back at the fire and shook his head. "I'm not sure this is going to catch."

"Does it matter?"

"Yes." He held out his hand. "Come sit with me."

She took his hand—that now familiar, large, rough hand—and sat down beside him in front of the fire, her thigh next to his. If she wanted to, she could put her head on his shoulder. Instead, she drew her knees up and looked at the smoking kindling. "Maybe some newspaper?"

"It'll catch," he promised, taking the poker in his free hand and stabbing at the logs. Flickers of orange and yellow flames erupted from under the stacked kindling. "There," he declared. "That's better." He leaned the poker by the hearth and turned to Phoebe, taking her chin by one finger until she faced him. "We could pretend it's New Year's Eve."

"No. I'm through pretending," she told him, and his hand caressed her cheek and brushed her hair back behind her ear. She shivered when he bent to touch her earlobe with his lips. "That's going to be another New Year's resolution."

She heard him chuckle softly as he lifted his head. "Are there any others I should know about?"

"I think that about does it."

Phoebe expected the kiss, but she didn't expect to dissolve into a mindless blob because of it. She didn't expect to be in his arms and on her back and loving every second of wanting him. He took off most of her clothes and she struggled with his until they both laughed in between kisses.

"We could take our time," he said, hooking his thumb into the waistband of her bikini underwear.

"I don't think I can wait." And she couldn't, because even though she considered herself a sensible woman, there was something about this man that made her need to have him inside of her. Where he belonged.

She wasn't wrong. They wouldn't have made it to the bed if she hadn't heard him yelp when his knee hit the wood floor.

"The bed," she said, wriggling out from underneath him. "The perfect place for injured rodeo men."

"Men?"

Phoebe hurried to get under the covers. "A figure of speech."

He joined her, his body sleek and strong, stretched out next to hers. And soon he was inside of her, thank goodness. She couldn't have waited much longer.

SHE TOURED HIS BODY with gentle hands that stopped a few inches above his waist. "This?"

"Two broken ribs," he said. "At Salt Lake in '96. Or '97. I can't remember."

"This?" She ran her fingers along a ten-inch scar on his side.

"That's why I don't ride bulls anymore."

"Thank God." Phoebe bent and kissed a ridge below his abdomen.

"Sweetheart..." The touch of her mouth threatened to kill him. She dragged her lips lower.

"Tell me."

"A fall. From a horse called Bag Lady." He groaned as she dipped lower, her lips finding him. "Vegas, '89."

She lifted her head and her hair swept over him, an erotic sensation that did nothing for his self-control. "Is there any place where you haven't been hurt?"

"Well," he drawled, wishing he could stay in this bed, with her, for the rest of his life, "you'll break my heart if you don't climb on top of me right this minute."

"Flirt." But she slid over him, cradling his body between her thighs.

He reached up and smoothed her hair from her face. What was such a beautiful woman doing with a broken-down bronc rider? "How long will Ian sleep?"

"An hour. Two if he's really tired."

"So how much time do we have left?"

"How much time do you need?" She wriggled against him, which made him clench his jaw.

"Not a whole lot," he admitted. "I could embarrass myself any minute now."

Her witchy smile made him laugh. "Then I should leave you alone?"

Will wrapped his arms around her waist. "Oh, sweetheart, not unless you want to see a man in pain."

SHE TOLD NO ONE what had happened. Not Kim. Not her mother, though both had called to talk about the weather and New Year's weekend. She cleaned her house and played with Ian, and when he wanted her to read the cowboy book, she pretended she'd lost it when all the time it was hidden in his pajama drawer.

Phoebe didn't want to think about cowboys.

"You could come with me," Will had said after making love the last time, half an hour before he took the two o'clock bus north. And what had she replied?

I can't. It had been hard to think, hard to stay awake when she was so warm. She would have been content to stay in bed for the rest of her life if he was there, too, enfolding her in all of that male heat. *I can't* were the last words she remembered murmuring before she fell asleep. And when she woke, he was gone.

He had asked her...what? To come with him to the rodeo? To come with him for the rest of the season? To come with him for the rest of his life? If she'd been more awake, she could have asked what he meant. She'd give a lot to know exactly what he was asking.

And what more could she have said? Phoebe washed sheets and vacuumed rugs and polished the silver candlesticks that sat on the dining-room table. She bought groceries and cleaned out her refrigerator and sprinkled sand on the front walk. And all the time she wondered what she should have told Will. I can't because I have a son? Because I have responsibilities and a business?

Or…because I'm in love with you and scared to death that someday you'll get in your car and drive off and not come back except to be buried? Ted didn't ride broncs or have a single scar or once-broken ribs. He'd been driving home from work when a car ran a red light. Bad things happened. A man didn't need to tempt fate by jumping bareback on wild animals.

Phoebe baked another lasagna for the freezer and watched too much television and opened another bottle of French wine. She refused a dinner invitation at Kim's, promised her mother she'd think about visiting her and told Ian that his cowboy book was still lost.

And when the phone rang and Sarah Knight said, "Phoebe, I got us tickets to the rodeo. Can you come to Denver?", Phoebe wondered if she'd been given a second chance.

"I sure can," she heard herself say. "I sure can."

THE NINETY-FOURTH ANNUAL National Western Stock Show held little interest for Will Briggs. He'd skipped the parties, the bars, the poker games and the dancing. He didn't feel like talking to anyone. He just paced and waited for Friday night's bronc-riding event. And he hoped luck would be with him so a fat chunk of prize money would end up in his pocket.

He figured that might ease some of the misery of leaving Phoebe and her boy, might make it seem like it was worth it, but all along he knew nothing could make up for what he'd almost had. Oh, sure, he'd needed to go back to his life, his world, his work. And Phoebe would remain in that beautiful polished home where she so obviously belonged. What did he have to offer her? Not much. A savings account and the prospect of owning a small ranch one day. A husband with a bad knee and a good horse.

Husband. Now there was a word he never thought he'd use to describe himself. But he'd be one if he stayed because he was in love with her. What would he do there in that town, in her husband's house? He'd asked Phoebe to come with him, but he'd gotten the answer he'd expected, dammit all. And she had been right to say no.

He just hadn't known how much it would hurt to hear the words.

"I SENT A NOTE ROUND to Will, to tell him Jack and I were here," Sarah stated, leaning on Jack's arm as they went down the steps to front row seats. "I didn't tell him you and Ian would be watching, too. Won't he be surprised?"

"Well…" Phoebe wanted to turn around and run out of the building. Especially when she realized that Jack was leading them to a row of reserved seats in the front row. She hesitated, watching Jack and Sarah greet the other people there as if they were long-lost friends, and then she and Ian were introduced to a whole row of people who wore enormous diamond pinkie rings, brand-new Stetsons and name badges sporting multicolored ribbons.

"We're all old friends," Sarah whispered. "Jack's grandfather was pretty well-known in Colorado before he started ranching down in Texas." And Phoebe nodded, all the while listening to the conversation that swirled around her.

"I see." But she really didn't. She heard the men talking in terms of millions of dollars and thousands of acres.

"See the man over there in the white suit? He always gives a party when the Denver Broncos make the play-offs. I was so glad we got here in time to go to it. Would you or Ian like some ice cream?"

"No, thank you, Sarah." She was so nervous she was afraid she'd be sick. What if he wasn't happy to see them? What if the horse tossed him off and he got hurt?

Her heart was in her throat by the time Will's name was announced. He burst out of the chute on the back of a monster horse the announcer called Old Dan, an animal that seemed determined to break every bone in Will's body as it jumped and bucked and spun.

Phoebe didn't know eight seconds could last so long, but her heart resumed beating when the buzzer sounded and Will was able to jump free of the animal. She watched him dust himself off, pick up his hat and put it on his head before giving the appreciative crowd a wave. He was less than twenty feet away and yet it felt like miles because she wanted to throw herself in his arms and sob with relief.

"Cow!" Ian shouted, bouncing in his mother's lap. "Cow! Cow!"

Will froze when his gaze met hers. She saw

his eyebrows go up, questioning, waiting. And then he strode toward her while the rodeo clowns shooed the still-bucking horse through a gate. Will climbed right over the barriers and dropped into the front row. He shook Jack's hand, waved at the rest of the cattlemen and winked at Sarah before squatting down in front of Ian.

"Cow," Ian crowed. Will removed his hat and dropped it on the boy's head before turning his gaze to Phoebe.

"This is a surprise," he said, his face smudged with dirt.

"You asked me to come," she said, her knees bumping his.

"I asked you to come with me," he said. "I didn't mean just to Denver."

The crowd cheered again as another rider came out of the chute, but Phoebe didn't pay attention to anyone but the man in front of her. He put his hands on her knees to steady himself.

"I don't have much to offer, Phoebe. But everything I have is yours."

"But you wouldn't be happy in Colorado City."

Will took a deep breath. "No. I'm ready to

quit the rodeo circuit after this season, but I'd rather go into ranching than the hotel business.''

''Ian wants to be a cowboy.''

Those dark eyes held hers. ''And his mother? What does she want?''

''You.'' The eight-second buzzer sounded as he leaned forward and took her in his arms. ''Only you.''

NO ONE PAID MUCH ATTENTION to the cowboy and the dark-haired woman who held his hand. They looked like any of hundreds of couples strolling toward the parking lot, the baby in the man's arms sporting a toddler-size Stetson that matched his daddy's. The elderly couple walking slowly behind them smiled at the baby waving to them over the cowboy's shoulder.

The old man figured he would make a pretty damn good manager for all three of his cattle ranches, which had gotten awfully big for an old codger without children to manage alone. If their Johnny had lived to be a man, well, that would be different. But he'd be lucky to have that tall cowboy taking over things.

The elderly lady who clung to her husband's arm thought that the baby would make a fine grandson to spoil. And the young woman would sure know how to spruce up the old ranch house, all nineteen rooms. When she got home to Texas, she was going to start baking cookies again.

And the woman, well, the dark-haired woman only had eyes for the cowboy. Which was a good thing since he was holding on to her hand as if he never intended to release it. She didn't look like she minded. In fact, she looked content to let the cowboy take her wherever he wanted to go.

ONE-NIGHT-STAND BABY

Bobby Hutchinson

For Patricia Gibson, who asks what you need,
and then does everything in her power to supply it.
Thank you, my dear and treasured friend,
for always being there.

CHAPTER ONE

ABIGAIL MARTIN SQUINTED through the cracked windshield of her secondhand Ford and pumped the brakes frantically as the car ahead of her suddenly stopped. Abby came to a halt only inches from its back bumper.

The incident sent a rush of adrenaline through her weary body. It seemed Vancouver was planning to usher in the millennium with a record downpour, and the dark city streets were busy, slick, and treacherous.

"Only five hours and forty-five minutes left in this century," the hyped voice of the radio announcer bleated. "Y2K is almost here, are you *ready out there?*"

Y2K was the least of her concerns. Eyes on the car ahead of her, Abby fumbled for the control and turned the sound down. Her trembling hand brushed the bulky drugstore bag containing diapers, wipes, sanitary supplies and a prescription the pediatrician hoped might ease Robert's colic.

She was exhausted, worn out from lack of sleep, and he must be too, poor sweet baby.

For the entire three weeks of his life, her son had cried. The sound of his plaintive voice echoed in her ears, even though he wasn't in the car seat behind her. She'd left him at home with her sister.

It was the first time Abby had been separated from him, and even though she knew it was ridiculous—she'd been gone not more than forty-five minutes—still she felt anxious, almost desperate to get back to him. Faye, even though her intentions were the best, wasn't very good with babies.

"For cripes' sake, Abby, will you just go to the damned drugstore and leave me here with him? I know I'm not Mother Teresa, but surely I can take care of my own rotten nephew for an hour," Faye had stormed at her, bouncing a wailing Robert on her shoulder in a way that made Abby long to snatch him back. "You need a break—you haven't been out of this place in days. I still say you should find a baby-sitter who'll take him for a few hours so you can sleep. I know you need stuff, but I really don't feel like driving back across town to find the only drugstore that's open. I'm sick of battling traffic—it's a zoo out there, where the hell is everyone going in the *afternoon?* New Year's isn't happening for hours yet.''

Still, Abby had hesitated. ''There's breast milk in a little bottle in the fridge—warm it up before you give it to him...''

''Would you just *go,* already? I'll feed him the bottle, anything to shut him up for a while, but I'm also gonna make the cup of tea I came here for and call Harry—he's probably frantic by now wondering where the hell I am—I said I'd be home hours ago. I never dreamed it would take three hours to have a facial. A person could die of old age trying to look younger.''

Abby smiled and shook her head, thinking of her sister. Faye was four years older than Abby, which made her thirty-five now. Their mother had always said the two were as different as night and day. Faye, aggressive and outgoing, had always been Abby's fierce and loyal protector. Unlike herself, Faye was never at a loss for words, which meant she was ideally suited for her career in law.

Abby had chosen psychiatric nursing, a profession that Faye found inconceivable.

"I work with nutcases too, but at least I get paid royally for it and there's usually no feces involved, unless it's metaphorical," she stated.

Faye was honest to a point that sometimes made Abby cringe. For instance, her sister had told Harry Weaver before they were married, in Abby's presence, that she hated cooking, didn't want kids and couldn't stand decorating. If those things were important to him, he had the wrong sister; Abby was the one he should marry. Besides, Faye had added with a wink, anyone with eyes could see that Abby was the pretty one.

But unassuming Harry loved Faye just as she was, and as far as Abby could tell, it was a good marriage.

But then, what did she know about marriage? The only man she'd ever believed she loved had hurt her so deeply she'd thought she would die of the pain. And she couldn't seem to put him out of her mind, mostly because she had a beautiful little boy who looked just like him.

The red light at the next intersection turned green just as Abby reached it. She stepped on the gas, aware that her breasts had the familiar ache that meant it was time to feed Robert. Underneath her jacket she could feel her milk soaking the front of her blouse.

A sudden blur of lights to her left made her turn her head sharply, but her brain had no time to register the fact that a truck was about to hit her.

The impact was thunderous. She was aware of glass shattering and fireworks exploding in her brain. Pain burst inside of her. Somewhere a horn was stuck and the monotonous sound seemed to guide her down a long chute and into blessed darkness.

"WELL, WHERE'S MS. SHWARTZ?" Dr. Conrad Banfield, head of the psychiatric unit at St. Joseph's Hospital, tapped his umbrella impatiently against his leg, realizing too late that it was soaking his pants. Conrad scowled and slammed the thing down on the ER admissions desk. Raindrops sprayed in all directions, and a nurse making entries on the computer jumped.

"Couldn't the psych resident handle this?" Conrad removed his tinted glasses, pulled a pristine handkerchief from his pocket and polished the lenses. "I don't appreciate being called out at this hour on New Year's Eve. I'm quite sure it could have waited until morning," he snapped at Leslie Yates, the triage nurse, as he put his glasses back on.

"And a Happy New Year to you too, Iceman." The sotto-voce comment came from behind him, but when Conrad turned the person responsible was already hurrying away, and all he could identify was a shapely green-clad backside, obviously feminine, pushing a patient in a wheelchair.

He knew most of the nurses called him the Iceman. The moniker had stung at first, but then he'd reasoned that it could also be interpreted as a compliment, referring to his greatest strengths: his ability to deal with every situation from a cool, rational, intellectually sound premise. Those same attributes, he reminded himself, had helped him become the head of the Department of Psychiatrists at St. Joe's at the age of only thirty-eight.

He turned back to Leslie, and she answered him in a level tone. "As you know, Doctor, we need two signatures to certify Ms. Shwartz is hypomanic. She's in Room 3, we've used restraints. Dr. Murdoch and the police are with her," Yates related. "They picked her up in Gastown, nude and climbing on car roofs. She refuses to stay willingly. And you *are* on call tonight, Doctor," she concluded with a bright, phony smile.

Conrad turned on his heel and marched toward the examining room she'd indicated. A glance at his wrist confirmed that it was twenty minutes to twelve, twenty minutes before the much-touted Millennium dawned, and it was obvious the hysteria associated with the turning of the century was causing problems. The ER was bedlam tonight, the waiting area full, the treatment rooms all in use, the staff racing from one area to the next. The only indication that it was New Year's Eve were the balloons tied to an IV pole by the nursing station.

Conrad knew, however, that a hospital staff party was going on at that moment upstairs in the staff lounge. He'd received a personal invitation to the party, but he certainly hadn't for one moment considered attending. He'd told the chairperson of the social committee exactly that, which was how he came to be on call New Year's Eve.

He didn't agree with social events being incorporated into the hospital routine and he'd been vocal about his feelings. It was both distracting and unprofessional.

"So you won't mind being on call that night, Doctor? I'll notify scheduling," the wily secretary had chirped, and too late, he'd realized he'd been tricked.

He didn't like to admit, even to himself, that the real reason he disliked social events so intensely was because they made him uncomfortable. He'd never mastered the art of nonsensical conversation.

Inside the treatment room, it took him less than five minutes to confirm that Ms. Shwartz, a bipolar patient of his, needed to be admitted. Normally a quiet high school teacher, she was at this moment doing her best to verbally seduce the Psych resident in between screaming obscenities at the two RCMP constables who'd brought her in.

She quieted a little when Conrad came in, giving him flirtatious looks and insisting that she wasn't off her meds, then begging him not to lock her up.

Conrad spoke with her gently, taking his time, assuring her that in his opinion she needed to stay in hospital, promising that he'd be in to see her soon. He completed the second pink certificate and wrote medication orders for her.

"Well, if I have to stay, at least I have the hottest looking doc in the place," Ms. Shwartz babbled to the nurse. "He's single, too, which doesn't say much for you stupid cows. What's wrong with you, don't you have eyes in your head?''

The nurse carefully avoided glancing at Conrad, and he sighed with relief as the police officers and an orderly escorted Shwartz upstairs to Psychiatry.

He was reclaiming his umbrella from behind the nursing station when a sharp increase in the noise level in Emerg told him many of the revelers had decided to greet the year 2000 among their co-workers.

"Happy New Year, Dr. Banfield." Leslie Yates, smiling cheerfully, came hurrying over to him. "There's a woman waiting to speak to you, her name's Faye Weaver. Her sister was in a car crash a couple hours ago. She's over there."

Conrad felt a slight twinge of alarm. "What does she want with me?"

Yates shrugged. "You got me. Maybe she needs a consultation."

Conrad waited, more irritated that ever at this new delay. He wanted nothing more than to drive back to his house and maybe catch the ending of the television program he'd been watching.

"Dr. Banfield?" She was carrying a plastic

baby contraption with handles, and the blanket-wrapped bundle inside was crying. She was blonde, only a few inches shorter than his six feet, with broad shoulders and features that were strong rather than attractive. She was dressed casually in slacks and a blue sweater. As she came close to him, Conrad could see mascara smeared under both eyes in raccoonlike circles. It was obvious she'd been crying.

He was certain he'd never seen her before. She had a cherry-red raincoat over one arm, and a large quilted diaper bag was looped over her shoulder.

"You *are* Conrad Banfield, chief of psychiatry here at St. Joseph's?" She had a loud and aggressive voice, and she raised it considerably to be heard over the baby's wails. Conrad realized that several staff members were glancing at them, hovering within earshot, and he cleared his throat uncomfortably.

"I am Dr. Banfield, yes," he confirmed in the quiet steady tone he used to calm disturbed patients. "How may I help you, Ms., umm, Weaver?" He was impatient, although he did his best to conceal it. What could this woman possibly want with him?

"Do you have ID, Doctor?"

"That's ridiculous." He scowled at her, to no avail.

"I need to see some ID." She was getting louder, and she was very insistent. He hated scenes. Other nurses were openly watching now, as was an intern. The noise from the crowd of parties was increasing.

Conrad decided to humor her. He sighed and reached in his pocket, pulling out his wallet, flipping it open to reveal his driver's license.

She studied it carefully and then nodded. "Okay, so that's settled. Here you go."

Before he realized what she was about to do, she'd shoved the baby carrier at him.

Conrad stepped back quickly, and she set the thing on the floor directly in front of him.

"What…what exactly do you think you're doing?" In the background through his shock, he heard the crowd begin to count down.

"Meet your son, Dr. Banfield. He's three weeks old," she pronounced in a steely tone and then paused as the revellers reached a crescendo with One! The woman smiled with grim satisfaction. "Happy New Year. As of right now you're responsible for the baby. His mother is my sister, Abigail Martin. I assume you do remember that name?"

Shock almost overwhelmed him. He could feel his face turning crimson, and he felt rooted to the spot.

"Rings a bell, huh?" Her voice dripped with sarcasm that quickly gave way to emotion when she added in a trembling voice, "Not that you give a tinker's damn, but Abby's upstairs in the operating room. Nobody's sure if she's even going to live, her car was totaled by some damn drunk. Thank God the kid was home with me. But I can't keep him. I'm a lawyer—I have a trial. And he *is* your son, like it or not, so you're responsible for his care—there's nobody else. Poor little sprout, to have a father like you." Her eyes blazed at him through a sheen of tears, telegraphing her disgust and outrage. "I told Abby she oughta let me take you to court, nail you to the wall good and proper. And that's exactly what I'll do now if you refuse to take care of your own son. I'll have your DNA tested, I'll drag this case through the press, I'll crucify you and your precious reputation here. You can scream vasectomy till hell freezes over, but if Abby says you're her baby's father, you are, and DNA will prove it. My sister doesn't lie. It would give me a real kick to take you to court, Doctor."

CHAPTER TWO

HER SHOCKING WORDS were like bullets, penetrating the shield he usually maintained around himself.

Conrad felt paralyzed. He stood like a stone with the squalling baby at his feet as images he thought he'd erased tumbled one over another inside his head, all in an instant.

The softness of Abby's body beneath his on that single fateful night, the sense of oneness he'd experienced when he made love to her, unlike anything he'd ever felt before, the laughter they'd shared.

The expression on her face weeks later when he told her the truth, that her pregnancy could have nothing to do with him.

How could it? As this woman had just announced at the top of her lungs, Conrad had undergone a vasectomy to prevent this very situation.

And now Abby was in surgery? Suddenly he couldn't seem to draw in a satisfactory breath.

The strident voice was still going on. "His name's Robert Martin-Banfield, I told Abby she was crazy to give him even so much as your name, but she insisted. Here's his stuff." She dumped the diaper bag on the floor beside the baby and pulled a small bottle of milk out of her purse.

"She's nursing him, this is..." Her voice broke and her face crumbled for an instant. "This is her milk. I guess you're gonna have to get some formula for him, she's in no shape to feed him. If she makes it through surgery."

She set the bottle on top of the bag and turned on her heel, hurrying off in the direction of the elevators.

Conrad made a move to follow her, and stumbled over the diaper bag. He staggered, off balance, taking two giant steps as he instinctively tried to avoid the seat holding the baby, whose monotonous cries had now become agitated shrieks.

"Careful there, Doctor." A nurse made a move to steady him and he jerked away, mortified when he realized that at least half a dozen staff members were openly staring. They'd just heard intimate details about his personal life. It was his worst nightmare come true.

"Take...this...child." He lifted the carrier and tried to hand it to the nurse, but she had quick reflexes. She moved out of arm's reach, shaking her head.

"Sorry, Doctor, we have a multiple MVA arriving, gotta run."

Bodies moved quickly away, and suddenly Conrad was an island with nothing but empty space surrounding him and the crying baby.

Calm down, Banfield. There's a solution here, you just need to think it through in a rational manner.

The hospital nursery, of course. He'd take the baby up there. Relief flooded through him as he shoved the nursing bottle in the diaper bag, shouldered it, and took a firm hold on the baby carrier.

He headed for the elevators. He had to check the directory to find Obstetrics; he'd never been on that floor. The baby was becoming even more agitated, and by the time the elevator stopped, Conrad was sweating. What happened if a baby cried too long? Could it choke? What was the clinical procedure for resuscitation for something this small? He'd been a psychiatrist for ten years; he couldn't remember details like that from his intern days.

He almost raced along the corridor to the nursing station. There was no one behind the desk. Here, too, it looked as if a major emergency was in progress. Nurses and doctors were hurrying to and fro, carts loaded with supplies stood everywhere, chilling screams escaped as doors opened and closed, and men with desperate eyes and haphazard clothing walked slowly up and down beside big-bellied women who stopped every so often to lean against the wall and made frightening noises.

Conrad remembered his brief, nightmarish stint in OB during internship and felt nauseous. He hammered on the bell at the desk, and at long last a harried nurse appeared, her green scrubs liberally stained with bodily fluids.

"I'm Dr. Banfield from Psychiatry," he explained rapidly. "A woman just left this baby with me, the mother's been in a car crash and there's no one to care for it so I'm leaving it here with you. The mother's name is Abigail Martin—she's presently in the O.R." He held the bundle out to her.

"Oh, no you don't, Doctor." The nurse was shaking her head before he finished speaking.

"Absolutely not. This isn't even the nursery, that's over in the east wing in Maternity, but I assure you they won't take that baby either—the only babies there are our newborns. And the Children's Ward only admits patients, so don't even bother going up there. You'd best contact social services, they'll know what to do. It's bedlam around here. Every woman in Vancouver wanted to have the Millennium baby. They're popping 'em out like gumballs tonight. The city must have been on fire last April with all the coupling going on."

Another nurse came racing past. "Maisie, Mrs. Littlejohn's crowning."

"Be right there."

"Stop!" Conrad was feeling frantic again. "Please, surely you could at least keep it overnight? It's New Year's Eve, it's unlikely anyone is available at social services." He thought of the explanations that would be necessary if a social worker became involved. He'd have to spell out what had prompted that woman to give him the baby in the first place. Everything in him shrank at the thought.

Maisie shrugged. It wasn't her problem. "There'll certainly be someone available in the morning, Dr. Banfield."

"But I'm a bachelor, for God's sake, I can't take care of a baby overnight. It's preposterous."

The nurse grinned. "It's amazing what we can do if we put our minds to it, Doctor. Now, if you'll excuse me."

Conrad considered sneaking along the hall to Maternity, putting the baby down on the first available surface and making a run for it, but he'd already revealed who he was to Maisie—she'd remember his name.

His sense of panic began to escalate. They'd track him down, and because of that Weaver woman the publicity would be horrendous. He knew how the tabloids worked—he'd be accused of abandoning his child, and even when he proved otherwise no one would believe him. The publicity would damage his career.

And besides all that, this was Abby's baby, a nagging voice kept reminding him. Abby, who at this moment was undergoing who knew what at the hands of the surgeons.

He had no relatives to call on. He certainly had no friends who'd take a baby at midnight on New Year's Eve. There was nothing to do except keep it. His stomach sank as quickly as the elevator descended to the parking level.

He opened the door of his two-seater sports car and tried to figure out the complexities of attaching the baby seat to the seat belt. He finally got the thing anchored, getting more anxious with every passing moment. The baby was still screaming, wrinkled face scarlet, wrappings loose now so that two tiny legs protruded, covered in yellow terry cloth and kicking frenetically.

Maybe it was cold. He turned on the heater. And how long had it been since it ate? Babies had very small digestive systems. He fumbled in the diaper bag for the bottle of milk and put it into the wide-open mouth. It took a moment, but the crying stopped and the baby sucked hard, gulping the milk so fast it choked, turning purple and struggling for breath.

Conrad frantically undid the straps and grabbed the child in his arms, tipping it forward, patting the tiny back. The choking stopped. The baby gasped for air, and then the crying began again, outraged now, and the sound was an enormous relief.

Trembling, Conrad held it on his lap at a forty-five-degree angle and stuck the nipple in its mouth again. Gulp, swallow, thresh, choke, scream. By the time the bottle was half-empty,

Conrad was sweating profusely. He felt as if he'd been in the parking garage for more than half his life. At one point the baby stopped screaming, turned bright red in the face, and strained hard, and an unmistakable noise erupted from its bottom end, amazingly loud and prolonged for one so small.

After that the small limbs relaxed and the eyes closed. The sucking continued sporadically until the bottle was almost empty. Conrad eased it away and cautiously put the baby back in the carrier. This time it slept, slumped into a tiny ball.

Conrad strapped it in and drove out of the parking garage, wondering how long it would be before the baby needed to eat again. He felt panicked at the thought of the crying starting all over again and remembered the instructions about formula. There was an all-night drugstore a few blocks away.

He parked in front and considered leaving the baby in the car, but reluctantly decided it was a bad idea. He undid the seat, doing his clumsy best to get the sleeping baby and the blue shawl integrated, then hurried through the downpour into the drugstore.

There was a daunting array of choices when

it came to baby formula. With the help of a sleepy female clerk, Conrad settled on one type and bought ten cans. That ought to get him through till morning.

"You okay for diapers?"

Damn. He remembered the sound effects and realized he was going to have to deal with the results. Were there diapers in the diaper bag?

The clerk glanced at the blue-swathed lump in the carrier and smiled. "Newborn size, of course. Boy or girl?"

He had no idea it made a difference. "Boy."

"How old?"

"Three weeks." He was surprised that he'd remembered.

"You need wipes?"

"Wipes. Yes, I suppose so." He had no idea what they were, but they sounded necessary.

"You haven't done this much yet, huh?" She found the proper packages and rang up his purchases. "Where's your wife?"

"My wife?" The concept was totally foreign and he stared at her blankly. He wasn't accustomed to having conversations with clerks.

"Yeah. The baby's mother?" Now she was giving him a narrow-eyed suspicious look.

"The baby's mother. Oh, yes. Abby." Again

he had that peculiar sensation, the feeling that he couldn't draw a deep breath. "She's in hospital. She was in a car accident," he blurted.

"Oh, that's just awful. I'm so sorry." Sympathy and concern replaced suspicion. "You take care, now," she called as he wrestled baby carrier and packages out of the store.

As soon as he had everything stowed in the car, he snapped open his cell phone and dialed the hospital, identifying himself and demanding to be put through to the surgical ward.

"Ms. Martin is now in Recovery. She came through the surgery very well, Dr. Banfield. If you hold on, I can find Dr. Haskell."

After a wait, Haskell came on the line and cheerfully explained that Abby had suffered a head injury but her skull had fortunately not been fractured. Due to blunt abdominal trauma, namely the steering wheel, she'd fractured several ribs and ruptured her spleen, so Haskell had removed it. Although she'd been in a life-threatening situation when she was brought in, the surgery had corrected the problem, and Haskell felt she was no longer in danger.

Conrad slumped back against the seat and intense relief spilled through him, warming the icy fear that had wrapped like tentacles around his heart. Abby was going to live. Conrad whispered thank you to a God he hadn't prayed to in years.

Halfway home, the baby woke and began crying again. Conrad pulled into his driveway and managed somehow to get packages, diaper bag and howling baby inside the house.

He parked the carrier on the kitchen table, shucked off his raincoat and sports jacket, and after reading the directions on one of the cans of formula, sloshed some in the feeding bottle.

But this time the baby refused it. After repeated attempts, Conrad faced the fact that milk wasn't going to do it this time. He'd have to resort to the diapers.

Ripping open the package, he wrestled the baby out of the carrier and with great difficulty undid the minute clothing and then stared in disbelieving horror at the mess he'd revealed. A greenish yellow mess was smeared all over the baby's clothing and toothpick legs, and now dripped onto the blue shawl. A small foot kicked, smearing Conrad's shirtsleeve.

With an exclamation of horror, he tore the lid from the plastic container of wipes and balled up a handful, but the baby still had several layers of clothing on. By the time he'd figured out the complexities of a sort of union suit beneath the pajamas and then deciphered the Velcro diaper fasteners, the mess had spread.

"Stop kicking," Conrad ordered, but the baby paid no attention. "Please," he heard himself begging as the disaster worsened and his gag reflex kicked in. He finally got the union suit loosened and the diaper off.

Naked, the baby's arms flew up and its cry changed to one of terror. Its body was unbelievably small and fragile. Terrified himself, Conrad tried to hurry, concentrating on cleaning the bottom end, and it was only when he managed at last to secure a diaper that he turned his attention to the top portion of the soiled union suit.

Twenty-three agonizing minutes later, the baby was clean and dressed, wearing fresh pajamas found by tipping the contents of the entire diaper bag on the floor.

Also on the floor were Conrad's trousers, shirt and shoes, along with every stitch the baby had been wearing, as well as the remains of two diapers whose tabs had fallen off, more than half the box of wipes and several dish towels he'd snatched up in desperation.

A glance at the clock confirmed that it was now two full hours into the Millennium. The previously spotless kitchen was a shambles,

Conrad was naked except for navy boxer shorts and an undershirt, and the baby was still crying.

Conrad was in a state of shock. He leaned his hands on the table on either side of the howling baby and stared down into the crumbled, angry little face, studying the ears that lay flat against the well-shaped skull, noting the unusual way the ear curved in on itself along the back rim.

His ears were flat to his skull, curved exactly like that.

It had to be a coincidence, nothing more, but his heart was hammering all the same.

The baby had long dark hair, and it grew in a double swirl at the crown of the head.

Conrad too, had a complicated double crown. Barbers always commented on it.

There was an upward slant to the barely discernable eyebrows. The tiny chin had a definite cleft.

He had a cleft exactly like that. His eyebrows tilted up at the outer edges.

This baby looked like him. He turned the boy over, the entire body nearly small enough to cup in one hand. He touched with a fingertip the deep indentation at the back of the neck. At last he took one tiny fist in his own and uncurled it, studying the extraordinarily long fingers, the minute fingernails, and when he released it, Conrad studied his own hand, admitting that there was a definite similarity in shape. His fingers, too, were unusually long. In spite of his own skepticism, physical evidence had to be considered. One characteristic, even two, might possibly be coincidence, but there were more than one or two. Even the long, narrow shape of the baby's head was his in miniature.

He felt short of breath, dizzy. He'd give anything to believe otherwise, but his scientific training was too deeply ingrained. It forced upon his mind the only possible conclusion.

Vasectomy or no vasectomy, Robert Martin-Banfield was Conrad's son.

He gulped and groped for a chair. Here, threshing and protesting at the top of his Lilliputian lungs was the one thing in all the world that Conrad had vowed he would never produce…a child with his genes.

He remembered now that after the vasectomy the surgeon had told him to come back after three months for a test, to confirm that the procedure had been successful. Conrad had forgotten to go for the test.

He remembered as well the terrible confrontation with Abby when she'd insisted her pregnancy was the result of the one night they'd spent together. She'd cried and screamed at him, and he'd lost his temper and said things he was ashamed of afterward, although he'd never quite admitted that to himself until now.

"You *are* my son," he whispered to the baby. He cleared the lump in his throat, tried the words in a louder voice. "You're my son."

Was it only his imagination, or did Robert Martin-Banfield look up at him and then scream louder than ever?

CHAPTER THREE

"Ms. MARTIN, CAN you hear me? Abby, it's
time for you to wake up now. Your surgery's
over, everything went well, you're in recovery,
wake up now. Abby?"

Cold. Icy cold. And with awareness came terrible pain, shocking and all encompassing. Several times, Abby slid back into the darkness
rather than bear it, but some nagging part of her
brain insisted she needed to surface, needed to
ask....

"Ms. Martin, can you answer me? Abby,
open your eyes."

The disembodied voice kept nagging at her,
asking her questions, demanding answers. It
wasn't quiet where she was—people were talking, there was activity. At last, with an incredible
effort of will, Abby forced her eyes to open and
stay open.

"Abby, hello there." Someone in a green

scrub suit smiled down at her. "Your surgery went very well—you're in Recovery."

Surgery?

"Hurts. Side...hurts." She fought against the pain, struggling to stay above the darkness. There was something she needed to ask, something urgent...

"You fractured several ribs and ruptured your spleen. The surgeon removed it—that's what's causing the pain. We'll give you something for it. You hit your head as well, nothing serious, but you're probably going to have a granddaddy of a headache. Do you remember the accident?"

Exploding glass, a car horn...panic seized her.

"My...baby. Where's...my...baby?"

"He wasn't in the car, Ms. Martin. You were alone. Your sister's here, I'll let you speak to her for a moment."

Abby fought hard against the darkness and the confusion in her brain.

"Abby?" Faye's voice and form shimmered in and out. "Abby, oh, honey, thank God you're okay. You're gonna be fine. I talked to the surgeon, he said you're gonna be fine, it'll just take time."

Faye was crying. Faye never cried. Abby got scared.

"Robert?"

"He's okay, he's being well taken care of. Don't you worry about a single thing, it's all under control. All you have to do is rest and get well."

"I need…to nurse…Robert."

"Sure you do, but not right now, sweetie. It's the middle of the night, you've had anaesthetic. We'll figure all that out tomorrow. Right now you just rest and don't worry about a thing. Robert's fine. I'll be here early tomorrow morning and we'll figure everything out then, okay, Abby?"

There was something Faye wasn't saying, but the struggle to stay on the surface was too enormous. Abby gave in and the darkness was there, waiting.

ALL THROUGH THE endless night, Conrad tried everything he could think of to stop the baby's crying—another bottle of milk, another bout of diapers, music, conversation. He even tried crooning a western ballad. He wrapped Robert in a soft terry bath sheet in case he was cold. He took it off in case he was warm. He jiggled him up and down in his arms and walked fast through all the rooms of the house. Nothing worked.

For the first time in years, Conrad found himself wishing desperately he had relatives, close friends, someone—anyone—whom he could phone for advice and support. But he'd chosen a reclusive lifestyle.

His mother, with whom he'd never had a close relationship, had died when he was twenty-three. He'd grown up an only child as his sister drowned when he was eight. He'd never developed the knack of making friends; until this moment, he'd felt it unnecessary, a disruption in the careful orderliness of his life.

During the long predawn hours, he had to use every technique he'd ever used on patients in order to stay calm as the incessant wailing went on and on, and by four-twenty he was desperate enough to call the hospital. He didn't identify himself. The call was routed to the ER, and one of the interns came on the line.

"Sounds like colic to me," he said in a weary voice after Conrad had explained the baby's behavior. "It's not a serious condition, colicky babies usually thrive very well, but they can wear you down. There's several things you can try, but basically it's a matter of the baby's digestive system maturing. Colic seldom persists after six weeks.''

''What can I do *right* now?'' Conrad's patience was hanging by a narrow thread.

''Make sure you burp him thoroughly after he eats, for starters.''

''Burp him?''

''Hold him over your shoulder and gently pat his back to help him release gas,'' the intern instructed in a tone that indicated he thought he was dealing with an imbecile. ''If he's bottle-fed, you could also try changing the kind of formula—some babies are allergic to dairy-based formula and do better on soy. And make sure you're not giving him formula that's too cold or too warm. Test it on your wrist, it oughta be body temperature.''

Conrad scribbled notes on a pad he kept by the phone.

''Isn't there any medication?''

''We try to avoid medicating. You'd have to check with your pediatrician on that.''

Robert was in the carrier on the kitchen table, thrashing his arms and legs and screaming. Conrad hung up and warmed the formula, tested its temperature on his wrist and finally the baby gulped it down. Then Conrad picked him up and held him over his shoulder, patting his back, astounded at the ferocity and frequency of the burps that erupted.

At five-thirty, after yet another diaper change and more formula, Robert sighed, closed his eyes, and went limp.

Conrad pressed a trembling finger to the baby's throat, searching for a pulse, certain he was dying. When he knew for certain the baby was just asleep, he put the carrier on the floor beside the sofa, wrapped the bath sheet snugly around baby and chair, found himself a blanket, fell down on the cushions and went instantly to sleep.

At six-fifteen, the phone rang. Conrad didn't stir. It rang again at seven, and he heard it from far away and let it ring. It rang again at seven-forty-five. This time Conrad became dimly aware that the baby was fussing.

Incensed, he staggered to his feet, snatched up the receiver, and bellowed into it, "You woke the baby, you bloody idiot."

"Tough."

Conrad immediately recognized the brassy female voice. It was Abby's sister. His heart sank.

"It's about time you answered," she went on before he could say another word. "You're gonna take Robert to the hospital this morning so that Abby can see him. She's been asking for him ever since she came to after the operation, and the nurse phoned me because she's getting herself in a state, so the sooner you get there the better. She's nursing him, she insists she's gonna go on doing it. I dunno what the doctors will say, but she's pretty stubborn when she sets her mind on something. And whatever's gonna help her get better is my main priority, so if that means breast-feeding her kid every five minutes, then that's what we're gonna arrange. So get up and get moving, Doctor.'' Her voice dropped an octave. "And so help me, if I get any inkling that you've been anything but supportive to her or nurturing to Robert, you'll answer to me and a judge.''

"Don't you threaten me.'' Conrad had had too little sleep and too much of this woman's attitude. "Don't you think for one second that your attempts at intimidation have the slightest effect on me. I intend to do whatever it takes to help Abigail, but I'd advise you to stay out of my way.'' He slammed the receiver down and felt victorious for all of three seconds. He still had the baby to cope with when all he wanted to do was fall into bed and sleep for eight more hours.

Robert complained intermittently as Conrad tried to feed him, diaper him, burp him, and somehow get showered and shaved and dressed himself. The constant noise on top of his lack of sleep was nerve wracking. It took an hour and a half to get them both cleaned and into the car, and thanks to some miracle, the baby fell asleep as soon as the car began to move.

It gave Conrad time to think, and by the time he reached the hospital, he'd made up his mind that Abby would have to find someone else to care for the baby. After all, he had a responsible position, patients to attend to; he was due at work at nine the following morning.

Of course, alternate arrangements would simply be made, he assured himself as he made his way up to the Intensive Care unit. It was inconceivable that he, Dr. Conrad Banfield, appear on the Psychiatric Ward with a baby. There had to be a workable solution.

But his first view of Abigail sent all other concerns out of his mind. The bruised, bandaged, fragile woman lying helplessly in the hospital bed, connected to IV lines and monitors, barely resembled the woman indelibly imprinted on his mind. He pictured a quietly vibrant, lovely woman with the wide, crooked smile, the rich mane of chestnut hair, the sparkling coffee-colored eyes.

"Hello, Abby."

She turned her head slightly toward him. One of her eyes was swollen shut, and she had a huge bruise on her temple. Squinting at him, she saw the baby carrier.

"Con...rad? What...what are you...doing here?"

"I brought the baby." His throat was constricted, and he longed to touch her. "Your sister gave him to me last night, after...while you were in surgery."

Disbelief was evident on her face, and then she made a soft, whimpering sound in her throat. Her thick, soft shoulder-length hair was matted with blood, stuck to her skull in places. Her delicate features were swollen grotesquely and it was evident that every slightest movement must be excruciating.

"You...have...my...baby?"

"Your sister brought him to me last night," he repeated. Suddenly, it became imperative that he reassure her. "Abigail, the vasectomy...

there's a possibility that maybe it didn't work.''

Too late, he realized that she'd known long before now, and he felt his skin burn with embarrassment, with shame for the accusations he'd made.

CHAPTER FOUR

ABBY WASN'T PAYING attention to his words
anyway.

"Faye…gave my baby…to *you?*" There was
disbelief and anguish in her tone. "How *could*
she…do that?"

It was the question Conrad had asked himself
most of the night, but now he felt defensive.

"I took good care of him, Abby, the best I
could. He cried a lot, but I fed him. He's not
hungry, look, he's sleeping now." He held the
carrier up for her to see.

"I don't…want you…to have him." Tears
were trickling down her cheeks. "When I told
you…you denied him." Her weak voice wa-
vered, her chin trembled, and he felt terrible.

He mustn't upset her further. He lifted up the
carrier and set it on the bed. "Your sister said
you wanted to feed him. Should I get a nurse?"

"Can't…until the anaesthetic…is out…of my
body."

"Of course. Your sister told me that this morning. I forgot."

"Could you...take him out of there, so I can hold him?" The longing she felt for her baby was evident in her voice.

Conrad hurried to do her bidding, carefully laying the sleeping baby in the crook of her arm, on her uninjured side.

Abby gazed at her son, tears pouring down her cheeks. "Did you...give him formula?"

Conrad nodded.

"What kind?"

He told her, adding in an apologetic tone, "He cried most of the night, maybe it was the wrong kind."

"He...has colic." For some reason, that admission brought on another flood of tears, and all Conrad could do was dab helplessly at her cheeks with tissues from the box on the bedside table. In the midst of that, a buxom nurse bustled in.

"What's going on here?" She scowled at Conrad. "Why is she crying? You take that baby and go now. I'm going to give her an injection and it'll make her sleep."

She turned her attention to Abby, gently scolding her. "You're not in any shape to care for your baby yet, Ms. Martin, but if you rest today, you'll find by tomorrow you'll be much stronger.''

''I...want to...nurse him,'' Abby sobbed.

''You can, but not until tomorrow. Daddy will bring baby to you tomorrow morning, isn't that right?'' The nurse gave Conrad a meaningful look, and he glared at her and then, as Abby's sobs continued, heard himself meekly agree.

''Six, he needs to eat...at six,'' Abby insisted, and again Conrad agreed. Desperate to be out of there, he stuffed Robert into the carrier. He was in the car again when he realized that he hadn't even brought up the matter of alternate care for the baby.

Well, there must be nurseries, day-care centers, any number of places where he could drop the baby. But today was New Year's Day, he remembered, and none of them would be open. And he'd promised to bring Abby the baby before dawn tomorrow. Conrad groaned.

Robert opened his eyes, stretched, and gazed around for a moment. Then, as usual, he began to cry.

The rest of the day and the endless night to come stretched ahead of Conrad like a glimpse into purgatory.

IT WAS TWENTY-FIVE past seven the following morning when Conrad finally arrived at the hospital. Then it took fifteen minutes with Robert screaming desperately the entire time, to locate Abby; she'd been moved the evening before from Intensive Care down to Orthopedics on four.

"She's in a state—she's been waiting for this baby since five a.m. I called you several times," the birdlike nurse at the desk snapped at him. "What did you do, Doctor, disconnect your telephone?"

That's exactly what he'd done. Robert had screamed steadily from five in the afternoon until four-thirty in the morning, and when he finally fell asleep Conrad had, in a frenzy, pulled every phone jack out of the wall. He remembered Faye and her persistent calls the previous morning.

You won't do that to me a second time, he vowed.

Then he'd tumbled into bed for three measly hours, until the baby woke him again. He hadn't had time to do more than grab a cup of instant coffee and splash his face with cold water. Diapering, washing, dressing and trying to give

Robert enough milk to shut him up until he could get him to Abby had taken forever.

Conrad felt as if he was struggling through a fog. He hadn't been this sleep deprived since he was an intern, and his temper was hanging by a thread.

"I'm leaving the baby here with Abby, I have rounds at eight," he snapped at the nurse.

Her eyes narrowed. "The moment this child is done nursing, doctor, we will page you. If you don't reply immediately, one of the aides will bring the baby up to Psychiatry. This is a medical ward, not a baby-sitting agency. Is that understood?"

Conrad wanted to lacerate her with his tongue. He wanted to reduce her to a quivering heap, the way he'd done routinely in the past with nurses on his own ward who dared to challenge his orders.

But he had no jurisdiction here. And Abby was at the mercy of this sharp-tongued crow, he reminded himself. He choked back a retort, shoved the baby carrier into her hands, and turned to head up to Psychiatry.

"Just one moment, doctor." Her tone was imperious. "I expect you to deliver this baby to its mother to nurse at an interval of every three hours today,'' the nurse ordered.

Every three hours? He'd spend his entire day ferrying Robert from Psychiatry on the tenth floor down here to the fourth. He ground his teeth and growled that he'd try.

"Trying is not good enough. The mother says this baby has colic. In my opinion, absolutely regular feeding will solve that problem.''

Conrad opened his mouth to contradict her, to sarcastically ask where she'd gotten that idea; at midnight last night, with Robert screaming on his shoulder, Conrad had looked up colic on the Internet and found at least twenty solutions, which meant that there wasn't any one certain answer.

But again, he held his tongue. A glance at his wristwatch told him he was already twelve minutes late for rounds, which horrified him. In ten years, he'd never been late once, a statistic he used to his advantage whenever he was up-braiding any of his staff for tardiness, which seemed a daily occurrence.

By the time the elevator reached ten, he was fifteen minutes late, fuming mad and feeling defensive.

"Happy New Year, Dr. Banfield.'' His plump

young secretary, Bunny Kowalski, had changed her hair color again over the holidays; her short spikes were now a florescent orange. And the skirt she was wearing barely cleared her crotch. He could swear she did such things just to annoy him.

"So what d'ya think of the Millennium?"

He thought looking after the baby was a bad way to begin, but he wasn't about to tell Bunny that. She was the latest in a long parade of secretaries, and she was lasting longer than most; she'd been with him almost a year. She had a bold attitude and a quick mouth that irked him, but she never cried when he upbraided her, and try as he might, he couldn't really fault her work; apart from sometimes being slow at updating files, she was efficient.

"You're sixteen minutes late, Doctor," she said in a smug tone. "The staff's waiting for you in the conference room." She seemed to be studying him intently, and with a sense of unease he wondered if his hair was standing on end, or he had something on his face. But that was impossible; he hadn't had any breakfast.

"I was detained in traffic." Conrad gave her a filthy look and smoothed a hand over his head as he hurried into the regular morning meeting.

He thought he heard her giggle behind his back, but when he glanced back she was focused on her computer.

Six pairs of nurses' eyes turned to him as he opened the door, as well as those of the social worker, the psychologist and the occupational therapist. Conrad nodded formally and sat down in his regular seat. He'd always maintained a distance between his staff and himself, so no one commented on the fact that he was late, but he was aware of sidelong glances and curious stares that made him uncomfortable.

One by one, using the charts and the Kardex files, the nurses brought him up to date on what was happening with his patients, who was sleeping well with the medications he'd prescribed, who'd been admitted over the holidays, how the patients on long-term stay were responding to treatment.

"Tillie Lauderdale has asked for an overnight pass again," one of the nurses reported. "She wants to spend the night with her daughter."

Tillie Lauderdale was a middle-aged housewife whose husband left her for a younger woman. She'd swallowed a barrage of pills, and would have died if a neighbor hadn't found her.

Conrad frowned. "You just told me she refused medication yesterday."

"That was because the meds were making her dizzy," the nurse said.

"If she can't follow what I order, then she certainly isn't going out on the weekend. Request denied," Conrad said in a tone that he hoped bridged no argument.

"I disagree," the nurse said, and although her face turned bright pink when Conrad scowled at her, she went on in a determined tone, "Mrs. Lauderdale is doing very well. She's been on the ward for six weeks now and she's a model patient. I think it would do her the world of good to spend a couple of nights off the ward."

"Mrs. Lauderdale has to learn that while she's my patient, she follows my orders to the letter." Conrad gave the nurse an icy look and raised his voice. "*No one* reviews my orders, Nurse. I thought I'd made that abundantly clear?"

The nurse didn't say any more, but the look she gave Conrad spoke volumes.

He was well aware that the nurses didn't like him. He'd lost his temper and yelled at nearly all of them at one time or another, and several times they'd made complaints through official channels that he invaded their territory, which was nonsense. He simply made certain that his orders were being carried out.

The meeting was almost over when Bunny knocked at the door and then walked in, and Conrad's stomach contracted when he saw that she was carrying Robert.

"Someone from Orthopedics just dropped this baby off, she said he was yours, Dr. Banfield." Her green eyes were bright with excitement, and her voice was two octaves higher than normal. "He's the spitting image of you, too, aren't you, baby?"

The silence was absolute. Everyone studied Conrad, and then the baby. He tried to maintain a professional expression and act as if it was entirely normal to have a baby arrive during rounds.

"Just keep him with you for the time being, Bunny." Robert was sleeping, which was a blessing.

"Sorry, sir, baby-sitting isn't in my job description," Bunny had the audacity to say as she set the carrier down gently beside Conrad. "He's sure cute, though. He's got that same cleft chin you have." She scurried out and closed the door behind her.

The staff got to their feet, not one of them

saying a word. They shot surreptitious glances at Conrad and the baby as they filed out. The door closed behind the last one and then Conrad clearly heard the outer office erupt in waves of female merriment and excited, muted whispers.

They knew. Hot waves of indignation and anger rolled over him as he realized that the grapevine must have done its usual efficient job at broadcasting every detail of the New Year's Eve scene in the ER. By now every last living person in St. Joe's, from the administrator down to the cleaning staff, probably knew all the intimate and embarrassing details of his life.

He took his tinted glasses off and buried his face in his hands. He wanted nothing more than to lay his head down on the table and just go to sleep, but Robert's face puckered and he began twitching, making restless movements and grumpy noises that meant he was about to wake up.

He would find someone to take care of this baby, Conrad vowed. *He couldn't go through another day with him. Especially he couldn't make it through another night.*

Conrad saw that the baby had a note pinned to his blanket.

''Robert is to be delivered at precisely eleven-forty-five and two-forty-five for feedings,'' it read. ''And Ms. Martin asks that you use a Snugli for him instead of this chair—he needs to be held constantly. It eases his colic.''

What the hell was a Snugli? And, damn it to blazes, who would he ever find to baby-sit if they had to keep taking Robert to Abby every couple of hours?

A tap on the door, and Bunny stuck her head in.

''Dr. Demetrius is on line one.''

Demetrius was a brilliant young psychiatrist in private practice whom Conrad suspected of lusting after his own position at St. Joe's.

''Tell him I'm not available at the moment.''

''But I just told him you were right here, he's holding for you.'' Bunny gave him an innocent look that made him want to shake her.

He snatched Robert's carrier up and stalked out to the phone. Robert began to wail, and it was hard to hear, but Conrad finally figured out that Demetrius wanted a consult about a patient.

''I hear a baby crying,'' Demetrius said when they'd arranged a time. ''Not yours, is it, Doctor?'' He laughed, and Conrad instantly concluded that he, too, had heard the story.

''Actually, he is mine,'' Conrad said as evenly

as he could manage. "I'm caring for him while his mother recovers. She was in a serious accident."

Dead silence, and then in a totally different tone, Demetrius said, "God, Banfield, I'm so sorry. I was joking, I had no idea. If there's any way I can help, perhaps cover for you for a few days, just let me know."

"Thanks, I'll keep that in mind." *As if he'd ever let Demetrius take over his turf.*

Bunny didn't even pretend she hadn't been listening.

"How's Abby doing, anyhow? We were all really upset about her accident. We're all gonna go see her."

Conrad had pretended, months before, when Abby abruptly transferred from St. Joe's over to West Memorial Hospital, that no one except he and she knew the real reason. Now, he suspected he'd been naive. It was entirely possible that the entire nursing staff had known even then that she was pregnant with his baby.

If it had ever been a secret, it certainly wasn't anymore. And that was freeing, in a way. There was absolutely nothing left to hide. His entire sorry life was an open book.

And Robert was still crying.

CHAPTER FIVE

"BUNNY, WHAT'S A Snugli?"

She didn't even look surprised. "It's a thing you wear on your chest to carry a baby. It leaves your hands free to do things. They sell them downstairs in the gift shop."

He opened his mouth to order her to go buy one, and then remembered that such a chore wasn't covered in her job description either.

"I can go get you one, if you want. If you don't mind me being away from my desk for a few minutes, that is."

The offer was unexpected. "Put the machine on. And hurry back." He reached in his pocket and extracted his wallet, handing her several bills.

"What color do you want?"

"I don't care. Just not pink."

"I'll get something dark." She was grinning. "It'll match the bags under your eyes, Doctor.

You must have left your glasses in the conference room.''

She was pushing him beyond his limits. This whole scenario was pushing him beyond his limits. Robert was screaming. He had orders to write, patients to see, a meeting with the planning committee, and he was so tired his brain felt as if it were wrapped in cotton wool.

''By the way, did you know you're wearing two different shoes, Dr. Banfield?''

He thought for a moment it was some kind of twisted joke, but when he looked down at his feet he saw to his horror that she was right. He'd somehow put a black loafer on one foot and a black oxford on the other.

And Bunny was giggling, *at him, Conrad Banfield, M.D., Ph.D., F.R.C.P.*

He'd become a laughing stock in his own department, an object of ridicule. Bunny must have seen something ominous in his expression, because she sobered quickly and all but ran out the door.

Conrad looked at his shoes and cursed under his breath. He'd have to get through the rest of the day hoping that no one would notice. He hurried into the conference room and reclaimed his glasses.

Bunny was back in less than fifteen minutes with the Snugli, and she helped him strap on the green corduroy contraption. With great difficulty, Conrad fitted Robert into it. It was rather like wearing a baby instead of a vest. He was accustomed by now to holding Robert in his arms, and he had to admit that the device was an improvement, although Robert didn't seem to think so. He went on crying vigorously, but at least Conrad could do more this way.

The majority of his patients were women. His specialty was depression and eating disorders. He had a number of outpatients who came to his office in the hospital every day to see him, several of whom were now lined up waiting.

Bunny sent them in one by one, and Conrad spoke with them, doing his best to maintain professional dignity over Robert's squalls. Every single patient gaped at him and said, in tones of utter amazement, "Is that *your* baby, Doctor?" Then they'd take a closer look and say, "He sure looks like you."

Conrad was forced to explain about the accident, over and over again. But in some inexplicable fashion, the baby's noisy presence seemed to make each consultation more relaxed than ever before. Patients who normally hardly spoke opened up. One woman, particularly withdrawn and acutely depressed, actually smiled at the baby.

Robert grew more and more agitated as the morning progressed, and by eleven-thirty, Conrad's nerves were stretched to the limit. His own stomach was grumbling; since Robert's appearance in his life, he'd subsisted on toast and tins of beans or spaghetti. For the first time ever, he was actually salivating at the thought of eating in the hospital cafeteria.

The bossy nurse was nowhere to be seen, so Conrad headed into Abby's room.

"You got a Snugli," she said when she saw him. Each word was still an effort, her voice hardly more than a whisper, but she looked a little better than she had the previous day.

"Yes. It does make holding him easier." Conrad unzipped the thing and extracted Robert, writhing and screaming.

"Have you changed him?"

"Sorry. Between patients and phone calls, I forgot." He felt guilty, stupid and negligent.

"Could you do it?"

Conrad thought of calling the nurse and decided against it. She'd undoubtedly lecture him. So, with an ease he was a little proud of, he divested the wriggling baby of a wet diaper and strapped on a fresh one.

"The thick part goes to the front, Conrad."

Why hadn't that rational idea occurred to him before now? He undid the fastenings and turned the diaper around.

"Has he been crying all morning?" Abby stroked the baby's hair and cheek, her forehead creased in a worried frown.

"He slept quite a while," Conrad lied. The pale transparency of her skin, the violent bruise on her cheek and forehead, her general air of fragility, made him want to comfort her any way he could.

"He must be starving. I usually feed him on demand, every couple of hours."

"The nurse said to bring him only after three," Conrad related. "She has some theories about colic, I gather."

"She's a know-it-all," Abby whispered. "It wears me down, listening to her tell me how to cure colic. I've tried everything, and as far as I can tell, nothing really works."

"I think that's right. I looked it up on the Internet." Conrad began to explain about the different theories, but he could see that Abby wasn't really listening. She was anxious to feed Robert.

"I'll go now. I'll pick him up in, what, an hour? Hour and a half?"

"*Where* is that nurse?" Abby sounded on the verge of tears. "I need to prop him and me up on pillows. I can't turn by myself because of my ribs and the incision. Could you help me, please?"

He absolutely didn't want to. It would mean touching her skin, leaning close to her. It would mean physical intimacy, but what choice did he have? She was injured, he was a doctor. Almost in a panic, he went to the door and glanced up and down the hallway, but the nurse was nowhere in sight.

"Tell me what to do."

With her guiding him, he propped pillows, turned her gently...she gave an involuntary gasp of pain, and beads of sweat broke out on his forehead. He'd never broken ribs himself, but he'd heard that they were the most painful of injuries. And she must also be refusing pain medication, so that it wouldn't transfer to her milk.

He hated seeing her hurt. "Abby, wouldn't it just be easier if you put him on formula?"

"Of course it would." Her soft eyes were filled with reproach. "But it wouldn't be the best thing for him. I want him to have the best start possible." She closed her eyes and struggled silently for a moment. "This will get easier, it just has to."

"Of course it will." He wondered if, under similar circumstances, he'd have the courage to undergo acute pain for the benefit of another person. It was an area in which he'd never been tested.

The skin on her bare arm was soft and silky, the bone beneath fragile. The hollow at the base of her throat forced a memory of the way his lips had once rested there. He recalled the sweet taste of her, the fullness of her lips beneath his, the way her agile body had responded as if it were made as a match for his. He could almost smell the faint perfume she'd worn that night.

Today she smelled of hospital soap and medications, but underneath was still the delicate, intimate fragrance that was purely Abby. There was another subtle aroma as well that Conrad recognized from holding Robert.

Milk. She smelled sweetly of human milk, the milk she fed the baby.

Their baby.

A shudder ran down his spine. For the first time, Conrad sensed the power of the living bond two people created between them when they had a child.

After enduring his awkward efforts, Abby finally said she was comfortable. Robert, writhing and furious, was lying on several pillows. Abby's gown fastened behind her neck, and Conrad could see that she certainly wasn't going to be able to undo it herself. He was beginning to really worry about the logistics of the rest of the procedure when the nurse came hurrying in.

"So we're nearly all prepared, are we? Good. You will collect the baby in exactly forty-five minutes, Doctor."

Conrad escaped, but as he wolfed down meat loaf and overcooked vegetables in the cafeteria, he kept imagining that Abby's essence clung to his fingertips. The night they'd spent together replayed itself in his mind as if it had just happened.

As head of the department of Psychiatry, he'd been forced to attend a fund-raiser that mild March night. Always awkward and nervous at social functions, he'd made the mistake of taking an Atavan capsule before the party. The strong tranquilizer had worked so well that he'd relaxed his rigid rules about liquor. Instead of his usual two drinks, he'd had at least four.

Abby was a relative newcomer to his department. Pretty, funny, vibrant, she was wearing a blue dress that night that swirled in gossamer layers around her slender figure. She asked him to dance. She made him laugh. With her in his arms, he was less clumsy than usual on the dance floor. She'd reached up and slipped off his tinted glasses and tucked them in his suit pocket. She wanted to see his soul, she explained. When he took her home after the party, making love with her was the most natural, exquisite thing in the world. Afterward, lost in a sensual dream, he'd told her he wanted to take her to dinner and the symphony the following week.

And then dawn arrived and Conrad was horrified. He'd been intimate with a staff member, which violated a rule he'd always been strict about.

She'd looked so young and innocently sensual the next morning, wearing a short cotton nightshirt that bared her shapely legs. She'd made him coffee, eggs, toast, which made it all the more difficult when he'd told her that it was impossible for him to go on seeing her except in a professional capacity. He'd respected the dignity and poise that almost hid her disappointment.

During the six weeks that followed, he'd fantasized about her, dreaming of her at night, trying to hide the hot rush of acute awareness that came over him whenever he saw her at work.

And then she'd come to his office and said she was pregnant.

Conrad's lunch abruptly lost its appeal. He shoved the plate away, sickened by the memory of how unfair he'd been to Abby. At that time, he at least should have gone and had the test to confirm whether or not the vasectomy had been successful before he accused her of anything. Instead, he'd convinced himself she was a liar, that she was trying to trick him into either marriage or support for her child.

He'd been an idiot, a cruel, heartless idiot. He stared at the half-eaten plate of food and wondered if there was any possible way he could ever make up for his cruelty.

There was silence from her room when he went to collect the baby a short while later, and he peered hesitantly around the door.

She was still nursing Robert. She was propped up, and the baby lay on a bundle of bedding, pressed against one delicate swollen breast.

Abby was gazing down at her son, a tender half smile on her lips.

Conrad tried to turn away and couldn't. There was a mesmerizing beauty about the scene that enchanted him.

Abby glanced up and saw him, and her face turned pink. "He's finished, he's asleep," she said, moving Robert and tugging her gown to cover her exposed breast.

"Could you burp him for me, please?"

Conrad took the limp baby and propped him on his shoulder, and after a few minutes an outrageously loud belch erupted. Abby's eyes met Conrad's. His eyebrows lifted in amazement, and then they both smiled. For just an instant, there was a companionable sharing between them.

AFTER CONRAD LEFT, Abby did her best to eat the soup and Jell-O pudding the nurse brought her, but pain, exhaustion and a confused welter of emotions made eating impossible.

She fought back tears. Feeding Robert was agonizingly painful, and trying not to reveal to anyone how difficult it was took every ounce of courage and fortitude she possessed. If she admitted she could hardly bear the pain it caused her to nurse him, the staff would insist she wean him.

Abby was determined not to let that happen, but the physical problems combined with the overwhelming anger, hurt and sense of betrayal she felt toward Faye were wearing her thin.

She'd told Faye how she felt, the moment the anaesthetic had worn off and her brain began to function. Surely Faye could have taken a week off and cared for Robert instead of handing him over to Conrad, of all people.

Faye didn't see it that way. She had an important trial, and what better person to care for a baby than its own father, she countered in that reasonable tone that made Abby want to scream.

There *must* be someone else she could get to care for her baby, but Abby had racked her brain all morning.

Her mother was dead, her father didn't live in Vancouver. All her friends worked. Those with children had complicated arrangements with either relatives or day-care centers. Taking on the care of a tiny baby was an enormous responsibility, and the fact that she was nursing Robert made the situation even more difficult. There was no one she could ask.

Each time she was forced to see Conrad, Abby

remembered the terrible day she'd gone to his office and explained that she was pregnant with his child.

Even thinking about it, all the awful emotions she'd experienced that day came flooding back. He'd called her a liar and a cheat, in a cold, dispassionate tone that was infinitely worse than any hollering could have been. He told her that he'd had a vasectomy, and went on to say she was trying to trick him.

Sick and scared and humiliated, she'd lost control, screaming that he was the only one she'd been with, that the baby was absolutely his. She'd told him that her fellow nurses called him the Iceman, and that she'd been the only one who'd believed they were mistaken. But she'd been so wrong, she told him. Iceman was far too kind a description of him.

The very worst part of it was the genuine feelings that she'd had for Conrad. She'd been half in love with him for weeks, and the night of the party, she'd fantasized as she dressed that he would dance with her, that the stern and forbidding façade he maintained at work would slip away and she'd see the appealing man beneath the protective façade.

She'd known he'd had too much to drink that

night, but the alcohol had allowed what she'd thought was his real self to show—an endearing, clumsy, painfully shy introvert, convinced that unless he maintained an iron grip, his world would collapse. He'd known exactly how to love her.

The passion they'd shared was genuine. Even now, she couldn't refute that. In the midst of their lovemaking, he'd told her of places he wanted to take her, things he wanted them to do together.

She'd wanted to see him again, more than anything in the world, so when morning came and he haltingly told her that he had rigid rules about dating a staff member, it was all she could do not to burst into tears.

But, fool that she was, she'd gone on believing that he'd come to his senses and realize that they'd shared something special, something real and rare and precious.

And then she'd told him she was pregnant.

And now, the Iceman had Robert.

CHAPTER SIX

THAT AFTERNOON, CONRAD visited the patients on the ward that were under close observation, doing his best to disregard the baby's wailing.

In what he was beginning to recognize as a pattern, Robert had slept soundly for half an hour after his feeding, and then woke up squirming, whimpering at first and then escalating to full-scale howling.

"Doctor, I'm lots better. Please can I spend a weekend away from the ward? My daughter would take responsibility—she's a responsible adult," Tillie Lauderdale was pleading in a loud voice.

"Not quite yet, let's give it another week or two. You must follow your drug doses to the letter before I can consider a weekend pass," Conrad said, raising his own voice considerably in order to be heard.

"Please, please, Doctor? I promise I'll take my meds, you know I'm not suicidal anymore, you know that.'' Tillie was begging now, even though they were all but shouting at one another and the effort to maintain a calm, firm and reasonable mask was telling on Conrad. He had an important meeting with the planning committee in less than an hour, and his nerves were frayed. Having to see Abby repeatedly was bringing up emotions he didn't want to feel.

''No.'' He drew in a deep breath to prevent himself from roaring, *''And that's the end of it.''* She didn't move or cry and he braced himself for another barrage of begging.

''Could I hold the baby? I'm very good with babies. What's his name?''

The meek request took him off guard. He stared at Tillie for a moment. She looked like a caricature of everyone's ideal concept of a grandmother: plump, kind, loving, gentle. She didn't smile much, but none of his depressed patients did. She certainly wasn't violent, and apart from the one episode of severe depression that had landed her here, she'd apparently lived an uneventful life as a homemaker.

''I...well, I...yes, I suppose so.'' The truth was Conrad was desperate for even a few moments' respite from Robert's screaming. His head ached, and every muscle in his body was tense. He unzipped the Snugli and extracted the baby, handing him over to Tillie, who smoothed down his rumpled clothing, settled him on her ample bosom, and began making soothing, non-sensical noises, calling the baby her little lamb and poopsie.

"His name is Robert."

To Conrad's astonishment, the baby's crying slackened. He burped loudly several times, threshed his arms and legs and writhed around for a moment and then went to sleep, limp and miraculously silent. Tillie cradled him lovingly.

"Poor wee poppet, he's got gas. I always found that letting them lay on my chest helped. It's the warmth of your body," Tillie explained.

Conrad, who'd been wearing Robert like a hair shirt all morning very close to his chest without any such effect, didn't bother to contradict her. There must be different types of body heat, he concluded groggily. Had anyone ever done a scientific study on that?

He wasn't about to. He sighed deeply, and his headache eased a little.

"Please, could I keep him for just a little while?" Tillie implored him, and Conrad hesitated and then nodded. He'd make sure the floor nurse kept an eye on things, but the idea of being able to attend his meeting without Robert roaring under his chin seemed like nirvana. He left the baby, the Snugli and the diaper bag and headed for his meeting.

He had to struggle hard to stay awake, and issues that he normally would have hotly challenged were passed by the committee without opposition, which meant that the meeting finished early. Conrad stumbled out and was passing an empty treatment room when temptation became overwhelming. The room had a cot and a pillow, and he told himself he'd lie down for half an hour; he had to take Robert to Abby at three.

He slipped in, closed the door, sank down on the bed, and instantly tumbled down into sleep.

"Dr. Banfield, Dr. Conrad Banfield, please report to Psychiatry at once. Dr. Banfield, please…"

The message incorporated into his dream at first, but then he came awake, struggling to a sitting position, slowly figuring out who he was and where. A glance at his watch confused him and then filled him with horror.

Four thirty-five? He'd left the baby with Tillie just after one. He was more than an hour late for

Robert's feeding. The baby would be screaming, the staff furious, Abby frantic.

Panicked, he staggered to his feet, splashed his face with cold water, and careened down the corridor.

"Where have you been?" Bunny scowled at him as he burst through the door. "My shift ended at four—I'm booking an hour's overtime because of this. Everybody's in an uproar looking for you. And where's the baby? We've had four calls from Ortho and a nasty visit from a snappy little widget of a nurse who wanted to know what kind of department we run down here."

Conrad didn't stop to answer her. He headed for the ward at a dead run, his heart hammering.

Tillie was in her room, sitting on a straight-backed chair and rocking Robert gently back and forth. She was talking to him in a soothing tone, and he was awake but not crying. She looked up at Conrad and for the first time he could remember, smiled at him.

"Your wee boy's getting a little hungry. I couldn't find a bottle, but I changed him."

Conrad had the presence of mind to thank her. He scooped up the baby and all his supplies and made a dash for the elevator.

"You're over an hour late, don't you know he has to eat on time?" Abby's eyes were red, and it was obvious she'd been crying.

Conrad felt like a worm. Silently, he handed Robert over.

"Is he all right? He's not crying, did you already give him a bottle, or...or..." Horror filled her voice. "You didn't give him some tranquilizer or something, did you?"

Shocked that she would think such a thing, Conrad shook his head in vehement denial.

"He..." She had to stop repeatedly and catch her breath between words. "He has to be starving...by now and he's not even crying. I knew I shouldn't trust you with him. You're not capable of...of caring for a baby. Babies need to be loved, that's not...not something you know anything about." The words tumbled out, and Conrad couldn't think of a defense. Every word she said was true.

"If only I had someone, *anyone,* who'd take care of him for me," she wailed.

Conrad's pride was stung. He wasn't exactly a nonentity, after all. "I am doing my best," he said in a haughty, defensive tone. "I've just never had any experience with babies before, but I'm learning."

"I don't want...you practicing on my son," Abby declared, trembling as she struggled in vain to arrange herself and the baby for the feeding.

On cue, Robert went from silent to screaming in under a minute. Conrad made a move to help, but Abby slapped weakly at his hand.

"Don't you dare touch me. Get a nurse."

Conrad's self-control snapped. "He's my baby too, Abigail. Would I do anything to deliberately harm my own child? I'm taking the best care of him I know how."

The look she gave him was incredulous. "*Your* child? Since when? You called me a liar and a cheat. You all but threw me out of your office." Her short, stertorous breathing was labored, and Conrad's own chest hurt just hearing it. Or maybe it was her words.

"I went through the whole pregnancy...and his birth all by myself." She looked daggers at him. "You're not to be trusted...with people's babies..." her voice broke "...any more than you are with their hearts."

There was something in that statement that he needed to think about, but the nurse appeared just then.

"What's going on in here? And where have

you been, Doctor? I distinctly told you exactly when this baby was expected for feedings, and now you have mother upset, which transfers directly to the milk.''

Conrad gave the nurse a look of utter loathing, which troubled her not at all.

"Leave, if you please," she ordered. "And be back here in exactly forty minutes for this child. This is not a day-care center.''

Conrad slunk off to the cafeteria again and bolted down something slimy masquerading as macaroni and cheese.

It had dawned on him that an entire day had gone by, and he hadn't found anyone to take on Robert's care, and it was too late in the day to start interviewing anyone for the job, even if he knew where to find someone to interview.

Now he faced another endless night of fifteen-minute naps interspersed with three hours of torture, walking up and down with a squalling baby in his arms.

One thing about his son, he thought with grudging admiration, was this amazing ability to cry for hours on end. Any lesser child would collapse in exhaustion, but not Robert. He'd obviously inherited his father's determination as well as his double crown.

Conrad felt a rush of something very much like pride just before he realized that twice in the past hour, he'd accepted the fact that he had a son.

JUST AS HE'D FEARED, that miserable night was a repeat of the previous one. Conrad estimated he had maybe two hours of sleep, and the following morning, in a groggy rush to get Robert to Abby and not be late for morning rounds a second time, he managed to somehow lock his keys in the car...with the motor running. Fortunately, it happened in the hospital parkade and he'd taken Robert out of the car, but of course Bunny overheard him calling the automobile association, and he had no doubt that within minutes everyone in the department knew about this latest mishap. They'd all be laughing at him...again. He was too exhausted to care.

In spite of it all, rounds went well. The nurses didn't seem as combative as usual, and one of them actually told a joke that Conrad found funny.

And when he went to pick up Robert, Abby told him with a catch in her voice that she'd found someone else to take care of the baby.

"Who is it?" Conrad knew that he should be

feeling only profound relief instead of this strange combination of concern and mistrust.

"One of the nurses has a sister who does day care out of her home." Abby was obviously struggling to keep her voice even, and she wouldn't look at him. "The woman's name is Margery, she came in to see me last night. She seems very loving, she has excellent references. The only problem is Robert will have to have bottle feedings during the day. She can only bring him to me in the evenings as she takes care of two other kids. She's coming to pick him up this afternoon, after his four o'clock feeding."

"Two other youngsters as well as Robert?" Conrad was trying to sort out the mixed emotions running through him. How could anyone human care for three small children?

"How do you feel about this, Abby?"

"Don't you dare psychoanalyze me," she flared. "You couldn't care less what I feel, so don't pretend. This is a way out for you. And it keeps me from having to see you every day."

Her angry words stung. "If that's your decision, fine." He loaded Robert into the Snugli and stalked out.

Tillie Lauderdale, with a nurse in tow, was waiting in his office and Conrad sighed and braced himself for yet another round of pleading for a weekend pass.

"Oh, Doctor, would it be possible for me to hold the baby again?"

Robert wasn't crying yet, but he was beginning to wriggle, a sure indication that any moment he'd begin, and Conrad had to interview an applicant, a psychologist, for a position opening in his department, a procedure that required all his attention. And Tillie seemed to have some ability to comfort the baby which he hadn't developed yet, he admitted.

"I suppose you may," Conrad conceded, guiltily aware that it was his own best interests he was thinking of.

But a huge smile spread across Tillie's features, and the nurse also smiled…at Conrad. He couldn't remember that happening before. He and the nurses on his service seemed to be perpetually at war over one thing or the other. He managed a grimace in return and handed over the Snugli and diaper bag, assuring himself that he absolutely trusted Tillie with Robert. After all, he knew her extremely well; he'd been her doctor for several months, she'd spent hours revealing her innermost thoughts and feelings to him.

On the other hand, he was not prepared at all to trust this Margery person. After all, what did Abby really know about her? He'd heard from news reports that one had to be ultracautious in handing over a helpless, innocent child to just anyone to care for.

He'd just have to make time today to find either a reputable nursery that met his standards or a nanny with impeccable qualifications.

He was familiar with hiring staff, after all. How hard could it be to find a suitable situation for a baby?

CHAPTER SEVEN

BUT FINDING SOMEONE Conrad trusted enough to care for Robert wasn't easy. By afternoon, he doubted that it was even possible.

Forcing himself to stay out of the empty treatment room and forgo the nap he craved while Abby was giving Robert his lunch, Conrad looked up day care on the Internet. There were several pages of warnings and questions to ask prospective baby-sitters.

He then called a list of nurseries in the yellow pages, only to find that most of them had a long waiting list, which made him instantly suspicious of the ones that didn't. He spoke with three women who advertised in the paper as experienced nannies. Two were ridiculously young and flippant, and the third sounded so much like the obnoxious nurse on Abby's floor that he had to wonder if the two women were related.

Tillie had kept Robert all morning, and although she asked to have him again in the afternoon, Conrad felt that he was taking advantage of her. Consequently, he'd spent the afternoon trying to write community referrals for several patients with Robert bawling and writhing on his chest. In the half hour when the baby fell into an exhausted slumber, Conrad's own head nodded and he fell asleep slumped in his chair. Bunny came in and woke him when he didn't respond to the intercom. It was time for Robert's feeding, and he hurried to the elevator.

As he took Robert out of the Snugli and handed him to Abby a few moments later, Conrad reminded himself that it was the last time he'd have to struggle with the infernal contraption. There'd be no crying baby tonight, no messy diapers. He'd drive straight home and fall into bed. Or maybe he'd stop first at his favorite restaurant and have a decent meal and a half liter of wine. And tomorrow he'd take the mountain of soiled clothing he'd accumulated in the past few days to the laundry, and call the cleaning service to do something about the disastrous mess in the apartment.

Yes indeed, he assured himself as Abby cuddled the screaming baby, life could return to normal now.

He'd just meet Margery first to set his mind at rest.

He spent forty minutes in the TV room with two ambulatory Ortho patients who were watching Oprah talk to a woman furious with her best friend for sleeping with her teenage son. The friend couldn't figure out what the problem was. Conrad slept through the second half hour, missing the advice the expert psychologist gave.

When he returned to Abby's room, a small red-headed woman in black tights and a snug top was changing Robert's diaper while Abby stroked his head and crooned to him.

"Conrad, what are you doing here? This isn't any of your business." Abby's greeting was anything but welcoming, but Conrad ignored it.

"I'm Dr. Conrad Banfield, the baby's father," he introduced himself to the woman, who looked to him as if she drank. She had several small broken blood vessels on the side of her nose, and he thought her eyes might be bloodshot. "You must be Margery."

"Yeah, how d'ya do." She was chewing gum, a habit Conrad despised.

"And what qualifications do you have?"

"What d'ya mean, qualifications?"

"I mean, what training have you had in infant care?"

"Training?" Margery laughed. "Good old experience. I've got four of my own, and I've taken care of dozens of other people's kids."

Conrad didn't consider that being qualified.

"But you haven't taken any courses, you have no documentation that you're equipped to care for an infant?"

Abby said, "Conrad, this is ridiculous. What are you trying to prove?"

"I simply want assurance that Robert will be cared for properly."

"Of course he will be. I'm licensed by the city," Margery said in a defensive tone.

Conrad knew for a fact that the city would license almost anything as long as one paid an exorbitant fee—look at the number of squalid pubs and second-rate restaurants around. Couldn't Abby see how ill equipped this woman was to care for Robert?

"What sort of environment will you provide for the baby?"

"What d'ya mean, environment?" Margery frowned at him. "There's cribs, toys, high chairs."

"And what stimulation will you provide for him?"

"Stimulation?" She turned to Abby. "Listen, I don't think this is gonna work out after all. My sister said this kid's got colic, that's tough enough to deal with without this guy on my case. I thought I was doing you a favor. I didn't expect to get the third degree here. You'll have to find somebody else, sorry." She picked up a worn handbag from the floor and hurried out the door.

Robert was starting to fuss again, and Abby's voice was almost a shriek. "Conrad, what is *wrong* with you? Now what am I going to do? There's no one else to take care of him."

"I'll take care of him." The words surprised Conrad as much as they did Abby. "I know you don't want to see me, so I'll try and arrange for an aide to bring Robert here for feedings. You need to just calm down and concentrate on getting better, this stress isn't good for you." Conrad thrust his arms through the straps of the Snugli. He picked up Robert and stuffed him in. "Besides, you don't need somebody caring for Robert who thinks they're doing you a favor, Abby."

"Oh, and you don't think that, I suppose?"

Her voice dripped with sarcasm. "You just raced here the moment you heard I was in an accident and volunteered to take him, right? I know Faye, I bet she threatened you with a court case and DNA testing and publicity and anything else she could think of unless you took him."

Conrad wasn't about to confirm that. "It was a shock at first," he admitted with dignity. "But I'm getting over it. I'm getting used to him."

"*Used* to him? I suppose *you're* providing him with stimulation and a good environment?"

"I'm trying." The apartment resembled a war zone, and he thought of Tillie and felt uneasy. It was probable Abby wouldn't consider having Robert spend his days on a supervised mental ward in the care of a patient as the best possible environment for her son.

Their son.

"I played Mozart for him last night, I think it helped calm him down a little." It had certainly calmed Conrad, and taught him that it was possible to actually doze off while walking with a screaming baby. "I read up on breast milk today. It's definitely the best for him. Now you won't have to wean him to a bottle." He was impressed with his own mastery of the terminology involved. The Internet was a marvelous teaching device. "I know how hard it must be for you to keep on feeding him. You can't have the normal pain medication, you must have a lot of discomfort. But if you're tough enough to go on with it, then I think that's what you should do."

"I just don't understand you." She was on the verge of tears again and he was sorry. Why did he always manage to make her cry?

He shouldered the diaper bag. "Sometimes I don't understand me either." It had to be sleep deprivation that made him admit something like that, and it was certainly insane of him to bend over and kiss her on the forehead, just to the left of the enormous bruise. Her skin was velvet beneath his lips. "Night, Abby. Sleep well. I'll take good care of Robert, I promise."

AFTER HE'D GONE, Abby felt as if she was in shock.

Without the benefit of either liquor or a gun to his head, Conrad Banfield had kissed her and volunteered to care for Robert. And the most amazing thing about it all was that she was relieved. There was something about Margery that bothered her, and it had taken Conrad to point it out; colic or no colic, taking Robert wasn't a favor. It was a privilege, one she'd planned to pay for generously.

Mozart. She thought about that, and to her own amazement, she actually giggled.

She went over in her mind the other things Conrad had said, and after a while she decided that in the morning, she'd have a nurse call him at home and tell him that she preferred to have him bring Robert to her for feedings. That way, she reasoned, she could ask him whether the baby had slept, or when he'd had his bath, and whether or not he'd been changed recently.

If he was going to care for Robert, she and Conrad had to communicate, didn't they?

Since the accident, nights had been agonizing for Abby, filled with overwhelming pain and worry about her baby. But that night, when she finished her dinner and closed her eyes, she slipped into a deep, healing sleep that lasted for hours.

CONRAD SPENT THE first portion of the night driving around the city with classical music blasting out of the car stereo. He'd discovered there was something about the motion of the car and the rhythm of the music that put Robert to sleep, and when he cautiously carried the baby into the house, he'd nap for a full two hours. Conrad had fallen into the pattern of his days as an intern, snatching every possible free moment to lie down on any horizontal surface and fall into a profound sleep.

When Robert awakened, Conrad went through the feeding, changing, burping, walking the floor routine, reminding himself when he got desperate that he'd deliberately chosen to do so.

He bought a crib and set it up in his bedroom, beside his bed, hoping that having his own bed would make Robert more prone to sleeping during the night. It didn't.

In the days that followed, Conrad found parenting a humbling experience. Sleep deprived, he wrote in the wrong charts and ordered meds for patients that weren't his. He then had to admit the mistakes to nurses whom he'd formerly reduced to tears for committing much less serious errors.

Always meticulous about his personal grooming, he forgot to take his suits and shirts to the laundry and was forced to come to work in corduroys and wash-and-wear checked shirts. On two occasions he discovered he was wearing socks of different colors.

Groggy and definitely not at his best, often with Robert shrieking as Conrad conducted appointments, it was extraordinary to discover that his patients were improving much more quickly than ever before. They opened up to him, spilling out things it would formerly have taken him months to discover. And as the days went on, the atmosphere in the entire ward subtly changed. Nurses whose antagonism toward him was once palpable began to pop into his office to find out how Abby was, or to make cooing noises to Robert. Days passed without a single confrontation; Conrad couldn't very well berate his staff for mistakes when he was having to rely on them to prevent his own blunders from having serious consequences.

At first, contact with Abby was minimal. He delivered Robert to her and, travel alarm stuck in his pocket, headed straight for the doctors' lounge to sleep for one blissful hour.

Whenever she was free, Tillie Lauderdale asked if she could hold the baby, and Conrad gratefully handed him over. The woman had an almost magical ability to calm and soothe. Robert could be crimson and shrieking, but after ten minutes with Tillie, he'd be either sleeping or peering around like a curious, nearsighted old man.

It was at three-forty-five on a particularly difficult Thursday night during the second week of the New Year that Conrad reached the point where he felt he had to either get a good night's sleep or commit himself to his own locked ward.

On Friday morning, swallowing any remnants of pride he still possessed, he humbly asked Tillie Lauderdale for a favor.

CHAPTER EIGHT

CONRAD WOULD GIVE Tillie a weekend pass if she and her daughter would come to his house and sleep in his guest room...with Robert.

Tillie's smile was radiant. She wasn't at all resentful of the terms. She phoned her daughter, and it was done.

Conrad called the Mop Squad Emergency team and a furniture store that promised quick delivery. By the time he got home, the house was clean, the laundry done, and within a half hour twin beds were delivered and set up in the spare bedroom that had formerly housed only his computer. He had the deliverymen move the crib in there as well, grateful that the room was large.

Tillie and her daughter Peggy arrived a short time later, and they brought bags of food; Conrad had overlooked that little detail. He'd been living on anything that could be delivered.

Peggy asked diffidently if he minded if she cooked; she was a vegetarian and believed in only fresh food, prepared at home. Tillie asked if she could give Robert his bath and his bottle, and Conrad stumbled to his bedroom, fell on the bed fully dressed, and slept for fourteen blissful hours, awakening just in time to take Robert to the hospital for his morning feeding. Tillie had him changed and dressed in fresh pajamas, and he wasn't crying as Conrad took him into Abby's room.

"You look better this morning," Conrad blurted as he handed the baby over to Abby. The swelling on her cheekbone was subsiding and her hair was freshly washed, soft and full around her face. She was wearing blue cotton pajamas instead of a hospital gown.

"Thanks, I slept a lot. And Faye brought me some clothes." She gathered Robert into the curve of her arm, and Conrad turned to go.

"Stay for a minute." She gave him a shy half smile. "Robert doesn't seem to be too hungry yet. Tell me how he spent the night, when he had a bottle, if he's still crying as much."

Surprised, Conrad sat down on the chair beside the bed. "I don't think he cried last night much at all."

She was instantly alarmed. "What do you mean, you don't *think* he did?"

So he was forced to tell her about Tillie. She listened as he stumbled through the whole story, and when he was done he steeled himself for an outburst.

"She sounds like a godsend."

Conrad waited, tense and defensive, for the *but* he figured was inevitable.

It didn't come. "I think it's a great idea to have her come and spend the weekend," Abby assured him. "I know exactly how worn down you get by having to be up all night. Colic has to be one of life's greatest tests."

"I agree," he said, relieved and overjoyed that she understood. "I haven't been as tired since I was an intern," he admitted.

Robert was starting to wriggle and fuss. "He's getting hungry." Conrad reluctantly got to his feet. "I'd better go. I'll come back for him in an hour."

There was a pause, and then Abby said in a small voice, "You can stay if you want. I mean, you don't have to or anything, I'm sure you have stuff to do..."

"No, I don't." He felt as if he'd been given a precious gift. "I'd like to stay. Can I help you get settled with him, or would you rather I called a nurse?"

"You can, if you don't mind."

Conrad felt richly honored. He gently turned her and settled the baby at her side the way he'd seen the nurses do. With no indication of shyness, she unfastened the buttons on her pajama top and Robert butted greedily against her. He then made great, rude, gulping noises as he drank.

Abby giggled. "Little glutton. He has a wonderful appetite, in spite of the colic. I think he's gaining weight, don't you?"

"I'm sure he is." Conrad's throat was constricted, and he struggled with a rush of emotion. Watching Abby feed the baby affected him the same way it had the first time he'd witnessed it, filling him with an overwhelming sense of wonder and tenderness. He cleared his throat.

"He's a fine physical specimen, very long legs and arms. He's probably going to be a tall man."

"He gets that from you. My family are mostly short, except for Faye." Abby was gazing down at the baby, her words matter of fact. "He looks a lot like you, don't you think? He has my eyes, but certainly his ears and the shape of his head and face are exactly like yours. And that cleft on his chin is identical to yours."

Her words confirmed what Conrad had secretly suspected, and a rush of outrageous pride filled him. He knew there was no rational reason to feel the way he did; he certainly hadn't deliberately willed any genetic advantages to this tiny boy. Instead, with the vasectomy, he'd done his best to prevent any such occurrence, but the reality, the perfection of the living baby filled him with an emotion he couldn't quite define.

"Tell me about your family, Abby." It was a question he always asked clients, but he wasn't using it this time as a tool. There was a hunger in him, as real as any he'd ever felt for food, to know her, know all about her...and thus know more about this scrap of humanity they'd so accidentally created together.

Her eyes lifted from the baby, and she gave Conrad a startled look. "My family? Well, Faye and I grew up on a small farm just outside of Vancouver. There were just the two of us kids...mom lost a baby, a little boy, who would have been in between us. There was never much money, but we managed okay. Mom took in sewing and Dad grew strawberries and fresh produce. Faye and I used to sell it at a roadside stand in the summer. Mom made our clothes. Nobody dared to tease us about them because

Faye would beat them up if they tried. She was a tough kid and always looked out for me. It was sort of like having my own personal bodyguard.''

She smiled and Conrad did too.

"Do your parents still live on the farm?"

Abby's eyes grew sad and she shook her head. "Mom and Dad never really had a holiday, so five years ago they decided to drive down to Mexico. They were in a bad car accident there. Mom died and Dad's pretty much an invalid. He lives with my uncle in Calgary." She stroked Robert's head with a finger. "He was horrified when I told him I was pregnant, he's very straitlaced." Her tone was sad. "He's never even acknowledged Robert's birth. I think he blames himself for Mom's death, and he takes out his anger on everybody."

"I'm sorry." For some reason he'd always envisioned Abby in the midst of a large, supportive family. He'd never stopped to consider what effect her pregnancy might have on those she was close to. It must have been very lonely for her, he realized now with an awful pang of guilt, going through pregnancy and Robert's birth alone. Unexpectedly he found himself grateful that Abby'd had Faye.

"What about you, Conrad? Are you close to your family?"

That amused him, and he smiled and shook his head. "Quite the opposite. I have almost no communication with my parents," he admitted. "They live in Florida." He got a Christmas card and a birthday greeting from them, and he did the same for them, but that was the extent of it.

"Do you have brothers and sisters?"

Again, he shook his head. "I grew up as an only child. I had a privileged childhood, my parents were extremely well-off." It was the rather pompous answer he always gave, but this time for some reason he couldn't explain, he elaborated. "I had an older sister, Rebecca. She doted on me. She was five when I was born. She drowned when I was eight. We'd gone swimming in the lake and I went out too far. She tried to save me."

He'd refused analysis during his own psychiatric training. He knew exactly how the combination of a domineering father, a mother unable to show her emotions, and the loss of a sister who'd called him her little angel, and who'd died trying to save him, had created the peculiarities of his personality. Further, he knew that intellectually recognizing a situation and being able to alter the behavior it produced were two very different things. He liked to think his own neurosis made him a better psychiatrist.

"I'm sorry about Rebecca," Abby said with a catch in her voice. "That must have been really hard on you."

"At first, perhaps." Conrad kept his voice brisk and impersonal. "Soon I was able to bury myself in my studies. I was sent away to a very good private school. Academia became my passion."

Robert was making the wheezing noises that meant he had to burp. Conrad automatically picked him up and tipped him over his shoulder, patting the tiny back with unthinking expertise. He did his best not to look at the apricot-colored skin on Abby's neck and throat and breast.

"The mind can be used to control emotion, to protect and guard against emotional pain and disorder," he explained. "It's all a matter of self-control and training."

Abby gave him a disbelieving look. She shook her head, and then groaned and held her hand to her bruised temple. "You're so wrong, Doctor," she said quietly. "In my books, lack of love is at the basis of every emotional disorder, and controlling emotion doesn't change that basic need, it only hides it. Babies have no self-control at all, and yet if they're not loved unconditionally, they don't do well. I believe adults aren't that different.''

Robert burped and spit up all over Conrad's shirt. He mopped at the mess, but he wasn't bothered by it; by now Robert had spat up on almost every shirt he owned as well as every rug in his house. He pondered Abby's statement. He'd been the champion of the debating team at university, but at this moment he couldn't think of one thing to refute her words.

An undeniable fact, one that he hadn't admitted to himself until this moment, was slowly dawning on him.

Sometime between the New Year Millennium and this moment in time, he, Conrad Banfield, had fallen in love with the small, messy, cranky boy he held in his arms. And the love he felt for this difficult little bundle of humanity was both unconditional and overwhelming. It was more powerful and consuming than anything Conrad had ever felt before. It was a love that called for an incredible amount of giving, yet demanded nothing in return. In fact, it was *all* about giving.

Robert was turning red in the face and grunting, giving his usual dramatic indication that a bowel movement was underway and a diaper change imminent.

Conrad caught Abby's eye, and they both burst into laughter. From the diaper bag he unearthed the supplies needed to change the baby. He spread them across the bottom of the bed and began to loosen Robert's clothing.

"Well, it's nice to see everyone getting along so well." Faye stood in the doorway, arms loaded with magazines and a bouquet of flowers, eyes narrowed suspiciously on Conrad as she took in the scene. "Just one big happy family, are we?" The words hung in the air.

The defensive guard that had slipped away as he talked with Abby reasserted itself, and Conrad hurriedly changed the baby, uncomfortably aware of Faye's critical scrutiny. The moment Robert was dressed again, Conrad put him in the carrier.

"Bye, Abby." He nodded at Faye and hurried out.

There was tense silence in the room for a long moment.

"Did you have to be so nasty, Faye?" Abby's voice trembled, and the rest of what she was feeling burst from her.

"He *is* taking care of Robert, which is more than you were willing to do."

CHAPTER NINE

FAYE WAS SHOVING the flowers any which way into a stainless steel container she'd found in a cupboard. She set them forcefully on the bedside table, sloshing water across the surface and absently rubbing at it with her sleeve.

"I know you're pissed at me for not taking care of him myself, Abby, but the simple truth is I'm hopeless with babies. They scare me to death. I'm okay for an hour or maybe two at the outside, but after that, I can't do it. You oughta know that. I never baby-sat for anyone but you when we were kids." She tossed the magazines down beside the flowers. "And excuse me for not greeting with open arms the man who all but called my sister a slut when she told him she was pregnant with his kid. Or have you chosen to forget that nasty little scene?"

Abby hadn't. But during the past couple of hours, talking with Conrad, the memory had faded, replaced by a feeling of companionship over the baby.

"He's doing the best he can with Robert," she told Faye, "and I appreciate that. I expect you to be civil to him when you happen to be in here together."

Faye made a disgusted noise in her throat. "I'd like to be civil to him, all right, in a courtroom. It makes me furious to watch you struggling financially, when he ought to be paying you generous support." Faye's voice became heated. "I'd go after him in a minute if you'd just let me. You said he's admitted Robert is his. I could get you generous support and money for the baby supplies you've had to buy. He's a doctor, he's single, he's got money," she counted on her fingers, "and you haven't. When you get out of here, you're going to need help. You're not in any shape to care for Robert alone, and your benefits will only last so long. And remember, too, when you finally do go back to work, good day care is going to eat up a huge chunk of your wages. Banfield ought to be paying through the nose for what he's put you through."

"He's offered to talk about finances."

"Well, if he does it again, call me. Don't say

a word or agree to anything unless I'm present,"
Faye ordered. "We'll get it in writing with wit-
nesses and nail the bastard."

Abby looked at her sister. "Being a lawyer
has changed you, Faye. You're hard and cyni-
cal."

Faye gave a bark of laughter. "I haven't
changed at all. I'm a realist, little sister. I always
was, just like you've always been a dreamer. I
love you dearly, but you're way too soft. You
need someone like me to protect you from the
Banfields of this world. And my professional
opinion is, don't sit around waiting for him to
suggest some paltry amount. You need a legal
agreement. Remember, financial support from a
parent isn't a gift; it's Robert's birthright."

Abby felt utterly exhausted, confused and
downhearted by the time Faye left. Was her sister right? Was she a gullible fool when it came
to Conrad?

She thought about the things he'd revealed
about his childhood that morning, and the other,
more important things he'd left unsaid. Her heart
had overflowed with compassion for the little
boy who'd lost his beloved sister in such a tragic
fashion, and once she envisioned him as a little
boy...a little boy very much like Robert would

be in a few years…it had become impossible to see him as cold and calculating. He was gentle with their son. He was gentle with her when he touched her.

And when he did touch her, all the old feelings came rushing back. The single night they'd spent together, he'd made love to her with a passion and a depth of tenderness, a kind of yearning intensity, that had captured her heart.

But Faye was right about one thing; Abby's meager savings weren't going to be enough to get her through the next months. She'd had to move before she had Robert; the small studio apartment she'd been living in wasn't suitable for a baby, and the new one was a lot more expensive. Her small old car had died just before Robert was born, and she'd bought the newer, larger Ford sedan, realizing that she needed space for car seats and strollers, which even secondhand had cost a lot. Because of the accident, the car was a total write-off, so now she had no transportation, and Faye had learned that the vehicle that struck her was stolen, the driver underage. Faye was taking care of her legal rights, but it was going to take time for the insurance company to make a settlement.

Worry settled over Abby like a black shroud.

Maybe Faye was right after all. Maybe she should do what Faye suggested and demand a financial settlement from Conrad, no matter how distasteful the idea was to her. As the years went on, Robert was going to need more than she could provide, that much was certain.

When Conrad brought Robert for his afternoon feeding, the easy camaraderie they'd shared that morning was gone. Conrad seemed distant and formal. He put Robert down on the bed beside Abby and hurriedly left, muttering about errands he needed to do.

When he came to pick the baby up, he diapered him in near silence and again left quickly. Abby spent the afternoon dozing fitfully and worrying more and more about the future.

HAVING TILLIE AND Peggy staying for the weekend meant that Conrad had time to do things like check his e-mail and go for a run. He'd finished two miles on the track and was beginning the third when he finally dared to examine the unfamiliar multitude of feelings that had welled up in him while he was with Abby, and which made him self-conscious and ill at ease now with her.

Physical desire was part of it. He couldn't be around her without remembering how it had

been to make love to her. But she stirred something else in him, something far beyond the
physical. When she'd talked about her childhood, he'd wanted her to go on and on, tell him
every detail. He longed to really know her, know
how she felt about everything, find out what
things delighted her. What were her dreams?
What did she really want from her life?

It had shocked him profoundly to acknowledge the depth of his feelings for his son. He'd
guarded his heart all his life, avoiding relationships that he felt would inevitably result in pain.
The love he felt for Robert had happened without his conscious awareness, and there didn't
seem to be anything to do about it. It was like
a fire, burning out of control in his heart.

He pounded around the track, going faster and
faster, trying to outrun the fact that his love for
Robert included Abby as well. Had he always
had these feelings for her, and hid them from
himself?

Knowing he cared about her made him much
less comfortable when he set out to deliver Robert to her on Sunday morning. He thought of
stopping and buying her something, but he
couldn't figure out what; her viper-tongued sister
had already brought flowers, and there'd been a

huge basket of fruit from the nurses she worked with. He finally settled on chocolates, racing into a drugstore, Robert screaming in his arms. He bought the largest box they had and shoved it into the diaper bag.

To his horror, Abby's room was full of women when he got there. She introduced them, a neighbor from her old apartment, two nurses from the hospital where she now worked, a friend she'd met at prenatal classes.

"So *you're* Robert's father," that young woman said, narrowing her eyes at him in a judgmental fashion. "It's a pleasure to finally meet you." But she didn't sound as if she meant it, and Conrad felt that every pair of female eyes in the room, with the exception of Abby's, were measuring him and finding him wanting.

He handed Robert to Abby and hurried out, going up to his office to catch up on paperwork. He had to steel himself to return when the hour was up. The women were still there, and they watched silently as he loaded Robert into the Snugli. When he got home, the box of chocolates was still in the diaper bag. Losing his nerve, he gave it to Tillie, along with a generous check, when he drove her back to the hospital that afternoon.

On the Orthopedic floor, he could again hear female voices and laughter floating down the corridor from the direction of Abby's room. Although he knew it was cowardly, he handed Robert to a nursing student at the desk and watched as she took him in. When the time came to retrieve him, Conrad sent the same young woman in to get the baby.

ABBY WAS EXHAUSTED by the time the day ended. She'd had company all day, and although she was grateful to have such good friends, their presence and animated conversation had tired her out.

Because they were her friends, she'd confided in them while she was pregnant. As a result, they all knew what had occurred with Conrad, and they were all astonished to learn that he was now caring for Robert. But they were clear and definite in their opinions about him; they all urged Abby to follow Faye's advice and go after financial support for her child. Each of them had some horror story that reinforced men's unreliable actions when it came to financially supporting women and children.

With all her heart and soul, Abby wanted to believe that Conrad would voluntarily provide for his son, but her sister had told her often enough how naive she was, how unrealistic.

And so when Faye came by just before visiting hours ended that evening, Abby wearily told her to go ahead and do whatever was necessary.

"MORNING, DR. BANFIELD. Morning, Sir Robert, aren't you a cutie in that hat?"

It was Monday morning, and Bunny greeted Conrad with a wide smile and put a finger into one of Robert's fists, giving him a mock handshake. "How was your weekend, Doctor?"

"Very good, thanks. Tillie works like a tranquilizer on this fellow, and I managed to catch up on my sleep and get him here early for his breakfast."

Of course Bunny knew all about the arrangement he'd made with Tillie; he'd come to the realization that there were few, if any, secrets among the staff, and instead of being appalled by it, he simply accepted it now. Wondering exactly when he and Bunny had become friends instead of adversaries, he said politely, "And how was your weekend, Bunny?"

He expected a standard reply, but instead she wrinkled her snub nose and rolled her eyes. "It was the pits. This guy I'm seeing, Zachary? Well, he's real passive-aggressive.''

Conrad hid a smile at the professional diagnosis. Before Robert had come into his life, it would have infuriated him that Bunny had absorbed the psychiatric jargon from working in the department. Now, he just found it amusing.

''I dunno if I can take it much longer. I went out with my girlfriend Saturday instead of watching him play squash, and that made him mad, so then he comes an hour late for our date. What d'ya think's the best way of dealing with somebody like that, Doctor?''

Conrad was both amazed that she'd confide in him and flattered that she'd ask his opinion. ''It's tough. Have you tried confronting him with it?''

She shook her head. ''It never dawns on me what's happening until afterward. But I think I'll do what you say. We're going out tonight. I'll just bring it up and see what he says.''

''People are often unaware that they're being passive-aggressive, remember. He might not realize what he's doing.''

''Time he found out, then, right? Thanks a lot, Doctor. Hey, you want me to hold Robert while you return these phone calls?'' She handed him a stack of pink reminders. "I'm pretty much caught up around here."

The unexpected offer surprised him. "Yes, please, Bunny. That's most kind of you."

"No problem. C'mere, squirt." She took Robert, babbling away to him.

He finished the calls in peace, reclaimed Robert, who was squalling as usual, and headed into the conference room for rounds. All the nurses smiled and said good morning, and several asked how Abby was and how Robert was doing.

Someone had heard of an herbal remedy for colic, and she'd made up a batch to try on Robert. Another told a risqué joke and everyone, including Conrad, laughed. The discussion about patients went well, and everyone seemed to be in an exceptionally good mood. Rounds had often been stressful, but today they were enjoyable.

When the time came to deliver Robert to Abby for his noon feeding, Conrad was feeling cheerful and relaxed.

"How are you doing, Abby? Feeling stronger today?" He took Robert out of the Snugli and placed him beside her, conscious as always of the feel of her skin as his hand brushed her arm.

She smelled sweet, of some gentle, flowery perfume.

She gave him a slight smile that didn't reach as far as her eyes. "I must be doing okay because Dr. Foster says I can go home tomorrow."

Even though he should have expected such news, Conrad was taken by surprise, and he was overcome with a confused jumble of emotions. He was glad she was healing, of course. But the thought of not seeing her every day left a hollow feeling in the pit of his stomach. And Robert...he wouldn't have Robert with him any longer.

A sense of devastation and a feeling of total emptiness overwhelmed him.

CHAPTER TEN

"IT SEEMS A BIT soon to me," he said to Abby at last. "Are you sure you're well enough?"

"My doctor seems to think I am." But Abby didn't sound at all certain, and all of a sudden a wild idea popped into Conrad's head.

His heart hammered, and excitement filled him. Did he dare suggest she come and stay at his house until she was completely recovered? He'd hire someone to take care of her during the day, the spare bedroom was already equipped, he'd take care of Robert during the evenings so that she could rest...

"I'm going to stay with Faye and her husband Harry until I'm stronger," Abby added, and Conrad's heart sank.

"She's arranging for a home-care nurse for the first little while. It should only take a week or two for me to get well enough to be on my own with Robert." Her voice was wistful. "I can't wait to get back to my own apartment. It's so hard to stay with relatives. Faye and Harry aren't used to babies.''

It was his cue, and he missed it. He was worrying over the intricacies of family feelings, whether Abby might think he was only trying to get back at her sister if he suggested she come to his house.

''So if you could bring all Robert's stuff when you come in the morning...?''

''Certainly.''

''You know you can come and visit him any time you want, Conrad.''

''Thank you.'' Didn't she understand that it was out of the question to imagine he'd go anywhere near Faye's house, even to visit his son?

Agitated, he went back to the ward, and for the next hour, he mulled the situation over. He'd been wrong, he decided, in not giving Abby a choice as to where she'd prefer to stay while she recuperated. When he collected Robert, he'd casually suggest that she come to him; after all, Robert was familiar with his house. Hadn't he read somewhere that babies, even very small ones, reacted negatively to a change of environment? And he was Robert's father, they had a joint interest in making things as easy for their child as they could, didn't they? There were also a number of financial issues they had to discuss concerning Robert's future and Abby's comfort, for which they needed privacy and time.

But when he went to get the baby, the physiotherapist was there, involved in a complicated demonstration of exercises that Abby had to do.

Conrad waited for a while, but the consultation went on and on, and he had to get back to his own patients. He took Robert and left, consoling himself with the thought that there was still that afternoon to talk with her.

Conrad grew more and more nervous as the time approached for Robert's afternoon feeding. He racked his brain for logical reasons to present to Abby, and finally he wrote out what he wanted to say on a paper and tried to memorize it. Just in case, he tucked it his pocket as he headed for the elevator and Robert's three o'clock feeding.

Filled with determination, he hurried into Abby's room, only to find Faye sitting by her bed.

His first craven impulse was to hand Robert over and get out fast, but a voice inside of him disagreed.

Stay and make your position clear, it urged.

Don't let this obnoxious woman stop you from saying what you've planned to say.

He drew in a deep breath and tried to concentrate on his speech, but before he could get a word out, Faye whipped a legal document out of her briefcase and slapped it into his hand.

"This is a written statement of claim which includes a declaration that you are Robert's father. If that isn't evident to you, then an order is included for the submission of your blood for tissue typing, as well as an order for child support, a compensation order for related and incidental expenses relating to his birth, costs and a clear description of access rights. If you have any objections, have your solicitor get in touch with me. I should warn you, however, that if this goes to court, we won't have any difficulty at all proving our case."

It took a moment for all the ramifications to penetrate his numbed brain. Conrad didn't glance at the papers he held. Instead, he looked at Abby.

"You agreed to this?" He knew she must have, but he needed, so very much, to hear her deny it. "Without even talking to me first, you let *her*..." he jerked his head at Faye "go ahead with this?"

Abby wouldn't meet his eye. In a shaky voice, she said, "Yes. I—I told her to go ahead." Then her chin tilted up defiantly and she looked at Conrad, her arm tightening around the baby. "I want the very best for Robert. I..." She cleared her throat. "I can't provide that, especially not now. And I can't take any chances."

"Chances? What chances?" Anger and the bitter taste of betrayal made his voice cold and distant. "You must know that I want the best for him as well. There was no need to take legal action, Abigail. We could have talked it over between ourselves and come to an agreement. In fact, I'd planned we'd do exactly that."

"Yeah, right," Faye snorted. "The same way you talked over Abby's pregnancy, no doubt."

Conrad lost his temper, and he bellowed at Faye, "You stay out of this. This is between Abigail and me. It's no concern of yours."

Robert's wails changed from hunger to terror.

"Hush, you're scaring him," Abby accused, and Conrad felt terrible for hollering.

Faye had no such problem. Her voice was loud and shrill as she fumed, "The hell it isn't my concern." She stomped around the bed and came to stand inches from him.

"Who do you think was there for Abby when

she was so sick she couldn't make it to the bathroom in those early months? When she cried for days and couldn't even work after that little scene with you, when she started bleeding at seven months in the middle of the night and was scared out of her mind, when she needed someone to take her and the baby home from the hospital? *I* took care of her, I've always taken care of her, ever since we were little kids. She needs someone to watch out for her, and you sure as hell weren't around, Banfield. So don't give me any song and dance about trusting you to do the right thing. Your track record doesn't exactly inspire confidence.''

"Faye, please, please, stop." Abby looked on the verge of tears, and Robert was screaming.

Faye glanced at them and turned back to Conrad. "Obviously this scene isn't doing Abby or the baby any good, so maybe you'd better just leave.''

He thought of insisting she leave instead, but one look at Abby's stricken face told him not to make this ugly scene any worse.

Conrad turned on his heel without another word and walked out.

ABBY WAS SHAKING as she tried to settle Robert at her breast to nurse. She crooned to him, and stroked his head. It took a long time to quiet him, and when at last he began gulping her milk, she finally looked up at her sister.

"Well, we sure won that round, didn't we?" Faye's words were smug, but Abby detected a hint of uncertainty in her eyes.

"I'm going home to my own apartment tomorrow, Faye," Abby said quietly. "I've decided we need to be in our own home, Robert and I."

"What?" Faye bristled. "Don't be ridiculous. You can't take care of yourself yet, much less a baby. You need help, Abby."

"I'll get home care, I'll manage."

Faye's eyes flashed. "I suppose you're pissed off at me because I stood up for you with Banfield. Honestly, Abby, you've got to toughen up. The world's a rotten place, you have to learn to fight for your rights. You can't just let people walk all over you."

"I know that's how you feel, Faye. But it's not how I feel. It's not the way I want Robert to see the world, either." Abby looked down at her son, drawing strength from him, and then back up at her sister. "I've always let you boss me around, because I knew how much you needed to feel that you were in control. I know you love me and want to do your best for me. But I'm grown up now, and I need to take charge of my own life. I can take care of myself, Faye.''

"Since when? I can't believe I'm hearing this. You let that arrogant SOB walk all over you, and when I stand up for you, you get mad at me." Faye's face was scarlet.

"I'm not mad." Abby shook her head sadly. "I'm just aware, for the first time in my life, that my way of doing things is right for me. I should never have agreed to that order. I'm telling Conrad that it was a mistake."

"Well, go ahead and burn your bridges, just don't come crying to me afterward." Faye snatched her raincoat up and stalked out of the room.

Abby watched her go, feeling sorry that her declaration of independence was causing Faye pain. But she also knew that it was past time to take charge of her own life. And she was going to begin by apologizing to Conrad.

WHEN HE LEFT ABBY'S floor, Conrad went back to Psychiatry. He sat at his desk and stared blindly at neat stacks of paper, unable to work.

When it was time to go for Robert, he asked Bunny if she'd do it as a special favor to him.

"Only if you promise to give me some more pointers on dealing with Zachary."

He promised gladly. When she returned with the baby, she handed him over and said, "Abby says she wants to talk to you and could you maybe drop in to see her before you leave tonight?"

Conrad shook his head. "Call and tell her I'll see her first thing tomorrow morning, I'm not feeling too good and I'm going home early."

"Gee, I hope you aren't getting that stomach flu everybody's come down with," Bunny said. "Maybe try some ginger tea when you get home."

"Thanks, I will," he lied. The truth was Conrad couldn't face another confrontation with Abby. He bundled Robert up and staggered out of the hospital, feeling like the victim of a violent ambush.

For the first time, Robert slept throughout the evening, a small, relaxed ball in the middle of the large crib. In a frenzy of activity that Conrad hoped would keep him from thinking, he gathered the vast array of baby paraphernalia he'd collected during the past weeks and began loading it into the car, telling himself his life could get back to normal at last. Then he made himself pasta, which he couldn't eat, and waited impatiently for Robert to wake up and start crying so he wouldn't have to wonder how to fill in the empty hours.

Robert finally awakened at eleven, and Conrad snatched him up before he'd even gotten one good bellow out. Conrad changed and fed him, talking to him the way he'd fallen in the habit of doing, telling him about patients and their treatment.

He noticed while he was doing it how much Robert had changed just during the time Conrad had kept him. He was plumper, his features more defined. And if tonight was any indication, he was finally getting over colic; he seemed to actually listen as Conrad explained the intricacies of treating schizophrenia.

Robert gulped down most of his bottle and Conrad burped him, and when he lifted Robert from his shoulder and looked into his small face, the baby's eyes seemed to focus on him thoughtfully. He studied Conrad's face, and all of a sudden he smiled, a wide, goofy grin that caused his eyes to cross.

And for the first time in his adult life, Conrad began to cry.

CHAPTER ELEVEN

MORTIFIED BY SUCH a loss of control, Conrad wiped his eyes on a corner of Robert's blanket. His heart seemed swollen, so large it felt as if his chest wall couldn't contain it. He blew his nose on a tissue, and enormous pride welled up in him. He had the irrational urge to phone the hospital and tell Abby what a miraculous feat their brilliant child had just accomplished.

Then he remembered the court order and didn't call. Instead, he spent the next half hour trying to coax Robert to smile again, but the baby went to sleep instead. Conrad sat with him in his arms, knowing he ought to put him in his crib and go to bed, get some sleep before the colic reasserted itself.

One hour passed, and then two. Robert lay spread-eagled across Conrad's chest, and the familiar warm weight of the small body, the sweetly personal smell of the baby's breath and head, his fast, regular breathing, the tiny twitches of his arms and legs, the flickering of his eyelids, were all noted and filed away like precious snapshots in Conrad's memory.

He thought again of Abby and the legal papers, and he tried to locate the righteous anger that had always been near the surface, but it was gone. Instead his chest still hurt with every breath he drew, and he had a moment's panic, thinking maybe he was suffering a heart attack.

Alarmed, he got up and gently settled Robert into the nest of soft blankets in his crib, and then slowly stood upright, waiting for the pain to extend down his arm.

It didn't, and when he drew in another cautious deep breath, he understood that the sensation wasn't physical, although it was centered in his heart.

He spent several minutes trying to identify it, and at last he understood that what he was feeling was overwhelming love, profound sadness, intense regret.

He'd gained a son, but he'd lost the woman he loved, and it hurt.

So often, patients told him that they were in pain from their feelings. He'd never understood until right now how severe that pain could be, how very real.

Steeling himself, he opened his briefcase and took out the papers Faye had drawn up. He sat down at his desk and read them, making determined changes here and there, increasing substantially the amounts that Faye had stipulated. At last he signed them and stuffed them back in the side of the diaper bag.

ABBY GOT UP AT FIVE. With the nurse's help, she showered then dressed in a blue tracksuit. She put on lip gloss and curled her eyelashes. She was sitting in the large easy chair beside the bed when Conrad arrived at six-fifteen. She felt weak and shaky and frightened, but determined. She'd made up her mind she was going to tell Conrad exactly how she felt about him. If she was going to live her life her way, she needed to begin by being totally honest. She was going to tell the father of her child that she loved him, and find out whether there was any hope of a life together.

Robert was in the Snugli, and both Conrad's arms were loaded with baby supplies. He was dressed casually, in khaki slacks and a brown sweater, and she realized he wasn't wearing his tinted glasses. His dark wavy hair was longer than usual, and he looked slightly disheveled and breathtakingly handsome.

Abby had been trying to figure out exactly what to say to him since three in the morning. "Conrad, could you sit down for a minute?" She was so nervous she could hardly get the words out.

He unstrapped the Snugli and handed Robert to her. The baby was asleep. "Actually, there's more stuff in the car that I should bring up." He sounded friendly, but distant. He headed for the door.

"Conrad, wait." The urgency in her tone must have gotten through to him, because he turned and faced her.

"I have an early appointment, Abby, I really should go. The legal papers are signed, they're in the side compartment of the diaper bag. I made a few adjustments, but I'm sure you and your sister will find the changes acceptable."

"Conrad, please." She'd beg if she had to. "Please, we need to talk. I *need* to talk. Would you just shut the door and sit down?"

She could see he was wary, but he did as she asked, closing the door and taking a chair on the opposite side of the bed from where she sat.

"You're not wearing your glasses anymore."

It slipped out, and she could have kicked herself. It wasn't at all the way she'd wanted to begin.

"I lost them somewhere." He shrugged. "I guess I didn't really need them after all."

An awkward silence fell. Finally, she plunged into it. "I'm so sorry for having those darn papers drawn up," she blurted. "It was wrong of me, and I want you to know that I'm going to rip them up and throw them away. I feel awful about them." She gulped and added in a small voice, "I'm not blaming Faye, I should just have had enough confidence in myself to know what was right."

"Abby, please. Don't." He stumbled to his feet and came around the bed. "I've thought it over, and maybe it's a good idea for you to have things spelled out in black and white." He shook his head, and his voice became harsh. "Faye was right about one thing...you have absolutely no reason to trust me." He was staring down at Robert, and his expression was desolate. "Having a legal order makes good sense."

"I didn't trust you before."

He nodded agreement, his face stern. He wouldn't look at her.

"But I do now." She tried to put what she felt into her voice. "Conrad, you've taken wonderful care of our son. Whatever happened in the past doesn't matter now, because I know that you love him, that you'll go on taking care of him, with or without a stupid court order.''

His eyes slowly lifted and met hers, and the pain and longing she saw there made her own heart ache. ''You're absolutely right, Abby. But it's not just about Robert.''

Time seemed to stretch and fold in on itself. She could only wait, heart hammering, breath suspended, as he struggled, searching for unfamiliar words that she'd dreamed of hearing him say.

''I love you, Abby.'' The declaration seemed to come from deep inside of him.

Her breath rushed out, her ribs hurt like fury, her soul filled with joy.

''I'll never forgive myself for the way I treated you,'' he said in a rush. ''I've never had the chance to apologize to you for the way I acted, but I do now, from the bottom of my heart. I was a fool. I was afraid.'' He drew in a shuddering breath. ''Terrified, and too dumb to admit to myself what was going on. There was something special between us that night, and it scared the living hell out of me. I'd never felt anything that powerful. So like an idiot, like I've always done with emotions, I pretended it didn't exist. And I hurt you, I denied you.'' He motioned toward Robert and added in a near groan, ''And him as well, God help me. He's taught me so much. You both have.'' He crouched down beside her, took her hand in his. ''Abby, is there any chance you'd ever forgive me, let me try to make it up to you?''

She started to answer, to tell him that she loved him too, that the forgiving part was already behind them, but he rushed on, ''I know you're going to Faye's, but if there's anything you need or want, if you want me to take Robert, or...or go shopping, or anything...''

''But I'm not. I'm not going to stay with Faye.'' Abby shook her head. ''That's what else I wanted to tell you, part of it, anyway. I'm going back to my own apartment, you can come and see us there. I want you to visit us, Conrad.''

He stared up at her for a moment. Robert was beginning to squirm and whimper. She'd have to feed him in a minute, but there was so much she needed to say to his father.

''Abby.'' There was naked entreaty in his eyes and his voice. ''Abby, you said you trust me. Come home with me. Please. Let me prove to you that I can take care of you and Robert.''

Astounded, she started to refuse, but he interrupted with a rush of words. "I'll bring whatever you want from your apartment. I've got a spare bedroom, and a swing for him, and a high chair, and plenty of diapers, and we can move the crib so he's close to you. He knows the house, Abby. I think he likes it there. Your sister can come and visit, I'll be gracious and friendly to her even if it kills me. Please, Abby. It would give us a chance to get to know one another. I'll take holidays, I'll…why, I'll call on Demetrius, he'll take over my patients for me. You and I need time to talk. There's so many things we haven't discussed. I haven't even had a chance to tell you that Robert smiled at me last night, first time I've ever seen him smile. He knew me, Abby."

She'd been about to refuse, because if she was really going to be independent, she couldn't simply fall into Conrad's arms, could she? Couldn't she?

It was the fatuous pride in his tone when he told her of Robert's smile that made her decide for certain. It would be wrong to deny him the pleasure of seeing Robert smile a second time.

"Okay, Conrad," she heard herself whisper. "Okay, we'll come with you." She was about to add, *but about that spare bedroom*...when his arms came around her, and his mouth closed over hers in a kiss that made her forget how much her ribs hurt.

There'd be time to sort out the details later. There'd be plenty of time to tell Conrad that she loved him, that maybe they ought to think about getting married.

So that their son wouldn't be embarrassed by them.

Robert, sandwiched between his mother and his father, indignantly decided he'd had enough. He was being ignored, so he did what he was best at.

He opened his mouth wide and howled for his breakfast.

EPILOGUE

CONRAD SHIFTED from one foot to the other, his anxious gaze riveted on the entrance to St. Joe's tiny hospital chapel. The room was already overflowing, and still more people were squeezing in, many of them wearing surgical greens or hospital uniforms, all of them smiling.

Doctor Nikolo Demetrius, as perfectly tailored as Conrad, stood at his side, and whenever their eyes met, he winked reassuringly. Niko was taking his duties as best man very seriously. Before they entered the flower-decked chapel, he'd brushed flecks of invisible dust from the shoulders of Conrad's charcoal silk suit, straightened both their ties, and checked once again for the ring.

Abby was the one who had decided they would be married at the hospital. "We met at St. Joe's, Robert was born there, it's where you first told me you loved me," she'd said to him.

''And the space is just right because there won't be many people.''

That had been a gross miscalculation, because Bunny had posted the announcement of the wedding on the computer, and everyone who could slip away from their duties was in attendance, including Bunny, Tillie, nearly all the nurses from Psychiatry, and many of Conrad's patients.

Everyone was here except Abby. She was now—Conrad consulted his watch again—sixteen-and-a-half minutes late for their wedding. He felt icy-cold and nauseous, his heart hammering with fear. Abby and Robert had spent last night at Faye and Harry's house; apparently it wasn't proper for a bride to spend the night before the wedding with the man she was to marry.

It was the first night in three months they'd spent apart. Those months hadn't been easy for either of them. Learning to live together, learning to parent together, had taken enormous amounts of patience and understanding from each of them, and they'd had differences of opinion more than once. But through it all, Conrad knew exactly what he wanted. He wanted Abby beside him for the rest of his life as his partner, his spouse, his beloved.

But what if Abby'd changed her mind in the endless hours they'd been apart? What if Faye had convinced her that marriage to Conrad was a mistake? He'd thought Faye had begun to accept him, even like him a little, but maybe he'd been wrong. Conrad felt perspiration trickle down his temples even as a cold shiver ran down his spine. The room was too warm, too filled with bodies.

The minister who was to marry them leaned toward Conrad, and beneath the buzz of voices and the soft strumming of the classical guitarist—who was also the obstetrician who'd delivered Robert—she whispered, ''Brides are always late, just take a few deep breaths. You're awfully pale. You don't want to pass out here. Heaven knows what all these medical people would do.''

Conrad nodded, forced air into his lungs, and as he released it there was a sudden rustling at the door.

He turned. Faye came in first, but Conrad had eyes only for Abby, carrying his son. She was breathtakingly beautiful in a simple cream dress and a floppy straw hat, it's crown encircled with daises. Robert, five months old, peered around, dark eyes wide and curious and unafraid.

At Abby's side was an older man leaning

heavily on two canes, and Conrad breathed a silent prayer of gratitude, stepping forward to meet Abby's father, Louis Martin. Abby and Conrad had written and telephoned, inviting Louis, but Abby had concluded it would take a miracle for her father to decide to come to her wedding.

The miracle had happened. Abby had her father with her on her wedding day.

As they'd planned, Abby handed Robert over to Tillie. The baby beamed at his favourite babysitter and patted her cheek with one chubby hand.

At last, at last, the woman he loved stood at Conrad's side. "Sorry I'm late," she whispered. "I had to nurse Robert, you know how he gets when he's hungry."

Conrad did know. Their adorable, brilliant son became a tyrant, turning purple and holding his breath if a feeding didn't happen exactly when he felt it should. In fact, Robert seemed inclined to be just a trifle rigid and demanding, but Conrad knew a parent could guide a child by setting a good example.

The minister cleared her throat.

The guitarist strummed one last dramatic riff.

Conrad took Abby's hand in his.

"Dearly beloved…"

Conrad, Abby, Robert. Three people, with one life stretching before them. His family. Conrad felt joy and love and light flood his entire being.

BABY JANE DOE

Judith Arnold

To Tzivia

CHAPTER ONE

TERRY HADN'T INTENDED to throw her engagement ring into the toilet. She'd actually been aiming at Todd's head, but his timely flinch caused the ring to ricochet off the wall and drop into the toilet with a wet *plunk!*

If Terry could derive any pleasure from the moment, it came from knowing that Todd really, really wanted to fish the ring out, but he couldn't move without causing great embarrassment to both himself and Allegra DeCosta, the hostess of this swanky New Year's Eve party. Allegra was seated on the marble counter beside the sink, her elegant red velvet dress bunched up around her waist and her legs wrapped around Todd's hips. The trousers of his tuxedo drooped loose, but her legs kept them from falling to the floor. She had on stockings with glittering gold threads running through them. Her garter belt was the same lusty scarlet as her dress.

Terry had wandered into the wrong bathroom,

obviously. The powder room on the first floor of the duplex was occupied, which hadn't bothered her since all she'd wanted to do was touch up her lipstick. But Allegra's debonair silver-haired husband had seen her loitering outside the door and said, "There's another bathroom on the second floor." So she'd gone upstairs, happy for the opportunity to peek into a few more rooms in the luxurious Back Bay condo, to check out Allegra's decorating taste and the architectural flourishes she and her husband had lavished on their million-dollar pied-à-terre. Terry had found the bathroom, tapped on the door, swung it open—and discovered her fiancé and Allegra in an extremely compromising position on the sink counter.

Happy New Year, she thought grimly.

"It's not what you think," Todd protested, gazing toward her and simultaneously shielding the hostess from view. His expensive haircut looked fashionably disheveled. His narrow bow tie dangled limply from the collar of his silk shirt. She wondered if her unexpected intrusion had caused the rest of him to dangle limply, too.

"It's not?" she said with sarcastic cheer. "What a relief!"

"Terry," Todd said, his voice edged in panic,

"get the ring out of the toilet, would you? It's two and a half carats. I paid a fortune for it."

It was indeed a very large ring. Terry had given it back to Todd a couple of months ago, when she'd caught him messing around with a client at the consulting firm where he worked. But he'd begged for her forgiveness and promised it would never happen again. So she'd taken the ring back.

In her ball game, two strikes meant he was out.

"Please, Terry, get the ring out of the can."

She stepped farther into the bathroom. Allegra peeked out from behind Todd's shoulder, her makeup remarkably unmussed. Todd could be so impeccable even when he was performing tongue tonsillectomies. "Hi," she said to her hostess. "How's it going?"

Allegra had the good grace to duck her head.

Terry leaned over the toilet. Through the clear water, she saw the ring glinting at the bottom of the bowl. "It's in there all right," she said, then reached for the flusher and pressed it. "Oops! I'm so sorry!"

Todd cursed. Terry skipped out of the bathroom as quickly as she could in her dainty high-heeled sandals.

Only when she was downstairs, surrounded by

the hundred and fifty or so party guests, did her shock begin to wear off, allowing pain to set in. Todd, the man she'd decided to marry, the handsome, wealthy, charming executive who'd allegedly fallen in love with her when he'd hired her to redecorate his apartment last summer, had brought her to this posh farewell to the twentieth century so he could boff the hostess.

She was not going to start the new millennium by becoming Mrs. Todd Whitley. She was going to remain good old Terry Galvin for yet another year, or two, or ten.

Deftly avoiding Allegra's husband and the other guests, she detoured to the room off the kitchen where the guests' coats had been hung. She donned her lined raincoat, buttoned it and hurried out into the foyer. "Say, Terry, where are you going?" one of Todd's friends called out to her.

She shook her head, stalked to the door and let herself out without a word.

Only when she was standing outside on the sidewalk, light flurries of snow swirling around her, did she realize she hadn't thought out her departure very well. No surprise; she hadn't thought out her relationship with Todd too well, either.

Not a cab was in sight. As it was New Year's

Eve, 1999, no doubt most of Boston's cabdrivers were at their own New Year's Eve blasts right now. The few who weren't were probably downtown at Boston's traditional First Night festivities, shuttling revelers around the city.

She considered going back inside to telephone for a cab, then vetoed the idea. She couldn't go back in there and face all those rich, insouciant people. She couldn't look her kindly host in the eye, knowing his wife and Terry's fiancé—her *ex*-fiancé—were getting it on in the upstairs bathroom. She couldn't allow Todd's friends to question her. And while it might be amusing to see if Todd was going to attempt to summon a plumber to take the toilet apart just an hour before the stroke of midnight, that amusement wouldn't compensate for the humiliation of having been duped by the man she'd once imagined herself marrying.

She decided she would walk home. Her sandals weren't suitable and the snow stung her face, but the prospect of frostbite and blisters was vastly preferable to the embarrassment of returning to the party.

She lifted the collar of her coat around her neck and started off. The city streets were well lit but eerily quiet; everyone in Boston, if not the entire universe, was somewhere else, somewhere better, somewhere where the twenty-first century was going to be greeted with joyful anticipation.

Not Terry, though. Her major goal right now was to complete the three-mile walk to her apartment before the century ended.

Her sandals made clicking sounds on the pavement. At least the snow wasn't sticking as it danced down from the purple-gray clouds. Occasionally, she would hear a cheer or a swell of laughter spilling from an open window; at major cross streets, she would see rowdy carousers careering along the sidewalks, singing songs, blowing on plastic horns and ringing bells. As she skirted Boston Common, she ignored the swarms of celebrants mingling in the park, cheering and swaggering and applauding the jugglers and bundled-up musicians who performed as part of the city's traditional First Night celebration. Terry kept her face forward, her collar clutched at her throat, her purse tucked carefully into one of her coat's deep pockets.

Snowflakes clung to her hair and melted. The little slip of a dress she'd worn was as inappropriate to the weather as her sandals. Next New Year's Eve, she swore to herself, she would wear corduroy jeans and a wool sweater. And boots, just in case it snowed.

Next New Year's Eve, she would be blessedly, defiantly single. No more hasty engage-
ments. No more mistaking infatuation for love.
No more opening her heart to a two-timing
creep.

Compiling a list of resolutions kept her mind
off how cold and lonely she felt. No more dates
with unbearably good-looking men, she vowed.
No more worrying about whether spending a
Saturday night curled up in front of the VCR
with a Harrison Ford movie—any Harrison Ford
movie—and a pint of gourmet ice cream was a
sign that she was a social failure. No more fretting about her biological clock. She was only
twenty-nine. She had time. And no more letting
her mother nag her about how having children
was a woman's noble destiny. Maybe it wasn't.
Maybe Terry would skip the whole motherhood
thing and devote her life to her interior design
business and her friends.

She glanced at her wristwatch. She'd been
walking nearly an hour. Her nose and her toes
were numb, her throat felt scratchy from the raw
night air, but she was only a few blocks from
her South End loft. A car swept past her, the
windows open and the occupants blowing noisemakers that made her head hurt.

As soon as she got home, she would take a

hot bath. Then she'd bundle up in her flannel jammies and drink something alcoholic and grieve over the death of her engagement.

The snowfall intensified as she reached her block. A thin layer of white powdered the sidewalk, and she had to watch her step to avoid skidding. At least the snow made the street look prettier. She liked snow. She just didn't like it when she was wearing a skimpy dress and strappy heels, and when her ex-fiancé was a son of a bitch and it was the biggest New Year's Eve of her life and she was all alone.

Just outside the door to her building, she heard a faint mewing sound. A thought shot through her mind as sharp and sudden as a bullet: *You aren't all alone.*

Great. In her misery, was she going to be visited by God?

No. She heard the mewing sound again, coming from the alley between her building and the next. Unless God was a stray cat, she wasn't experiencing any sort of spiritual epiphany.

From an open window in the adjacent building, she heard the boisterous sounds of yet another party, whistles and applause and dozens of voices counting down the final minute of 1999. Then she heard the mewing sound again.

Maybe she ought to resolve to become one of

those eccentric spinsters who lived with cats. She'd never had a cat before, but she wasn't going to start the new year by letting some poor kitten freeze in the snowy alley.

"Ten, nine, eight..." Through the open window, the voices wafted down to her, ticking off the final seconds. Shrugging her coat more tightly around herself, she picked a cautious path into the alley and halted.

"Seven, six, five, four..."

Her gaze circled the area. Several Dumpsters were lined along one brick wall, but bits of trash had escaped them and lay at her feet. "Here, kitty, kitty," she murmured.

"Three, two..."

And then she saw it, a ragged bundle tucked between two Dumpsters. She hunkered down, pulled back the gray wool fabric—

"One, zero! Happy New Year!"

She barely heard the trumpeting noisemakers, the hoots and cheers and shrieks of delight coming from the party. She was too entranced by the sight before her: a baby. Tiny, pale, whimpering thinly and pushing at the blanket with its delicate little hands.

A baby.

"FINN? YOU'D BETTER take this one," Maggie shouted across the detective squad room.

Allen Finn took a swig of Coke, lowered his booted feet from his desk and sat up straight. Twenty minutes ago, he'd joined Maggie and the few other souls on the precinct's skeleton crew to count down the seconds to the year 2000 in the first-floor lounge, which had a TV. After they'd all drunk a toast with soft drinks and watched a few minutes of a televised fireworks display, he'd returned to his desk on the second floor, where Stephen King's latest bestseller awaited him.

Finn figured that in another half hour or so, the patrolmen out on the streets were going to have their hands full with D.W.I.s trying to make their way home from countless New Year's Eve parties across the city. But as a detective, he didn't have to deal with drunk drivers.

As it was, he hadn't had to deal with anything yet. It had turned out to be a damned good night to volunteer for overtime. The other guys in his squad had all had plans for New Year's Eve. Finn had had a standing invitation to join his sister and her family, but he'd decided to do his last good deed of the century and offered to man the detectives' squad room overnight. Someone had to do it—why not him?

So now Maggie was saying there was a call

that required the attention of a detective. He noticed the blinking red light on his phone console, pressed the button and lifted the receiver. "Detective Finn here."

"Yes? I—um—I found a baby."

"A baby." Not a D.W.I., he thought. Not a party out of control. Not a gathering where someone had been injured by a firecracker, or a husband high on something who'd decided to take out his frustrations on his wife.

A baby. He reached for a pen.

"She can't be more than a day or two old. I found her in an alley beside my building. She's…" The woman's voice dissolved into a sigh.

"Is she alive?" he asked, tugging his notepad closer.

"Oh—oh, yes! She's wonderful. She's radiant. And she seems healthy, and, oh, she's got the most adorable little mouth…" The woman sighed again. He realized it was a sound of ecstasy.

Radiant? The woman didn't sound drunk, but you never knew. Even if she wasn't drunk, well, there were plenty of loonies in Boston. It didn't take a great leap of faith to suspect that the arrival of a new millennium might lure a few of them out of their padded cells.

"I wouldn't have even called," she continued, "but I knew I had to. I mean, it was the right thing to do."

"Okay." He had to do the right thing, too. "Let me have your name and address."

"Terry Galvin," she told him. "Teresa, actually, but no one calls me that except my mother when I'm in trouble." She recited a South End address, then added, "The baby really seems fine. I probably shouldn't have dialed 9-1-1. It's not like this is an actual emergency or anything—"

"I'll be there in a couple of minutes," he told her, partly to put an end to her beatific chattering and partly because it was his job to forge out into the cold December night—make that the cold January morning—and take care of this wonderful, radiant newborn who'd been abandoned in an alley. As he hung up the phone, tucked his notebook into an inner pocket of his leather bomber jacket and slung his arms through the sleeves, it occurred to him that Teresa Galvin might be the mother of the baby. She could be that crazy. All alone on New Year's Eve, stuck at home with a newborn when she'd rather be out painting the town red... Who knew? Maybe she'd called the police emergency number because she was lonely.

Nearing the squad-room door, he stopped at Maggie's desk to tell her where he was going. "You'll start getting the drunk drivers soon," he predicted. "Enjoy the peace while you can." Then he headed downstairs and stepped outside.

A dry, fine snow filled the air like white dust. He jogged around to the side lot and unlocked one of the unmarked squad cars, then drove off into the night, alert for reckless drivers—and reckless pedestrians, too. You never knew what you'd run into on New Year's Eve.

He reached Terry Galvin's street in less than five minutes. It was part of a recently gentrified area of the South End; old warehouses converted into lofts, tenements spruced up so their rents could be doubled, trendy restaurants and boutiques aglow with Christmas lights. He parked the car in front of the alley next to the building bearing her address and wondered if that was where she'd found the baby—assuming she'd been telling him the truth on the phone.

He entered the building's vestibule, pressed the intercom button next to number 3 and heard her voice crackle through the speaker. "Yes?"

"It's Detective Finn."

"Okay. I'm on the second floor, on the left when you come out of the elevator." The inner door buzzed as its lock was released, and he entered the building.

She didn't sound flaky. A touch giddy, maybe, as if she'd had a glass or two of champagne, but not like a refugee from an asylum. He really, really hoped she wasn't some lonely loser looking to make friends with a cop during a long night of solitude.

The elevator was a huge industrial model, apparently a holdover from the building's previous life as a warehouse. While it creaked up a level, he dusted the snow from the shoulders of his jacket and finger-combed his hair. On the second floor, he got out, found her door and rang the bell.

She cracked the door open, using the safety chain. All he could see was a narrow sliver of creamy skin and one large hazel eye.

He held up his detective's shield. She stared at it for a minute, then shut the door and unhooked the chain. She opened the door fully and then backed down the short entry hall to the well-lit room at its end.

He entered, then halted as she moved into the light. His breath caught in his throat. That she was a beautiful woman meant nothing to him; he saw lots of beautiful women in his work and he knew better than to respond.

What stunned him was that she was nursing the baby.

She was a slender slip of a woman, dressed in a delicate gray dress that almost wasn't there—short, sleeveless and gossamer. She'd pulled one shoulder strap down to her elbow, letting the front of the dress fall away so the baby had access to her breast. She'd draped a towel around the baby and her chest, but he could see her smooth, pale skin, the sweet roundness of her breast, the shadow at the base of her throat—and the towel-wrapped bundle cradled against her bosom, not making a sound.

He lifted his gaze to her face. He hadn't misguessed when he'd thought she sounded beatific on the phone. Her heart-shaped face was framed in long, reddish-blond curls, her eyes were wide and her smile was blissful. She looked like a chic angel tripping on some drug he'd never heard of.

His gaze dipped back to her half-exposed breast, then up to her face once more. "Ms. Galvin?" he asked uncertainly. If the baby wasn't hers, how could she be nursing it?

She seemed to understand his confusion. "She's not getting any milk out of me," she said, moving farther into the living room, which he took as an invitation to follow her. "She was just fussing and fussing, and nothing else I did seemed to calm her. It's not like I've got pacifiers and bottles of formula lying around. She was fretting so much—the poor thing—so I thought I'd try this."

He swallowed, unsure why seeing a pretty woman calming a frantic baby with her breast should disturb him so much.

"I also checked her diaper," Terry Galvin continued, almost like a schoolgirl proudly describing her performance on a history test. "I stuck a sanitary pad in there so she wouldn't be so wet. If I could have run out and bought a package of diapers, I would have, but you know, midnight on New Year's Eve...or is it New Year's Day? Anyway, I improvised." She smiled sheepishly.

Her living room was a cavernous space broken up with red and black leather couches, oddly shaped tables, eccentric lamps, clean white walls and an expanse of windows. The floor was parquet covered with rugs patterned with bright geometric shapes. The art on the walls was abstract but colorful, too. Such a busy room ought to have given him a headache, but it didn't. It made him grin.

"I'm sorry I'm babbling," Terry Galvin said. "It's just that this is the most exciting thing that's happened to me in—I don't know, maybe my life.'' She had arching cheekbones and rosy lips. A silver necklace with a crescent-moon pendant hung around her neck, and star-shaped silver earrings dangled from her ears. She looked as if she was dressed for a fancy party—except for the absence of shoes and the fact that her dress was half off her so the baby could...well, whatever it was doing to her breast.

He realized his attention was lingering too long on the exposed skin, the curve of her arm cradling the infant, the spill of her hair over her bare shoulder. He ought to take the baby from her, but he wanted to keep his distance. She wasn't just a damned good-looking woman; she exuded a glow, part contentment, part a rapture so bright he almost feared it would burn him if he got too close.

He pulled out his notepad. ''Where did you find the baby?''

''Outside in the alley, between two Dumpsters.''

He took notes as he questioned her. ''What time was it, do you know?''

''Exactly midnight. I heard people at a party next door counting down the seconds.''

He really needed to have a look at the infant. If it had been outside on the cold ground at midnight, it could be suffering from hypothermia. "Was the baby crying or still?"

"She was kind of mewing. I thought she was a kitten at first."

"Was she wrapped in anything?"

"A blanket." With the baby still nestled snugly against her, she motioned with her head for Finn to follow her into a compact, efficient kitchen. On the clean stainless-steel counter lay a rumpled gray blanket. "She was wrapped in that," Terry said. "I unwrapped her once I got her inside because the blanket was so cold I thought it couldn't possibly be keeping her warm. I wrapped her up in these towels instead."

The small dimensions of the room forced him closer to her. She smelled of a musky perfume. "Were you on your way out when you found her?" he asked, keeping his eyes on the dirty blanket.

"On my way home," she said. "I'd left a party early."

"Why?"

She made a face. "I wasn't having a very good time," she said, her undertone leaving no doubt that she'd prefer not to discuss it.

He couldn't avoid checking out the baby any longer. If he eased the baby out of Terry's arms, maybe she could cover herself with the towel really fast. He was having enough trouble standing this close to her. If he saw her breast, he didn't know what might happen.

"I think..." His voice emerged rusty, and he cleared his throat. "We've got to get this baby to Mass General and let some medical professionals examine her," he said.

Terry looked concerned. "Oh, but she's fine. I'm sure she is."

"It's not for you or me to decide," he pointed out. "A doctor should look at her."

Terry mulled this over, then nodded reluctantly. "You're right, of course. That would be the best thing for her. It's just—" she gave another sheepish smile "—I can't bear to let her go. She's so precious. She just fits so perfectly in my arms." She peered up at Finn, her eyes shimmering with green and silver. "You probably think I'm crazy."

Not as crazy as he'd thought when she first called the precinct house, but he wasn't willing to dismiss the possibility that she was a few cards shy of a full deck. "One way or another, you're going to have to let her go, Ms. Galvin." He extended his hands, careful to leave a bit of space between the tips of his fingers and the baby's back so he wouldn't accidentally touch Terry.

Relenting with a sigh, she handed the infant to Finn. He glimpsed her breast so briefly it was like the flash of a camera snapping a photo— and the image was imprinted like a photo in his mind. He blinked and saw the gentle curve of flesh, the damp, swollen red tip. When he opened his eyes, the towel was concealing her as she slid the strap of her dress up her arm.

The baby immediately began to wail and squirm in his hands. She was so small her torso fitted in his palm. He knew instinctively to support her head with his other hand.

Terry Galvin was right; the baby did look healthy. Her skin tone was pink, her hair wispy, her eyes scrunched up and her tiny hands fisting. She had obviously found much more comfort in Terry's embrace than in his.

Then again, he didn't have a woman's consoling anatomy. "Okay," he murmured, adjusting the baby slightly as she whimpered. He rested her on the counter, continuing to cushion her head with his hand, and with his free hand pulled his cell phone from an inner pocket of his jacket. He poked the buttons with his thumb, then held the small phone to his ear.

"Mass General Emergency," said the woman who answered.

He identified himself, then told the clerk that he had an abandoned infant who needed ambulance transport to the hospital. "The baby doesn't seem to be in crisis, but she spent some time outdoors tonight. I'd like to get her over to you as quickly as possible."

"We'll send an EMT team right over," the woman promised.

Finn gave her the address, promised to meet the EMTs at the entry to the building and broke the connection.

"An ambulance?" Terry peered up at him, apparently troubled.

"Quicker and safer than my driving her."

"But—but it might frighten her. The sirens and lights, and all that equipment. She needs to be held, Detective Finn. She needs a woman's arms around her."

Don't we all. "The EMTs will take good care of her," Finn promised, wondering why Terry Galvin's loving, worried expression made him think he needed her arms around him, wondering whether a woman like her could comfort a man the way she could comfort a lost little baby. Wondering why a man who'd chosen to spend New Year's Eve working because there wasn't anyone special he'd wanted to spend it with was strangely pleased to be spending it with a beautiful but possibly deranged woman and a forsaken child.

CHAPTER TWO

SOMETHING HAD HAPPENED to her the moment she'd picked up the baby. She'd felt transformed, filled with a glowing warmth that melted her pain and anger at Todd and caused her heart to flower. Holding a tiny, vulnerable living creature in her hands, comforting her, bonding with her...

In that instant, Terry had forgotten all about her embarrassment and bitterness at the party, her exhaustion and the chill that had settled into her bones from her long walk home, her pangs of self-pity that she was going to spend New Year's Eve and possibly the rest of her life alone.

She *wasn't* alone. She had this baby.

It practically broke her heart to relinquish the baby to the emergency medical technicians, who arrived just minutes after Detective Finn had contacted the hospital. Having neglected to put on her shoes before they went downstairs to meet the ambulance, she was forced to stand in the vestibule, watching through the glass front door as the detective carried the baby to one of the EMTs, who strapped her into a clear-sided bassinet and lifted her up into the back of the vehicle. It looked so...medical, all that chrome, the startlingly white walls and that awful flashing red light shooting color onto the falling snowflakes.

Detective Finn talked for a minute with the driver, then turned and strolled back to the vestibule. When he stepped inside, she felt another change inside her, this one less sentimental, more physical. He was a large man, at least six feet tall and built like a long-distance runner, all muscle and sinew. While he looked nothing like Harrison Ford, he had a similarly rough-hewn, intriguing face. His eyes reflected weariness lightened with a hint of amusement. His nose was blunt and straight, and his mouth looked as if it had gotten worn out trying to smile, or perhaps to keep from smiling.

The vestibule filled with his smell—leather and soap and spice. ''I'd like to have a look at the area where you found the baby,'' he said, then pointedly stared at her shoeless feet.

Her toes curled under his scrutiny. ''Mind if

I slip into something more comfortable?'' she asked, then grinned at her choice of words.

He almost smiled. ''Go ahead,'' he said. ''I'll wait for you here.''

She got into the elevator and rode up, feeling doubly bereft without either the baby or the detective for company. Not that the detective meant anything to her. The baby had altered her in some indescribable way. She didn't see how a rugged, grim-faced man with thick brown hair and soulful eyes could alter her—although she bet he could alter a bed rather profoundly with his presence.

She had no interest in him in the context of her bed, of course. She was not very fond of men at the moment.

She headed straight for her bedroom, pulled off her dress and stockings and donned jeans, a wool sweater, thick socks and her lined snow boots. On her way out, she grabbed her parka, her ragg-wool mittens and her elegant evening purse, which still held her wallet and keys. As the elevator descended, she felt her spirits improve.

She assured herself that seeing Finn had nothing to do with it. She only wanted to get out of her empty, echoing apartment.

He was folding his cell phone and peering

through the glass front door as she joined him in the vestibule. He turned at her entrance, and his mouth settled into a wry smile. He pushed open the glass door and gestured for her to precede him outside.

She led him to the alley. Snow lay in a pale film on the ground. Before she could enter the narrow passageway, he clamped his hand around her arm to stop her. Through her jacket and sweater she felt the heat of his palm, the sharp imprint of his fingers. He wasn't squeezing, but she could feel strength in his grip, male power. He was the exact opposite of the baby, she thought: big and hard and invulnerable.

"Wait a second," he said, then released her arm and turned from her.

She watched him cross the sidewalk to the car parked in front of the alley. He unlocked the trunk and reached in. When he straightened up, he was holding a flashlight and an instant camera. He slammed the trunk shut and returned to her.

"This snow's a problem," he warned. "The less we disturb the scene, the better."

She nodded. Her heart pumped a little faster—from the excitement, she decided, not from Finn's nearness or his deep, gruff voice. It hadn't occurred to her until he'd used the word "scene" that this was a crime scene. When she'd phoned the police, she hadn't been thinking about a crime. She'd been thinking only that she didn't know what to do with the baby, and who besides the police would answer their phone on New Year's Eve?

But abandoning an infant was a crime. Abandoning one in a dark alley on a snowy night was more than just a crime. It was inhuman. The baby could have died.

Perhaps the person who'd left her there had *wanted* her to die.

Terry stifled a sob. Finn turned to her and snapped on his flashlight. The beam smacked her in the face. If she hadn't already been fighting tears, the harsh glare of the light would have filled her eyes.

"Are you okay?"

"I'm just worried about the baby. She's so small and—"

"The EMT said she looked okay. Good color, strong heartbeat..." He aimed the flashlight at her throat, sparing her eyes, and studied her. "You saved her life, you know."

She shuddered as that truth swept through her. "She's a precious little girl," she murmured. "I don't understand why anyone would have left her here."

He stared at her for a second longer, then swung the flashlight around so the beam struck the ground in a white oval. "Where exactly did you find her?"

"Between these two Dumpsters." She walked carefully toward the space separating the massive metal trash receptacles, letting Finn keep his flashlight's beam a step ahead of her. "Right here."

Handing her the flashlight, he lifted the camera to his eye and started snapping photos. Square after square of chemically treated paper cranked out of the bottom. He aimed at each Dumpster, aimed at the ground, aimed at the rough brick wall, tapping the shutter again and again. The flashbulb lit up the alley like a strobe light, flickering a silver-blue glow.

Sighing, he lowered the camera, pulled out the photos and tucked them into a pocket of his jacket. Then he took the flashlight from her. "Stand back," he said, squatting down and running the beam inch by inch over the ground.

"What are you looking for?" she asked.

"Anything." He moved the light this way and that. "A footprint, a thread, anything. With this snow…" He swore under his breath. Straightening, he lifted the lid on first one Dumpster and then the other, peering in at their contents. He wrinkled his nose and made a face.

"You think the person who left the baby would have thrown something in the trash?" she asked.

"Maybe." He ran a hand through his hair. It glittered where snowflakes had landed on it. "I'll cordon off the area. Maybe we'll find something in the daylight."

He started out of the alley. Lacking a better idea, she followed him. "What happens now?"

He paused to send her a quizzical look, then continued on to his car. "We'll inspect the area in the daylight," he repeated.

"No. I mean with the baby. And with me." For some reason, she felt as if one answer might cover both. She felt connected to the baby, as if their fates had merged.

He opened the trunk of his car, stashed the camera and flashlight and pulled out a spool of yellow crime-scene tape. "The hospital will keep her for a while and make sure she's okay. In the meantime, the mother might show up."

"What if she doesn't? She left her baby out here to die! Do you think she's going to have second thoughts?"

"Maybe. Or maybe it wasn't the mother who left her here. It could have been the father, or a baby-sitter. The baby could have been kidnapped. We don't know."

She watched him rope off the alley with yellow tape imprinted repeatedly with the words Police Investigation: Do Not Cross in ominous black letters. Anxiety nibbled at her. She couldn't bear the possibility that that lovely baby would lie in a hospital for days while Finn and his department picked through the contents of the Dumpsters and waited for some mystery mom to show up. Even though Terry had never had children, she knew they needed to be held and loved, especially when they were as young as this baby. "What if you don't find the mother?" she asked.

"The state will take custody," he said. "I've already notified DSS—the Department of Social Services. They'll have a caseworker over at the hospital tomorrow."

"But what happens tonight?" *Who's going to hold that baby? Who's going to sing to her and kiss her downy skin? Who's going to give her a breast to suckle when she cries?*

Finn crossed back to the car and tossed the spool of crime-scene ribbon into the trunk. He slammed it shut, then turned to face Terry. "She's safe where she is, Ms. Galvin. It's not your problem anymore."

"It *is* my problem," she argued, then bit her lip, aware that she must sound insane. Maybe she *was* insane. Maybe her brain had mutated when she'd lifted the baby into her arms, gray matter dissolving into maternal mush. If so, she didn't mind. She liked her brain better now than she had a half hour ago. "There's an old Chinese proverb that says if you save someone's life, you're responsible for that life forever."

"And there's an old Boston proverb that says thanks for calling the police, but we'll take it from here."

"But she's—I mean, I *found* her. If I'd found a wallet containing a lot of money and turned it over to the police, and no one claimed it—"

"This isn't a wallet. It's a baby."

"And until someone claims her, I feel responsible for her. I want to know how she is, and where she is, and what's going on with her."

He stood on the sidewalk, staring at her. He might be vexed, or he might be intrigued. She couldn't tell.

"You want to go to the hospital?" he asked.

The suggestion delighted her. "I'd love to! I can stay with her so she won't be alone. Imagine how scared she must be! I'll go sit with her and hold her and sing lullabies to her." She glanced past Finn at the dark, empty street and wondered if she'd have any more luck finding a cab here than she had outside the DeCostas' condo.

"I'll drive you," he offered.

"Oh—would you?" She hadn't dared to ask him. She'd assumed he would have to go back to the police station and organize a search for whoever had abandoned the baby.

She gazed into his face. Upstairs in her loft, she'd seen that he had brown eyes, but out here in the night they looked almost black. His hair looked darker, too, damp from the melting snow. His jaw was rough-hewn, and a narrow scar extended past his right eyebrow.

He was much better-looking than Harrison Ford, she realized. This extremely handsome detective was going to chauffeur her to the hospital. And here she'd thought she was going to be spending New Year's Eve like a spinster-in-training.

In all probability, he was willing to drive her because he'd rather do that than return to his desk to file a report. Or maybe he'd intended all along to go to the hospital, to continue his detective work there. He was just being nice to her because it fitted into his plans.

Even so, as she climbed into his car, she didn't mind pretending that she and Finn were actually *going* somewhere together. Like a genuine couple, a man and a woman who both cared about an infant foundling.

He said nothing during the drive. The wipers moved intermittently, clearing the melting snow from the windshield. In profile, he looked carved from granite, his jaw thick and hard, his nose cutting a sharp angle. His hands looked almost too large for the steering wheel. Seated beside him in the car's warmth, she could smell his masculine fragrance even more strongly.

The hospital's emergency wing was bright and bustling despite the holiday—or maybe because of it. Several ambulances were lined up in front of the awninged entrance, lights flashing and medical personnel rushing back and forth.

"This seems to be a hot spot," she observed.

"Drunk drivers," he explained, steering past the ambulances and finding a parking space not far from the door.

Terry shuddered and averted her eyes when they walked past the row of ambulances. They entered the building, sidestepping a gurney being pushed speedily through the corridor by a trio of interns. Again she looked away.

Finn pointed to a small waiting area. "Wait there. I'll see what I can find out."

Nodding, Terry took a seat in the alcove. She

closed her eyes and conjured up a memory of the baby, so soft and snuggly in her arms. She recalled unsnapping the baby's pink coverall, carefully opening the diaper and discovering it damp, then lining it with a fresh sanitary pad. The baby's legs had spun and shifted as if she was pedaling an invisible tricycle. Her toes had been so cold that Terry had closed her hands around the tiny feet until they felt less icy. Then she'd snapped her back into the coverall and lifted her. The baby had immediately nestled into her arms and pressed her face to Terry's bosom, seeking love and nourishment.

How could a mother abandon her child? Terry wasn't even the baby's mother, yet she'd given her breast without having to think about it. It was an instinct, a natural act. It was what a woman did for a hungry, frightened baby.

"Ms. Galvin?" Finn's voice broke into her reverie.

She opened her eyes and rose to her feet. His jacket hung open, revealing a thick flannel shirt, and beneath that a physique that invited the kind of thoughts Terry's mother always used to tell her good girls didn't have. She gave him a hesitant smile. "Is everything okay with the baby?" she asked. "Can I see her?"

"Yes and no."

"Why not? How is she? Where is she? I really ought to be with her, Detective Finn—"

"You can't see her now." He scruffed his hand through his hair, then gazed at his fingers as if surprised to feel the moisture of melted snow. Two women bundled up in sheepskin coats entered the small waiting area looking stricken and tearstained. The detective eyed them briefly, then took Terry's elbow, his touch light yet oddly commanding, and steered her out of the lounge.

Terry was moved by his sensitivity. Those women were obviously awaiting dire news about their loved ones; they deserved the lounge more than she did. She wanted to question Finn about where he was taking her, but she decided it didn't really matter. She wasn't going to leave the hospital until she got to see the baby, caress her cheek and kiss her belly and murmur that everything was going to be all right. The baby needed reassurance. So did Terry.

He ushered her down a hall, away from the flurry of emergency-room activity. She had to scamper three strides to his two to keep up with him. He didn't slow down until they reached a cafeteria, which was dark.

"Damn," he said.

"I'm not hungry."

"I was going to get some coffee." He thought for a moment, then touched her elbow again and led her around a bend in the corridor to an alcove filled with vending machines. "Would you like a cup?"

At—she checked her watch—one-fifteen in the morning, coffee was either a very good or a very bad idea. Coming from a vending machine, coffee was nearly always a bad idea. "Thanks, I would," she said.

He pulled two singles from his wallet, inserted one into the machine and gestured for her to make her selections. She punched the cream and sugar buttons. He bought a cup of black coffee for himself, then crossed the hall to a row of chairs and gestured for her to sit before taking a seat himself. An empty gurney stood against one wall, and a couple of nurses chatted at the intersection of two halls a short distance away. One of them glanced their way, grinned and waved. Finn waved back, but he didn't return her smile.

"A friend of yours?" Terry asked, letting her gaze stray briefly to his chest and then forcing it back to his mouth, which seemed equally capable of filling her mind with bad-girl thoughts.

Finn shook his head. "Work sometimes

brings me here. I've gotten to know a few of the staff nurses.''

"I see." She sipped her coffee, which was predictably wretched but welcome anyway. "Do you think maybe one of the nurses you know could get me in to see the baby?''

He smiled and shook his head again, apparently from amusement tinged with disbelief. ''You've got a one-track mind, don't you?''

Actually, no—she had a two-track mind. One track led resolutely to the baby, but the other track circled around the detective, veering toward his thick, callused hand wrapped around the waxed-cardboard cup that held his steaming coffee, then roaming past his taut, well-muscled thighs, then skimming up his chest to eyes as dark and strong as his coffee. Interesting that tonight of all nights—the first night of the new millennium and the last night of her engagement to Todd—all she could think about was the infant she'd found and the cop who'd responded to her call.

''Here's the story,'' he said, leaning back slightly in the vinyl chair, which seemed just a bit too small for him. ''The baby is in generally good health, but she's suffering from dehydration, mild hypothermia and a skin rash. The doctors are administering fluids and getting her body temperature up. They think she's going to be okay.''

"Could they figure out how old she was? Or who she was? Or what might have happened to her? She wasn't abused or anything, was she?''

"If you don't count being left in a cold alley to die abuse,'' he muttered. Anguish must have flashed across her face because he used his free hand to give her shoulder an awkward pat. "She's probably no more than two days old, and wherever she was before the alley, she was well taken care of. Her clothing was inadequate for the weather, but it wasn't torn or anything. We'll have the lab do some work on the blanket she was wrapped in. Maybe we can figure out where it came from.''

"I still don't see why I can't visit her.''

"Maybe you can,'' he said cryptically. "But first we've got some talking to do.''

She suffered a twinge of apprehension. His expression had altered slightly. He still looked both amused and bemused, but steel glinted in his eyes as he stared at her as if he might suspect her of something. She couldn't imagine what.

"How did you happen to come upon the baby?'' he asked.

"I was walking past the alley and I heard her

whimpering. I thought it sounded like a kitten, so I went to look."

"Who was with you?"

She blinked, confused. "No one. Except the baby, once I found her."

"You were all alone, walking down a street at midnight on New Year's Eve in a fancy silk party dress." Skepticism edged his voice.

She pulled herself straighter in her chair. How dare he doubt her? "As a matter of fact, I was," she snapped. "I told you, I left a party early."

"And walked home?"

"Yes." If he didn't believe her, she could strip off her boots and socks and show him the blisters.

"You've got to admit, it's a little strange."

"It's not strange. I caught my fiancé in a compromising position with the hostess of the party and I left. And walked home because I couldn't find a cab." She realized she had to force indignation into her tone. She was annoyed with Todd, and her ego was bruised, but she couldn't say she was devastated. Recalling the way she'd bank-shot her engagement ring into the toilet, she almost grinned.

Finn pulled a pad from the inner pocket of his jacket and started taking notes. "So you found the baby and...what? You just picked it up and brought it to your apartment?''

"It's a *her,* not an *it.*"

He conceded with a nod. "Her."

"I wish I knew her name," Terry added. She hated thinking of the baby as just *her*—or *the baby.* "We ought to give her a name until we find out what her real name is."

"Legally, she's Baby Jane Doe," he said.

Terry wrinkled her nose. That was worse than *her.* "I think we should call her Dawn. As in the dawn of a new century."

"Call her whatever you want," he said. "In my report, she's Baby Jane Doe."

Terry scowled but didn't belabor the point. In her mind, the baby had become Dawn. *Dawn Galvin,* she thought with a secret smile. "All right," she said, eyeing the pad and Finn's raised pen. "I didn't just pick Dawn up—" she caught the slight tug at the corner of his mouth, either a smile or a grimace at her use of that name "—because I was scared that whoever had left her might still be around. It doesn't take a Ph.D. to know that for a woman, a dark alley at midnight isn't the safest place to be. I looked around, then I went out of the alley and looked up and down the street, but I didn't see anyone. So I went back into the alley and bent over, and…'' She was going to sound daffy, but it was only the truth. "It was like the baby was reaching out to me. Her little arms were fighting the blanket, trying to break free and reach me. So I picked her up." And it had felt right. It had felt more right taking the baby in her arms than being engaged to Todd for four months. It had felt as if some empty place inside Terry was suddenly full, her hunger satisfied, her questions answered. "You probably won't understand this," she said, then took a sip of her coffee to fortify herself, "but there's a bond between that baby and me. I felt it right away."

He sighed, apparently too polite to tell her he thought she had a screw loose. "Ms. Galvin. There's no bond between you and the baby."

She bristled at his patronizing tone. "There is. I found her."

"You found her. Period."

"And saved her life. You said so."

"You're a good citizen. No question about that."

"I'm more than a good citizen. I'm…" *Bonded to her,* she wanted to say again, but he had no idea what she meant and she couldn't begin to explain. "What's going to happen to Dawn now?"

"DSS will assign her to a caseworker. She's

in state custody now. When the hospital releases her, she'll go into foster care. Meanwhile, I'll track down the mother.''

''What about the father?'' Terry asked, troubled that a caseworker was going to put the baby into some anonymous foster home when Terry knew, without logic or reason, just *knew* the baby belonged with her.

''In these kinds of cases, the father usually isn't in the picture.''

''In other words, you're assuming the baby was born out of wedlock and her mother dumped her.''

''It's a safe assumption.''

''I don't like this,'' she admitted. ''I don't like that poor little baby getting tossed into the state bureaucracy while you go off in search of her mother. I don't like your making 'a safe assumption'—''

''Ms. Galvin,'' he cut her off. ''Give me a little credit, okay? I've been a cop for a long time.''

''And I've been a woman all my life, and I know that baby shouldn't be farmed out to some strangers who are doing it for money!''

To his credit, he mulled over her assertion. His eyes seemed to soften slightly, although they didn't shift from her even when he lifted his cup to drink. "I'll make sure she's put in a good home," he said.

"How?"

He seemed to consider his reply for a long moment. Then he reached into his pocket for his cell phone, pulled it out and punched a few numbers. His gaze remained on her as he lifted the compact phone to his ear. "Hello? Pat?" He listened for a minute. "Yeah, I know what time it is, but it's New Year's Eve, so— Yeah, I'm sorry. Listen, I'm calling from Mass General. A newborn was found in an alley tonight. She's been admitted to the hospital, but I think they'll release her in a couple of days. I'll be talking to DSS tomorrow. Any chance you could take this one?" He listened. "It would mean a lot—" his gaze narrowed on Terry "—to me." He paused. "All right, I'll see what I can do. Happy New Year." He pushed the disconnect button and folded the phone shut. "Pat's my sister," he told Terry. "She's a registered nurse, currently home raising her kids, and she takes in foster children. Okay?"

It took all Terry's effort to keep her mouth from flapping open in astonishment. That Dawn was important to her was one thing, but that an experienced police detective would wake up his sister to make sure the child he thought of as

Baby Jane Doe could be placed in a good foster home went way above and beyond. If Terry had saved the baby by bringing it in out of the cold, Detective Finn was doing his part to save the baby, too.

"Thank you," she murmured, fighting off tears. The first tears of the night, she thought. Her first tears of the new century.

He gave a bashful shrug and looked away. "You want to find out if they'll let you see the baby now?"

"Yes," she whispered. Actually, she wanted much more. She wanted to hug Finn, to bury her face against his shoulder and weep for joy. Instead, she sniffled away her tears and said, "Let's go see her."

CHAPTER THREE

HE SHOULDN'T HAVE BEEN sitting in his car outside an office building on the edge of the theater district, watching for Terry Galvin. He was a cop, for crying out loud. A detective working to find and arrest whoever had abandoned an infant on a snowy New Year's Eve. He wasn't supposed to get involved.

Too late. He'd become involved the moment he'd seen Terry cradling that infant in her arms.

The hospital had released Baby Jane Doe that morning. Finn's sister, Pat, had brought the baby to her home in West Roxbury, where she had a spare room already set up as a nursery. Finn knew that if he didn't tell Terry the baby was at his sister's, she'd go back to the hospital.

She'd been there constantly, he had learned from a friend on the nursing staff. Terry had spent most of New Year's Day in the neonatal unit, sitting by the baby's isolette, holding her, feeding her bottles and singing to her. Since the hospital had only a skeleton staff on the holiday, the nurses were happy to let Terry help out. Finn thought it was a bad idea, allowing her to become more attached to the infant, but her attachment to the baby was no worse than his attachment to both of them.

He sat parked next to a fire hydrant—one of the advantages of being a cop was that you could park illegally without getting ticketed—and watched for her to emerge from her building. He couldn't bear the thought of her heading directly from work to the hospital and learning that the baby had been discharged. He had to tell her himself.

At five-thirty, rivers of people flowed out of the office building, bundled in tailored wool coats and puffy down parkas, their heads bowed against the evening chill. The sun had set a half hour ago, but Finn had perfect vision. Even if Terry had a wool hat pulled low over her head and a thick muffler wrapped to cover the bottom half of her face, he would know her. Hell, he could see her with his eyes closed.

He spotted her amid a swarm of workers leaving the building. She wasn't wearing a hat or a scarf, and he could see her heart-shaped face framed by her wild mane of curls. She wore a slim-fitting coat of red wool, a color that should have clashed with her hair. But it made her look—what was the word? *Radiant.*

He was about to get out of his car when her gaze zeroed in on him. He didn't know how she could see him in the gloomy interior of the vehicle, but suddenly she was waving, grinning like an angel who'd just gotten promoted to a higher cloud as she picked her way across the icy sidewalk in an elegant pair of high-heeled shoes. She wore black leather gloves; a purse on a strap hung over one shoulder and in her other hand she carried an oversize leather portfolio.

"Hi!" she shouted through the passenger-side window. He quickly turned on his engine and pushed the button to open it. "Hi," she said again, leaning down to peer in. Her smile warmed him like sunshine.

He couldn't speak for a minute. "Hi," he finally managed, feeling like a fool. He'd come to tell her something important. Why couldn't he spit out the words?

Because seeing her for the first time since the early hours of New Year's Day reminded him of the way she'd smiled when he'd sneaked her into the neonatal unit for a minute that morning, and she'd reached into the isolette, run her fingers gently through the baby's hair and cooed to her, and he'd felt something unfamiliar squeeze his heart. He wasn't crazy about kids, he'd re-minded himself then—and every time that mem-ory had reared up inside his head in the days since. He also didn't like flaky rich ladies who lived in avant-garde converted lofts and wore expensive silk dresses on New Year's Eve. Terry was not his type. Terry plus the baby was even less his type.

Yet he couldn't forget about her. And that was probably why he couldn't forget about the baby. He usually tried to put aside all thoughts of the victim when he was trying to solve a crime be-cause those thoughts distracted him. This time, though... He kept thinking about the baby. And the woman who'd saved the baby's life.

She was talking, he realized. Gazing into her bright hazel eyes, he'd been so entranced he'd forgotten to listen, but she was telling him about how wonderful he'd been to set things up with the hospital so she could visit the baby every day. "Yesterday, I could swear Dawn smiled at me after I gave her a bottle. She stared straight into my eyes and smiled. She knows me, Detec-tive Finn. She knows who I am."

"It's Finn," he said.

She hesitated. "Just Finn?"

"Yeah." He grinned. "Nobody calls me by my first name. Except my sister, sometimes."

"Okay," she said, smiling slowly. "Finn."

God, that smile of hers could stop a bullet. Once again, he had to force himself to speak. "I thought you'd want to know the baby's been released from the hospital. So there's no reason for you to go there anymore."

Her smile vanished in a blink. He saw a puff of vapor escape her on a sigh, and the light faded from her eyes. "They released Dawn?"

"My sister has her now. I didn't want you going all the way over to Mass General and finding out she was gone."

"Your sister has her." Terry lifted the strap of her purse higher on her shoulder. He could almost hear her brain ticking as she thought. "So she's all right?"

"The baby? Clean bill of health."

"Good." She bit her lip and did something with her eyes—he had no idea what, but he felt himself slipping under their spell again. "You probably think I'm crazy, Finn. *I* probably think I'm crazy...but if there was any way you could find out if your sister would mind my dropping by, just to see Dawn... I don't want to make a pest of myself, but you already know I'm a pest—"

"No, you're not," he assured her.

"And Dawn means so much to me, and I'm

afraid if I just disappear from her life, it will be like another abandonment. I know, I *am* crazy, but..." Her eyes shimmered with tears.

As alluring as her eyes were to begin with, they were impossible to resist when she was on the verge of weeping. He knew Pat wouldn't care one way or another if Terry visited. Pat was another of those women who was into kids in a big way. She and Terry would understand each other.

Still, he shouldn't get involved. And he shouldn't do anything to encourage Terry's obsession with the baby.

"Get in," he invited her, gesturing toward the empty passenger seat.

She hesitated for a moment, then opened the door and sat, balancing her portfolio against her knees as Finn pushed the button to shut the window. He told himself he wanted her in the car only because he was tired of craning his neck to view her through the window. But once she was settled next to him, her warmth and spirit filling the air, he thought about what a terrible liar he was, especially when it came to lying to himself.

He wanted her in the car so she'd be closer to him.

"If you'd just like to stop by and say hello to

the baby, it probably wouldn't be a problem,'' he said cautiously.

Fortunately, she didn't scream or freak out or kiss him in gratitude. He couldn't bear to have a woman like her kiss him in anything but passion—and he wasn't going to get involved with her, he reminded himself yet again. He was a cop, she was a witness, there was a case to be solved. Period.

''Your sister won't mind?'' she asked, sounding as wary as he felt.

''If she does, she'll let me know.'' He started the engine and eased away from the curb into the rush-hour traffic. He remembered the last time he'd had Terry in the seat beside him, on New Year's Eve. He'd been much too aware of her and annoyed at himself because he knew he ought to be thinking only of the case. He was still too aware of her, but the case wasn't as immediate. ''You haven't talked to the media, have you?'' he asked.

She shook her head. ''I saw a TV news report about Dawn the evening after I found her, but nobody's contacted me.''

''Good. I've kept your name out of it. It's in the police report, but I've told the press not to bother you. You don't want that kind of attention.''

"You're right. I don't." She smiled shyly. "Thank you."

"Once the story hit the news, DSS got close to fifty calls from families offering to adopt the baby," he continued, thinking she ought to get used to the idea that someday the little girl she called Dawn would no longer be a part of her life.

"Fifty families?" She looked appalled. "They haven't got any right to adopt her."

"Of course not. We've got to try to locate the parents first—"

"And I'm going to adopt her," Terry said with unnerving certainty.

He chuckled. "Don't hold your breath. You're a single woman. DSS will place her with a married couple."

"I don't think so," Terry said calmly. "She belongs with me."

He might have told her she was nuts—but she already seemed to know that. And she spoke not like a lunatic but simply like a woman who recognized the truth.

Stopped at a red light, he turned to her. "If you're going to get weird about this, Terry, I won't take you to my sister's."

"I'm not weird," Terry said, giving him a placid smile. "You're bringing me to your sister's because you know it's the best thing to do for Dawn as well as for me.''

Damn it, she was right.

FINN'S SISTER LIVED in a well-maintained Victorian on a tree-lined side street in West Roxbury, one of the quieter residential neighborhoods of Boston. Terry relaxed when she saw the house. Her baby was in a safe, cozy home. Not that she'd feared Finn's sister would be slovenly or irresponsible, but still... She wanted the best foster family for Dawn, just as she wanted the best police detective on the case.

Finn parked and they got out of the car. An inch of snow had fallen, but here the sidewalk had been shoveled clean, as had the short front walk that led to the porch. Terry would have been more comfortable in her boots, but she'd had to dress for a meeting with a new client that morning, and the tailored suit and leather pumps were part of her aren't-I-impressive look.

Finn rang the doorbell. Terry hung back a step, aware that, regardless of Finn's assurances, his sister might not be thrilled by the appearance of a stranger on her front porch. From behind Finn, she'd be able to gauge his sister's mood before she made her presence known.

Finn's sister didn't seem terribly surprised to

see him when she opened the door. She greeted him with a bear hug and a teasing hoot. "Well, look who's here! And right around dinnertime, too. Let me guess. You're hungry?"

He hugged her back, then turned and drew Terry forward. Despite his sister's friendly, curious smile, she felt awkward. Maybe his sister thought she was his girlfriend or something.

"Pat, this is Terry Galvin," Finn introduced them. "Terry, this is my sister, Pat Sweeney. Terry's the woman who found the baby," he explained.

Pat's expression changed slightly. She still looked friendly and curious, but there was something more in her dark eyes, something like understanding, or maybe admiration. "You're quite a heroine," she said, holding the door open wider. "Come in."

Terry felt her awkwardness evaporate. She stepped into the entry hall, savoring the warmth and light. "I think you're the heroine," Terry argued gently. "All I did was find her. You're the one taking care of her."

"Only since this morning. And she's a sweetheart. Here, let me take your coats." Pat already was sliding Terry's coat off her shoulders.

"I don't mean to stay long," Terry said quickly. "I just wanted to see the baby, and—"

"Hey, Uncle Finn!" A pretty teenage girl in baggy jeans and a baggier sweater skated down the hall in her socks and sent Finn an impish smile. "You gonna arrest me?"

"Only if you don't do your homework," he said, shrugging out of his leather jacket and tossing it over a hook on the coat tree near the door.

The girl rolled her eyes. "Sheesh. You and Mom."

"Yeah. Me and Mom. Where's your sister?"

"Where else? Basketball practice." The girl stomped up the stairs, still grinning.

She nearly collided with a small boy coming down the stairs, his hair tousled and his smile lopsided. "Hey, Unca Finn," he hooted, his pronunciation clumsy and halting.

"Hey, big guy! Give me five," Finn said, holding his hands out to the boy. They slapped palms in one direction and then the other. Then Finn slung his arm around the child's shoulders and headed down the hall with him, leaving Terry and Pat in the suddenly silent entry.

"That's Danny," Pat said. "He and Allen are special buddies."

Terry gazed toward the doorway through which they'd vanished. Unlike Pat's daughter, who looked like Pat and Finn both, Danny was fair-haired and had flat, slightly crooked features.

"He has Down's syndrome," Pat answered her unvoiced question. "We adopted him three years ago. He was placed here in foster care just a few weeks after he was born. We had him for four years, and then his birth parents decided they really couldn't deal with him, so we adopted him. Their loss," she said briskly. "Our gain. Come on, I'll show you the baby."

Terry wanted to say something: that she was glad Danny had been placed in a home like Pat's, that she was glad he and Finn were buddies. That she was sorry she was dressed so stodgily in this relaxed, bustling house. That as long as Dawn was with the Sweeneys, Terry knew the baby would be well cared for. That seeing Finn loop his arm around Danny had melted her heart. She knew she was already making a big mistake letting her heart respond to the baby without also letting it respond to Finn, but she couldn't help herself.

She and Pat wound up in a brightly lit kitchen redolent with the aroma of something rich and hearty simmering in a large pot on the stove. The room wasn't big but it was busy—knotty-pine cabinets, a large pine table, a refrigerator bedecked with schedules, shopping lists and re-

minders. Ski goggles sat on one counter, a trig-
onometry textbook on another. A stack of plates
on the table awaited distribution.

In a relatively quiet corner of the room stood
a cloth-sided portable crib. Pat took Terry's arm
and walked her over. "There's your princess,"
she said.

Dawn lay on her side, dressed in a one-piece
outfit, white with little yellow bunnies hopping
across the fabric. Her thumb was in her mouth,
her skin creamy soft, her silky hair tufted on her
scalp. She opened one eye and made a whimpering sound.

"Hello, darling!" Terry momentarily lost
track of Pat standing beside her, the room's
cheer, the appetizing smells wafting from the pot
on the stove. She was conscious of nothing but
her baby peering up at her. Without thinking, she
reached into the portable crib and scooped the
baby into her arms. "Hello, Dawn! Oh, you look
so good! So big and strong and healthy!" She
hugged the baby and planted a kiss on the crown
of her head.

"Dawn?" Pat asked.

Abruptly, Terry remembered she wasn't
alone. Still cradling the baby, she turned and
smiled sheepishly. "That was the name I gave
her because she entered my life at the dawn of

a new millennium.'' Pat's perplexed smile prompted her to add, ''She needed a name.''

''Finn calls her Baby Jane Doe.''

''I know. And that's awful.'' If Pat thought Terry was being presumptuous, she could say so. But when Terry had Dawn in her arms, she became a warrior goddess, prepared to fight to the death for this magnificent child, even if the fight was only about her name.

From an adjacent room she heard laughter—Finn's and Danny's. She carried Dawn to the doorway connecting the kitchen with a den, where Finn sat on the floor with his nephew, playing a video game. ''Danny keeps him out of trouble,'' Pat said, peering through the doorway and grinning. ''Why don't you stay for dinner? I know Allen wants to.'' She gestured toward the den.

''Oh, I don't want you going to any trouble—''

''I made tons of food. There's more than enough. And seriously, if he doesn't eat dinner here, he'll probably wind up buying takeout and zapping it in the microwave. And if you stay, you can keep Dawn occupied while I make a salad.''

Terry didn't need much persuading. ''Okay,'' she said, settling into one of the chairs at the table. Balancing Dawn on one arm, she slid her free arm out of the sleeve of her suit jacket, then transferred the baby and slid the other arm free.

Pat handed her a cloth diaper. "Here, put that on your lap under her just in case her diaper leaks," she said, then got busy pulling salad fixings from the refrigerator.

The next half hour passed in a haze of domestic congeniality. Pat prepared the salad while Terry cuddled the baby, and they talked. Pat told Terry that she'd loved being a nurse but wanted to work fewer hours after her two daughters were born, and when the hospital where she worked couldn't accommodate her schedule, she'd decided to stay home and take in foster children. More than thirty had passed through her home over the years, and she still kept in touch with some of them.

At some point, Pat's husband, Jim, walked through the back door into the kitchen, tracking snow onto the mat by the door, and Pat lambasted him before giving him a loud kiss on the cheek. "This is Terry," she said, waving her paring knife in Terry's direction. "She's a friend of Finn's."

A friend of Finn's. That wasn't exactly true, but Terry loved the sound of it.

Once Jim left the kitchen, Lizzie, Pat's older

daughter, entered in a warm-up suit, lugging a book pack and an athletic bag. "Great practice, Mom," she said, sparing Terry a quick smile before she bounded through the room.

"It's a zoo here," Pat said with a laugh. "But it's *my* zoo."

"I don't see any cages or bars," Terry commented. "That's the best kind of zoo."

"Yeah. The animals run wild. Hey, everybody!" she bellowed into the air. "Supper!"

The family spilled into the kitchen. Plates clattered as Sarah, the younger daughter, passed them around the table. Danny was put in charge of silverware, Lizzie of bringing salad dressing, butter and a gallon of milk to the table from the refrigerator. Jim and Finn got into a friendly argument about which teams were going to wind up in the Super Bowl and Pat interrupted frequently to issue orders—"You sit there, Terry. Danny, fold the napkins neatly. Liz, you're not in the gym anymore, so take it down a decibel."—until somehow they were all seated but Pat, who scooped Dawn out of Terry's lap and settled her back in her portable crib.

Terry glanced toward the crib to make sure the baby wasn't going to fuss. Turning back, she met Finn's gaze. He was seated across the table from her, and if the Sweeney family were less welcoming, she might have panicked to find herself so far from the only person in the room she'd known longer than an hour. But the Sweeney family *was* welcoming, and Finn's eyes were warm. He seemed to be communicating that she was doing fine, that bringing her to his sister's house uninvited had turned out to be a good move.

She smiled at him. He looked so attractive in his forest-green shirt and khaki trousers, his tie loosened and his hair mussed. His face was still rough-hewn, but there was a gentleness about it, a tender affection she hadn't seen when he'd been working New Year's Eve. Surrounded by family, pestered by two nieces and a nephew and facing the prospect of a home-cooked meal, he looked content.

Terry figured that sooner or later someone was bound to start grilling her. The interrogator turned out to be Jim, who confessed to being a lawyer when he wasn't doing more important stuff, like attending Lizzie's basketball games or Sarah's piano recitals. "Finn arrests 'em, and I get 'em off," Jim boasted with a laugh. "Between the two of us, we keep the wheels of justice turning at warp speed."

"He's lying," Finn said. "He's a patent lawyer. He has nothing to do with criminals."

"Nothing to do with criminals? Look who I'm eating dinner with—three hellions with larceny on their minds. Right, kids?" He winked and the girls pulled faces of pained tolerance. "So how about you, Terry? Do you have anything to do with criminals?"

"No. I'm an interior decorator."

"Oh, cool!" Lizzie bellowed. "Do something with this dump, would you?"

Terry smiled and explained to Lizzie that most of her clients lived in downtown apartments. "Besides, your house is lovely. I wouldn't change anything."

"Except the refrigerator," Pat suggested. "I'd like to redecorate it so it doesn't have all those car pool and practice schedules on it."

"That's beyond my range of expertise," Terry joked. "I never mess with anything stuck to a refrigerator with magnets."

The conversation moved blessedly away from her, centering on school, a colleague of Finn's who was recovering from heart surgery and a scandal linking a chemistry teacher at Sarah's middle school with the hostess at a local sports bar. Dawn dozed through most of the meal, but as Terry was polishing off the last of her salad, a thin cry arose from the crib.

In no time, Pat had a bottle filled with formula

and warmed. "Would you like to feed her?" she asked Terry.

"I'd love to," Terry said, her vision blurring with tears of gratitude. If her baby had to be anywhere other than with her, she was thrilled that Dawn should be staying with a woman as perceptive as Pat.

The children excused themselves, but the adults lingered around the table as Terry, her lap protected by the cloth diaper, gave Dawn her bottle. "You're good at that," Pat observed, relaxing in her chair. "Have you had a lot of practice?"

"None at all," Terry admitted. "I'm an only child, and I never baby-sat as a teenager. And I have no children of my own." She peered down at Dawn, watching the baby's round cheeks flex around the bottle's nipple. "This just feels natural to me, though. When I hold Dawn, it's like…I don't know. Like this was meant to be."

Pat smiled. "When I watch you holding her, I know what you mean. She's so peaceful in your arms."

"She sure isn't peaceful in mine," Jim remarked. "Whenever I pick her up, she screams bloody murder."

Terry smiled at him, then turned to Finn. He watched her intently, his dark gaze unmoving, his mouth hinting at a smile. God, he was handsome. It hit her with the force of a blinding light, one so fierce she actually forgot for a moment that she was nursing the baby. For that one moment, all she could think of was that Detective Allen Finn was the sexiest man she had ever seen.

She wondered if he'd felt the same cataclysmic awareness she'd felt in that instant. Did he know she found him shockingly attractive?

Of course not. To him, she was just a pleasantly deranged woman fixated on a baby. He'd brought her to his sister's house to humor her, to reassure her the baby was safe and well cared for.

"It's getting late," he murmured as soon as she'd set down the bottle and nursed a burp out of Dawn. "We should probably be on our way."

It wasn't that late, but Terry had already accepted too much of the Sweeneys' hospitality. She immediately rose to her feet, wobbling a little on her high heels, and handed the drowsy baby to Pat. "You've been so generous, opening your house to me. I don't know how to thank you."

Pat dismissed her thanks with a wave. "Any time you want to visit her, come on over. She obviously likes being with you."

Pat's invitation was more than Terry could have dreamed. "Oh, thank you! Thank you!" She wanted to hug Pat, but that would be too presumptuous, so she restricted herself to clasping Pat's hand in her own. "Thank you," she repeated with a smile to Jim.

"And you—" Pat sent her brother an affectionately scolding look "—stop by whenever you need real food."

"That would be every day," he teased back, giving Pat a kiss on the cheek. "Hey, Danny?" he called, moving toward the den. "I've got to go now." The little boy scampered into the kitchen and flung himself at Finn. Finn gave him a hug. "You gonna study your numbers for me?" he asked.

"Yeah."

"Adding and subtracting?"

"Yeah."

He slapped Danny five, and Danny slapped him back. "Say goodbye to the girls for us," he said to Pat. "I don't want to distract them from their homework."

Another minute of goodbyes and thank-yous, and Terry and Finn were outside on the porch in the frigid January night. A thin film of ice glazed the porch steps, and Finn took Terry's arm as they descended to the sidewalk. His hand remained on her until they reached his car, and he helped her onto the seat.

Like a gentleman, she thought, once again keenly aware of how handsome he was. Not handsome like a model or a movie star, but handsome like a man who knew who he was and where he was going. Handsome like a man who was strong and sure of himself.

She waited until he'd pulled away from the curb before speaking. "Thank you."

"No problem."

"You have a wonderful family."

"I know."

She recalled the easy warmth between him and his sister and brother-in-law. And the patience and genuine affection he showered on his nephew. If Terry couldn't have Dawn, the Sweeneys were the perfect family to take her in. And Finn was the perfect uncle.

He seemed lost in his own thoughts as he drove across town to her neighborhood. She wished she could guess what was on his mind. Was he pleased with how well the baby was doing? Did he think Pat had been an idiot to invite Terry to visit again? Did he think Terry was a first-class nuisance?

A few blocks from her home, he finally spoke.

"It's probably too late to warn you not to get involved with the baby."

She laughed sadly. "Way too late."

"Either I'll find the mother or the baby will be adopted."

"If the mother doesn't show up, I'll adopt her," Terry vowed.

"Not likely."

"But not impossible." She twisted in her seat to face him as he pulled to a halt in front of her building. "Dawn and I belong together. Even your sister could sense it."

He turned off the engine and turned to her. "I know how these things go, Terry. If the baby is freed for adoption, she'll go to a married couple. I just..." He sighed. "I don't want you getting your heart set on something that's not going to happen."

The same sweet protectiveness she'd seen in him when he was with his nephew was present now. Finn was concerned about her. He didn't want her hurt. He cared.

"You are the nicest man I've ever met," she declared, meaning every word. "I'm so glad you were the detective who answered my call." Impulsively, she leaned toward him to kiss his cheek.

Only, somehow, her lips missed their target. Somehow, her mouth met his—and everything changed forever.

CHAPTER FOUR

HE HADN'T MEANT to kiss her. But he'd just spent the past couple of hours with her, watching her snuggle and feed the baby, seeing her sparkle like a jewel, and it had been all he could do not to make a pass at her in front of his sister's family. As obsessed as she was with the baby, that was how obsessed he was becoming with her.

And there she was, leaning across the seat to kiss his cheek. The hell with his cheek. If she was going to present him with her mouth, he wasn't going to waste the opportunity.

Her lips tasted like honey, an intriguing sweetness that seeped through him like a drug. She gasped slightly when their mouths made contact. The merest hint of resistance and he'd back off faster than a street kid with something to hide.

But she didn't resist. Quite the opposite—she lifted her hand to his shoulder. He felt her touch through his jacket and shirt. He felt it through his entire body.

He wanted her. He'd wanted her from the moment he'd seen her holding the baby to her breast on New Year's Eve, and now that she was kissing him, he wanted her more.

He slid his hand under the thick tumble of her hair. It was surprisingly soft, a delicate mesh of coppery waves. Closing his eyes, he pictured her above him, naked, with her hair raining down onto his body, and the vision heated his blood. He felt as if his skin were emitting steam.

Reason rattled inside his skull. As a cop, he shouldn't be kissing a witness. But she tasted too good, and she felt even better. He brought his other hand to her throat, let his thumb skim the underside of her chin, and she sighed, her lips parting and allowing him entry.

Their tongues touched, and his temperature soared. No steam, he thought—he was emitting flames.

He heard her moan, an intoxicating whisper of sound. Closing his eyes, he imagined her moaning when she came. He pictured her body trembling above him, her thighs tight around his hips and her skin damp. With one small sound she had made him as hard as steel.

This was bad. It was wrong. He had to stop.

Drawing back from her had to be the most difficult thing he'd ever done. He observed her face as her eyes came into focus and she took a deep breath. Gradually, her fingers relaxed, and only then did he realize how tightly her hand had been clamped on his shoulder.

"There are rules against this," he murmured, wondering if he sounded as disappointed as he felt.

She flicked her tongue over her lips and he stifled a groan. She seemed unaware of the effect that one tiny gesture had on him. "What rules?"

"Police department rules. Rules about avoiding personal involvement in a case."

Her mouth curved in a smile that was both bashful and sly. "I bet those rules get broken all the time."

"Not by me."

She accepted his decision with a nod. He wished he could accept it himself.

"Well." She lifted her portfolio from the space under the glove compartment. "I'll try not to lead you astray, Detective." She was still smiling, but it was a sad, rueful smile. "I am really, really grateful to you," she said earnestly. "You are a prince, Finn." She looked as if she wanted to kiss him once more—or maybe that was his own yearning he saw in her eyes—but she turned and stepped out of the car before he could chuck the rules and haul her into his arms.

Through the window, he saw her cross the sidewalk to her building and disappear inside. His car—and his body—seemed to drop a good thirty degrees in temperature and he cursed. What an ass he was for being a good boy, following protocol, practicing proper ethics.

What an ass he was for getting involved.

SHE SAW DAWN EVERY DAY. Sometimes she'd manage to squeeze in a visit between appointments with clients; sometimes she'd make the trip to the Sweeney house after work. If it was evening, Pat invariably insisted that she stay for dinner, so Terry took to bringing food with her on those late visits: take-out Vietnamese, quiche and cold cuts from a neighborhood deli, fresh-baked bread or pastries from a local bakery. Pat always said the food gifts weren't necessary, but Terry believed they were the least she could offer when Pat was being so generous in letting her spend time with the baby.

"I'm not being generous," Pat often argued. "She behaves better for you than anyone else. She never frets when you're around. Besides, I don't mind taking a break from changing diapers."

"I want to adopt her," Terry said one unseasonably mild Saturday morning. They'd bundled

Dawn up in a fleece coverall that Terry had bought for her, tucked her beneath a fluffy blanket in a stroller and gone out for a walk in the winter sun.

"It's obvious you love her," Pat said.

"More than love her, Pat," Terry insisted. "It's like she's a part of me, a little pulse beat in my life."

She knew she sounded flaky, but so what? Her clients loved when she made outrageous recommendations, suggesting a sleek deco lamp — atop a chunky mission table next to an abstract Rothko print on the wall. If they thought her ideas were flaky, it didn't stop them from paying her far more than she was worth to implement those ideas at some of the city's most expensive addresses. Just that week, she'd signed a contract with a society matron who was overhauling a town house in Louisburg Square. The architects were still working on the interior, but Terry had spent the past two days drawing sketches of various rooms to give the client a sense of the possibilities.

She had to admit that some of her sketches were spectacularly flaky. But her client would consider them inspired. And maybe—just maybe—the Department of Social Services would consider the notion of Terry's adopting Dawn inspired, too.

"If Dawn becomes available for adoption," Pat said, "her caseworker will be looking for a married couple."

"I know. Finn told me." Terry sighed and tightened her hands on the stroller handle. She tried not to talk about Finn, or even think about him, especially around Pat. Whenever she thought about him, she remembered the taste and texture of his mouth on hers, the solid strength of his shoulder beneath her hand, his quiet, unshakable potency. She thought of where that one kiss could have led if he'd allowed it. She thought of how much she admired his ethics, and how much she wished he was just a little less ethical.

On several occasions, he'd shown up at Pat's house while Terry had been there. They'd exchanged a few words and a reserved smile or two, and then he'd gone off to tutor Danny in his numbers or rehash the most recent Celtics game with Lizzie. But Terry's awareness of him was a physical thing, a song in her bloodstream, a second pulse beat in her soul.

"It's really not fair that you have to be married to adopt a baby," she complained.

"Why aren't you married?" Pat asked so mildly she didn't seem nosy.

Terry laughed and steered the stroller around a corner. "I was engaged until I caught my fiancé fooling around with another woman at a New Year's Eve party. I guess if he'd been more discreet, I'd be a lot closer to getting married."

"You don't exactly seem heartbroken," Pat observed.

"I'm not. I'm relieved." She would never have fallen for Todd if she'd known there were men like Finn in the world. "But how am I supposed to find a husband in time to adopt Dawn? I haven't got a man in my life."

"No man in your life, huh?" Pat eyed her speculatively.

Terry reached into the stroller to smooth a corner of the blanket around Dawn's foot. "You want to know how pathetic my social life is? My closest male friend is Finn."

Pat didn't laugh. "You could do worse."

"I know. But...I'm sure I'm not the only female friend in his life."

"You're not. He's got me," Pat said. "And he's friendly with some of the women he works with. But they're not *friendly*, if you know what I mean."

Terry knew the risks of fishing for information. The biggest was indulging in the foolish fantasy that she and Finn might someday kiss again, and do more than kiss. But he was worth that risk. "Does he have a girlfriend?"

Pat shook her head. "He got a divorce three years ago. Nice woman, but she wanted more than a cop can give. She wanted security and safety, a husband who came home from work at five o'clock sharp every day. Not that I blame her—that's what I wanted, too, so I married a patent attorney. My father was a cop," she explained. "He was a good man, too. But I wouldn't want to be married to someone like him, or to have the father of my children come home late, too stressed-out or bitter about a case to want to talk about homework problems."

"I've seen Finn with your kids. He doesn't seem stressed-out or bitter with them."

Pat shrugged. "They're not his kids." She gestured that they should turn the next corner, which would bring them back to her house. "I think he'd be a great father, but he doesn't think so. He thinks he's too much like our dad."

"If your dad was a good man, then Finn is definitely like him," Terry said. She slowed to a halt when she saw the familiar car parked in front of Pat's house. "He's there."

Pat grinned. "He's been visiting us a lot more since you started coming around."

Terry pursed her lips. "Maybe he's been visiting because he likes to see Dawn."

"Maybe." Pat didn't sound convinced.

They resumed walking. As they neared the house, Terry saw the front door open and Finn step outside. Dressed in jeans and his leather jacket, he looked a bit raw, a bit rugged—utterly unlike Todd and his suave buddies. How could she have thought she could be happy with a man like Todd?

Finn descended from the porch to greet them, then lifted the stroller with Dawn in it and carried it up the steps. "You again," Pat teased. "It's too early for dinner. You must be here to mooch some lunch."

"I must be," he teased back, but his gaze was serious when it settled on Terry. The way he looked at her almost let her believe he hadn't come for food. He'd come because he knew she'd be there.

There *was* a man in her life whether or not he accepted it, whether or not he wished it. "Finn," she murmured as he deposited the stroller inside the house, "let me take you out for lunch. We need to talk."

She must have sounded awfully solemn because after scrutinizing her for a long moment, he said, "Okay."

Fifteen minutes later, after she'd kissed Dawn goodbye and promised Pat she'd be over tomorrow, Terry and Finn were seated across from each other at a local sandwich shop. "I didn't mean to take you away from Danny and the girls," she apologized.

"That's okay." He leaned back in his seat while the waitress delivered their order——a hamburger for him and a tuna melt for her. When the waitress departed, he busied himself with a bottle of ketchup. Obviously, he was waiting for her to speak her mind.

"How is the investigation going?" she began. If he'd found Dawn's mother, she could dismiss the crazy idea that had taken root in her mind.

"I assume you mean the baby? I'm working some other investigations, too." He bit into his burger, chewed, swallowed, then washed the food down with a swig of iced tea. "I've contacted every hospital in New England and eastern New York State. Mass General took a blood sample from her, but we haven't gotten a match with any hospital-born infant from late December. Either the baby was born in another part of the country or she wasn't born in a hospital." He took another bite, chewed and swallowed.

"I've put out information on a police computer Web site. We've also set up a phone number people can call if they have any information. We've gotten lots of crank calls and a few worth pursuing. So far, nothing's panned out."

"Which means Dawn will be freed for adoption?" Terry tried not to get too excited.

Finn shrugged. "Eventually, if nothing turns up. But—" he sent Terry a sharp look "—there's no way a single woman can have a shot at adopting her when there are married couples who want her."

Nodding, she lowered her sandwich and mustered her courage. "Finn, I know you think I'm a crackpot." He opened his mouth to object, but she cut him off before he could speak. "You're right—I *am* a crackpot. But if there were any way I could become Dawn's mother, I'd do it. Any legal way."

"Legal? I guess that means you aren't going to kidnap her," he joked.

"Will you marry me?"

He froze, his burger halfway to his lips for another bite. She recalled the way those lips had felt on her, the way one kiss from him had made her want so much more. But her proposal wasn't about sex. It was strictly practical. She wanted to adopt Dawn, she had to get married, and Finn was the only man in her life. He was unmarried and, as far as she could tell, decent and moral.

He lowered his burger and stared at her, obviously stunned. Sensing that he was about to say no, she continued talking. "I know this isn't romantic—but that's probably for the best. After I adopted Dawn, you'd be free to divorce me. And for the few months until the adoption was finalized, I think we could tolerate each other. I'd stay out of your way. I'm aware I'm kind of eccentric, but really, my apartment is huge. I've got three bedrooms plus a study. We'd hardly even have to see each other."

"You want me to marry you and we wouldn't see each other?" His voice sounded raspy, as if the very idea was strangling him.

"Unless you wanted to. See me, I mean. I'd be willing to accommodate you—oh, that didn't come out right," she muttered, feeling her cheeks grow warm. "What I mean is, this wouldn't have to be a real marriage. Just enough of a legal marriage to convince the Department of Social Services that I could make a good home for Dawn. *I* know I can make a good home for her with or without a husband. They're the ones with the hang-up about marriage. And there isn't any other man I can turn to."

"So you chose me out of desperation," he said wryly.

"I...well, yes. That sounds terrible, but..." She sighed. She was doing this all wrong. The way he was looking at her made her feel like a freak, someone he might want to arrest and bring to the state mental hospital for observation.

She searched his face for a sign that he wasn't planning to have her committed. "I know you care about Dawn. Not as much as I do—no one could care that much—but enough to want her to wind up in a good home. Well, no home could be better than mine. Ask your sister—even she says Dawn is happier when she's with me. We belong together. And it seems the only way we can ever be together is if I have a husband."

"Even if you had a husband, the odds of your getting her are slim to none," he pointed out. "There are couples who've been waiting for years to adopt."

"Yes, but if anyone cares about what's best for Dawn, they'll let me adopt her."

"You sound pretty damned sure about that."

"I am."

He regarded her thoughtfully, then reached for his iced tea and took a sip, his dark eyes never leaving her. "You haven't got any other guys you could marry? Someone you know better than me?''

''I broke up with my fiancé New Year's Eve,'' she reminded him. ''As for other guys I know, trust me—you're the best.''

He laughed without smiling. ''Somehow that doesn't sound like a compliment.''

''All right.'' Hope drained away. ''Forget it, Finn. I'm sorry I asked. It was just a crazy idea. Very crazy. I didn't mean to insult you.''

''I'm not insulted,'' he said quietly.

She brushed off his attempt to reassure her. ''Being a creative thinker works well in my business. But when it comes to interpersonal relationships—''

''Hey.'' He reached across the table and clamped his hand over hers, apparently aware that his touch would silence her. His hand was so much larger than hers, the palm warm and leathery smooth. ''I'm no champ when it comes to interpersonal relationships, either,'' he told her. ''I've already been divorced once. If I married you, I'd probably wind up oh-for-two.''

His pessimism fed her optimism. He'd said, ''If I married you…'' Was he actually considering it?

''Divorce would be up to you,'' she said. ''If that's what you want—no lawyers, no alimony, nothing like that. We could write a prenuptial agreement. We could even get the marriage annulled if you wanted to avoid an actual divorce.''

''I was thinking, maybe you wouldn't want to marry someone who's a failure at marriage.''

''You're way ahead of me, Finn. I'm a failure at engagement.'' She tried not to respond to the gentle pressure of his hand on hers, tried not to let herself think that in the marriage bed at least, Finn wouldn't be a failure. If they did get married—if—it would probably be in name only, just to keep things simple, to make the divorce easier. Finn would consider marriage to her only if the exit was clearly marked.

''The thing is…'' His thumb traced a circle on the back of her hand. ''I don't think marrying me is going to get Dawn for you.''

''With a husband, at least I have a chance. Without one, I don't.''

He patted her hand, then released it. Her fingers felt icy without his protective warmth. ''I'm a cop,'' he reminded her. ''That means lousy hours and lousy moods.''

She heard the message underlying his words: he wasn't flat out rejecting her. ''You can't scare me,'' she warned. ''If I didn't think we could make a go of this, I wouldn't have asked you. But I did ask. It's up to you to say yes or no."

He shook his head and laughed. The raspy sound was gone from his voice when he said, "Give me a few days. I've got to think about it."

She gripped the table to hold herself in her seat. She wanted to launch herself at him, leap into his arms, hug him and kiss him and thank him for not automatically nixing the idea. He wanted her to give him a few days, but he was the one giving her a few days—of hope. A few days to believe he might say yes even though the idea was insane.

For a few days, she could dream that Finn would marry her, Dawn would be their daughter, and together they would become a family.

WHAT THE HELL WAS WRONG with him? Why hadn't he just said no?

He spent that Saturday afternoon like most others: buying groceries, doing laundry, taking care of all the business he couldn't take care of during the week. A zillion times as he took care of that business, he found himself thinking not about how much detergent to pour into the coin-op machine in the basement of his apartment building or whether to buy the microwavable meat loaf or the microwavable lasagna, but about Terry. About her magical eyes and her dazzling smile and her fierce commitment to that baby.

And about the way her hand had felt in his, and the way she'd looked the first time he'd seen her New Year's Eve, with her dress drooping down and her creamy skin exposed and her hair falling in dizzying curls past her shoulders. If he married her, it wouldn't be because he wanted to sleep in a different bedroom from hers.

She wasn't looking for a real marriage—a good thing, given that his last attempt at a real marriage hadn't gone too well. But if he ended up doing something as irrational as marrying her, he'd want the sex part of it to be real.

There he was again, contemplating her proposal as if he might actually say yes.

"You wanna buy that loaf of bread or become one with it?" the cashier asked. She had three earrings in one ear, four in the other.

He realized he'd been standing in the checkout aisle holding the bread for several minutes instead of handing it to her to ring up. He set it on the counter and gave her a hard stare. He owed her no explanations for his distracted state.

He remained distracted while he carted his groceries home, lugged his clean laundry upstairs and put everything away. He remained distracted while he opened a bottle of beer, zapped the lasagna in the microwave and turned on the TV to a Celtics game. A few months ago, he wouldn't have been alone on a Saturday night. But he hadn't gone on a date in a while—not since he'd met Terry Galvin.

He'd seen her apartment. It was the opposite of his—airy and whimsical. His place was compact and functional. So was his life. How could he waste even a minute considering marriage to an airy, whimsical woman?

Especially one obsessed with Baby Jane Doe.

The TV sportscasters droned. The beer tasted stale. The lasagna was rubbery. He sat in solitude, telling himself to forget everything about the baby except the fact that it was his job to locate her mother. As if the woman who'd given birth to her deserved to be called a mother.

He'd already located Baby Jane Doe's mother, and that mother had named her daughter Dawn.

He reached for his phone, punched in Terry's number and said, "Okay. I'll marry you."

CHAPTER FIVE

TWO WEEKS LATER, Finn met her late Friday afternoon on the plaza outside City Hall, a bulky modern building of concrete geometry. Oddly, she'd seen Finn less often after they'd agreed to get married than she had before, when she'd been constantly running into him at Pat's house. They'd talked on the phone, making plans and sorting out details, but he'd been working his cases and she'd been finalizing the contract for her job at the town house on Louisburg Square, so they hadn't had a spare moment for personal meetings.

She'd seen him at Pat's last weekend, but that reunion had been awkward. He'd been reserved, holding back from her, and she hadn't dared to question his reticence. She was grateful he was willing to marry her. He didn't owe her any explanations.

She'd seen him again the previous Tuesday night, when he'd come to her apartment to drop off a suitcase filled with his things. He'd already told her he planned to keep his own apartment, and she'd said she thought that was a wise move. She and Finn weren't madly in love; this marriage wasn't likely to survive, and he would want his own place back once they parted ways.

The inevitability of that parting made her wistful. She didn't expect more—she couldn't. She hardly knew him. All she knew was that he was generous enough to take her as his wife, he was a loving uncle and brother and he was an honest, hardworking cop. And he was sinfully good-looking.

The last time she'd seen him had been yesterday at noon, when they'd met at Macy's to buy wedding rings. The clerk had asked if they'd like to have their bands engraved, but Finn had said no. Terry wanted to believe he'd been thinking only that there wasn't enough time to get their initials carved into the rings, but she couldn't help wondering whether he thought the marriage would be less permanent if they kept their rings anonymous.

She had brought her friend Nicole to City Hall with her. She'd known Nicole since college, and now Nicole oversaw the business end of Terry's decorating enterprise. As recently as ten minutes ago, when they emerged from the City Hall T station, Nicole had warned her that this wedding was by far the craziest thing Terry had ever done. But good friend that she was, she stood by Terry, holding a small bouquet of flowers.

Finn also dragged a friend with him, a man he introduced as his partner on the squad. "Finn's better than Todd at least," Nicole whispered, shoving the flowers into Terry's hand.

Terry reminded herself of the nature of this wedding—and admitted that she was going to have to remind herself regularly. Finn looked so handsome, so gallant and resolute as he took her hand and gave her a tentative smile. Foolish though it was, she wished theirs could be a true marriage, not just an arrangement that might make adopting Dawn easier.

They trooped en masse into the building, found the clerk's office and entered. Fifteen minutes later, after signing some papers and saying their "I do"s, Finn gave Terry a peck on the cheek and ushered her out of the office as his wife.

Maybe it *was* the craziest thing she'd ever done, marrying a near stranger because she wanted to be Dawn's mother. But that wasn't the only reason she'd married Finn. She'd married him because she trusted him, because he had integrity, because she knew intuitively that she would never stumble upon him having sex with another woman in a bathroom at a party. She'd married him because she hadn't been able to forget the kiss they'd shared—even though he'd given her no reason to think he would ever kiss her again.

"Well, kiddo, you're on your own," Nicole said, kissing the cheek Finn hadn't kissed. "This has been interesting. I'll talk to you Monday. Finn, great meeting you." She gave him a brisk handshake. "You, too, Jack," she added, shaking hands with Finn's partner. "I'm out of here."

Jack seemed mildly nonplussed by Nicole's flippant farewell. He gazed sheepishly at Finn. "I've gotta get home, too," he said. "The wife's waiting for me."

"Sure. Thanks for being my best man." They shook hands, and Jack eyed Terry curiously. "We'll be fine," Finn said, evidently reading doubt in Jack's expression.

"Yeah. Right. Well…good luck." And he was gone, trailing across the plaza after Nicole.

Alone amid a crush of rush-hour pedestrians spilling from the area's buildings, Finn turned to face Terry. His eyes were dark, beautiful but mystifying. Was he already regretting that they'd done this? Did he believe, like Nicole, that it was crazy? Did he think, like his colleague Jack, that they needed luck to make it work?

"How about some dinner?" he suggested.

She wasn't really hungry, but if they didn't eat she wasn't sure what they'd do. Nodding, she let him take her hand and lead her across the plaza. She felt the weight and texture of the plain gold band on her ring finger when his hand closed around hers.

They found an Italian place a few blocks away, modest and dimly lit, the tables small enough to be intimate. They sat facing each other, husband and wife. A profound silence stretched between them. They used to be able to talk pretty easily with each other, didn't they? How was she going to stay married to him if she couldn't even strike up a conversation with him?

They ordered dinner and Finn asked the waiter to bring them a bottle of Chianti. Another long silence settled over the table until Terry forced herself to speak.

"I met with Dawn's caseworker today," she said, then relaxed. Talking made her feel more comfortable. "Janet Chou. She knows you."

"More or less. Our paths have crossed," he confirmed.

"She's suspicious about our wedding."

He feigned surprise. "I wonder why."

Terry smiled even though Janet Chou's suspicions posed a challenge to everything Terry wanted. "She said she was concerned about conflict of interest. She thought that if you wanted to adopt the baby, you might not work as hard to find the birth mother."

Finn's eyebrows rose. "What did you say?"

"I said you were a good, ethical police officer and nothing was going to keep you from doing your job." Her answer seemed to please him. He drank some wine and grinned. "I also told her that even if you did find the birth mother, the likelihood was that the baby would be released for adoption anyway, because anyone who would abandon a baby on a snowy night obviously wasn't fit to be a mother."

Terry decided not to describe the rest: that the social worker had questioned the legitimacy of their hasty marriage, and Terry had explained that she and Finn had fallen in love with the baby and then with each other, and it was all of a piece. She'd told Janet Chou that she and Finn were marrying because they wanted to make a family with Dawn. She'd acknowledged that other couples on the adoption list might have been waiting longer for children, perhaps after trying unsuccessfully to conceive children on their own, but that Terry's desire to adopt Dawn wasn't about some abstract idea of "children." It was about one special baby girl with whom she'd bonded, one specific infant who belonged with Terry—and Finn, she'd insisted. Dawn belonged with them both.

"She'll want to observe us with the baby," Terry warned him. "I suggested that she set up a time with Pat and we'd be there."

"What if you get what you want?" he asked slowly.

What if? She almost blurted out that she *had* gotten what she wanted: Finn as her husband. But then she remembered she wanted Dawn, too. "I'll be thrilled," she said.

"What are you planning to do about your career?"

"Oh, I've figured that out," she said, relieved to focus on the baby so she wouldn't have to dwell on the strange notion that Finn was what she wanted. "I'm self-employed and flexible. My office is spacious. When I can't have her with me, I can hire a baby-sitter. I figure I can set up a little baby area right in my office. My clients won't mind. They already think I'm a nut. In fact, my nuttiness is why most of them hire me."

His smile was hesitant and surprisingly gentle.

Did he think she was a nut? Was that why he'd married her?

Over steaming plates of pasta and seafood, Finn told her a little about Jack, with whom he'd been partnered for three years. She told him about Nicole. They carefully avoided discussing what would happen that night or the following morning, what would happen when the food and wine were gone and they had to confront the reality of what they'd done.

But eventually the food and wine were gone. They tussled briefly over who was going to pay the bill, but Finn won. "You proposed," he pointed out. "You got the license, you made the arrangements, you picked out the rings. The least you could do is let me pay for dinner."

Feeling as if she'd already failed in a vital way, she let him pay. Was that how he saw her? Some demanding, controlling harridan? If it made him feel better, he could pay for all their food for as long as their marriage lasted.

As delicate as fairy dust, a light snow was falling when they left the restaurant. It reminded Terry of the snow that had fallen the night she'd found the baby—the night she'd met Finn.

He took her hand again, this time her right, and she felt the ring on his finger. She'd considered telling him he didn't have to wear a ring—

lots of married men didn't for a variety of reasons—but when she'd chosen her ring at the jewelry counter, he'd chosen the matching man's ring for himself.

They hadn't argued about who was going to pay for the rings, either. He'd paid for hers and she'd paid for his.

He walked with her to a public garage and across the echoing concrete floor to his car. Neither of them spoke as he drove outside into the snowy night. As in the restaurant, she thought their moods might be eased if she struck up a conversation. But he was driving her to her home—to *their* home—and she was too anxious to speak, too busy trying to guess what would happen once they got there. She'd made up one of the guest rooms for him, left his suitcase in there, laid out fresh towels in the guest bathroom as if he were a visitor. Would he be relieved or insulted?

She listened to the clack of the windshield wipers. She glimpsed his rugged profile whenever the headlights of an oncoming car illuminated his face. She worried, and tried to convince herself that worrying was what new brides always did. But most new brides were in love with their husbands. Most new brides didn't marry for crazy reasons.

He found a parking space not far from her building. Still, neither of them spoke as he pulled a small duffel from his trunk and locked up. More clothing? she wondered. Combined with his other suitcase, did he have enough clothing to last a week? Would their marriage outlast his wardrobe?

In the elevator, she found her voice long enough to say, "I've got a spare key for you upstairs."

He nodded.

She shouldn't have called it a "spare" key. She should have said, "I've got *your* key upstairs," so he wouldn't feel like a spare resident. She shouldn't have said anything at all, but instead should have simply handed him the extra key and said, "This is yours."

They entered her apartment and she flicked on a lamp. Finn blinked in the sudden light. He hated the room, she could tell. He hated the bright colors, the playful furnishings. He was probably calculating how long he'd have to stay in this sham of a marriage before he could escape. He was wondering what idiotic impulse had allowed him to be dragged into Terry's illogical scheme. He was thinking—

"Terry." His voice was low, hoarse, unbearably male.

"Yes?" Hers was faint.

"I know we didn't work all this stuff out, but..."

I'll get your key for you, she almost said. *And I've got a comfortable bed made up in the guest room. And...*

"Damn," he murmured, turning her to face him, his hand on her shoulder. "We're married," he said, some kind of explanation, and covered her mouth with his.

Sensation swamped her, sweet and warm. Desire, need, a longing so profound she didn't dare to name it.

He slid his hand down her back, then scooped her into his arms. Without breaking the kiss, he carried her through the living room to the hallway, nudging open one door and then another until he found her bedroom with its cozy double-bed. She heard a thud as he dropped his duffel bag, and then they were tumbling across the down comforter, his hands moving on her, easing off her coat, unbuttoning the jacket of the beige wool suit she'd worn for her wedding day.

Her hands were on him, too, tugging at garments, sweeping through his thick, silky hair, tracing the angles of his face. She didn't remember unbuttoning his shirt, but suddenly it fell open to reveal a pale gray T-shirt underneath.

She'd never realized how sexy a gray T-shirt could be.

Then again, anything Finn wore would be sexy. Anything he *didn't* wear would be even sexier, she thought, tearing at the T-shirt before he'd even wriggled out of his dress shirt. She wanted him naked. She wanted him inside her. She wanted *him,* her husband, all of him.

Her suit jacket sailed across the room. Her shoes fell to the floor, two thumps. He slid her skirt from her hips and tossed it aside, ran his hands over her nylons and peeled them down so he could run his hands over her legs. Her slip vanished. Her bra, her panties, and she was naked before this glorious man, completely exposed to his eyes, his hands, his lips—all of which seemed equally capable of arousing her.

God, what eyes. They burned with an inner fire, shimmered with a deep hunger as he stripped off what was left of his own clothing. His gaze was as exciting as the heat of his hands as they skimmed over her, as erotic as the pressure of his lips on her breasts, her throat, her belly. When he stroked his fingers between her legs, she moaned. Keys and bedrooms and the future didn't matter. All that mattered was Finn.

She touched him, too—his broad, strong back, the sleek muscles of his abdomen, the harsh edge of his jaw. She flattened her hands against his buttocks and he groaned; she arched beneath him and he groaned again. Drawing back, he reached over the edge of the bed to the duffel he'd brought in, unzipped it and pulled out a box of condoms. He must have known this would happen—or maybe he'd simply hoped.

She'd hoped, too. Without daring to acknowledge it, she'd hoped that this marriage, as contrived as it was, would include intimacy in some form, even if it was just being able to talk over breakfast or share a tube of toothpaste. She had hoped that Finn could be a real husband to her in some way, because... She was afraid to admit it, but she could fall in love with him. Maybe she'd already fallen.

He settled between her legs, dropped a light kiss on her lips and pressed deep into her. They moaned in unison. It felt so right to be bound to her husband this way, sealing their marriage, making it true. He surged inside her, telling her with each thrust that she was his, that the rings on their fingers weren't just jewelry, that the civil ceremony in the clerk's office wasn't just about getting Terry's name on the adoption list. More existed between them, and even if he didn't love her, he belonged to her as much as she belonged to him.

She arched, taking him deeper, letting him carry her higher and higher until the tension within her burst in a lush release. Above her, he froze for a moment and then let go, joining her in ecstasy. Sighing, he sank into her embrace, warm and heavy and damp with sweat.

She closed her arms around him, feeling oddly protective. She didn't know why. He was so much bigger than her, a cop, a man who carried a gun and knew how to use it. A man who solved crimes, unraveled mysteries, made the city a safer place. Yet he seemed utterly vulnerable right now, emotionally raw. At the instant he'd climaxed, she'd seen it in his eyes: fear and yearning, triumph and helplessness.

She continued to hold him until his breathing returned to normal. He leaned back, as if wanting to spare her his crushing weight, and she smiled up at him. "Would you like me to show you the guest room?" she asked mischievously.

His answering smile was wicked. "As a matter of fact, no."

"Good." Hooking her hands at his nape, she pulled herself up and kissed him. He kissed her back, and she knew that at least one aspect of this marriage was going to work out just fine.

CHAPTER SIX

"FINN?" MAGGIE CALLED from her desk near the squad-room door. "Line two."

Finn leaned back in his chair, punched the flashing button on his phone and lifted the receiver. "Detective Finn here," he said into the phone.

"Detective? This is Arthur Wellburn," a man drawled. "I'm a lieutenant in the Annandale, Virginia, Police Department."

Finn sat up straighter and jotted the man's name on a notepad. "What can I do for you?"

"Well, I've got a young lady here at the station house who says she abandoned her newborn in Boston on New Year's Eve. I found your name in my computer with regard to a Baby Jane Doe discovered in Boston on New Year's Eve, and I'm wondering if this might be the lady you're looking for."

Finn's fingers cramped around his pen. He took a deep breath and reminded himself that he was a detective and this was his case. "Could be," he said calmly. "Keep talking."

Lieutenant Wellburn from Annandale, Virginia, talked. Finn wrote down everything he said, nodding and inserting "uh-huh"'s when appropriate. He'd put his abandoned-baby report out on the wire as soon as he'd concluded that the mother was no longer in the region. He'd also alerted hospitals up and down the East Coast to inform him if a woman with complications from childbirth, but without a child, came in for emergency help.

That was in January. Now it was April. The tulips and daffodils in the Public Garden were poking through the newly thawed earth. Finn was married, and DSS was beginning the paperwork to release the baby for adoption.

To Terry and him. The caseworker had observed Dawn with them and noticed the strange, almost mystical bond between Terry and the little girl. "This is highly unusual," Janet Chou had muttered. "But we do like to act in the best interests of the child—and frankly, I don't see how any other parent could connect with this baby the way you do."

He remembered that day and the day, just recently, when Janet had phoned him to ask the status of Baby Jane Doe's case. "Static," he'd told her. "We've had no nibbles, no bites."

"She's been in foster care going on four months. I think we should consider getting her settled," Janet had said. "Tell your wife I'm putting the wheels in motion."

Your wife. The word still had the power to startle Finn. Two months didn't a relationship make, even if those two months were spent as husband and wife.

They were still learning about each other. Terry had learned that he didn't like idle chatter first thing in the morning, that he enjoyed fishing, and that given the choice between a ticket to a Celtics game and a year's supply of groceries, he'd starve and go to the game. He'd learned that she'd lost her father as a teenager and gone to college on a scholarship, and her associations with the city's elite arose from her work. He'd learned that she'd started her career working for an interior decorator who fired her for being too whimsical in her designs, and in desperation she'd called her friend Nicole, the business consultant, and said, "Help me set up my own company." He'd learned that she made significantly more money than he did—and that it didn't bother him to be outearned by his wife.

They had more to learn, more kinks to work

out and more compromises to make. But they were doing all right. They could disagree on politics and regard the world differently—Terry was much more optimistic than Finn—and still get along. As for sex…

He sighed. Just thinking about sex with Terry was enough to make him hard. He hadn't known a man could be so turned on by his wife. He'd thought that marriage lowered the flame. His last marriage had.

This marriage was a conflagration. No matter how vigorously they might be arguing over the mayor's latest initiative or the most recent move by Congress, no matter if Terry's request that he fold his bath towel a certain way and remember not to leave dirty dishes in the sink sounded a lot like nagging, the moment they kissed or touched or even looked at each other a certain way, he was lost. He wanted her. Constantly. Even when they were arguing and she was nagging, he wanted her. The flame was burning hot and wild.

But as much as he desired her, as much as she seemed to desire him, he knew why they'd gotten married: for the baby.

The baby whose mother seemed to have materialized, all of a sudden, in Annandale, Virginia.

According to Lieutenant Wellburn, the woman had waived extradition. She'd turned herself in to the Virginia police because guilt had been gnawing at her, and she was prepared to return to Boston to defend herself against criminal charges. She'd been suffering from postpartum depression, she'd claimed. She had abandoned her child because after giving birth, she'd temporarily lost her mind.

Baby Jane Doe had a way of making women lose their minds, he thought, terminating the call and pulling out the paperwork. Baby Jane Doe—aka Dawn—had certainly made Terry lose her mind.

He considered telephoning her with the news but decided to wait until he could see her in person. Instead, he called Janet Chou and told her someone from Virginia would be escorting the mother north to face charges of child abandonment. Then he spent the rest of the day working on his other cases and trying not to think about how Terry was going to react to the news.

He brought her roses.

"What's wrong?" she asked as he handed her the bouquet and closed the door behind him. She was dressed in slim-fitting white jeans and an oversize knit shirt that drooped slightly over one shoulder, offering a glimpse of a midnight-blue bra strap. That thin ribbon of satin lying smooth against her skin made his heart beat a little faster. Every time he entered her apartment—from the first night, when he'd found her attempting to console the frantic infant at her breast, until tonight—he got horny.

She fingered the roses and anxiously studied his face. "What makes you think something's wrong?" he asked, shrugging out of his jacket and hanging it in the closet because he knew that would please her.

"These." She dipped her nose to the blossoms and inhaled. "Either you're apologizing for something you did, or you're about to give me bad news."

"I'm not apologizing." He walked into the kitchen, irked by her perceptiveness. He'd taken half a shelf in her refrigerator for beer, and he pulled a bottle out now.

"Then tell me the bad news." She tossed the roses onto the counter, not bothering to put them in water.

"It's not bad news. Just…" He wrenched off the bottle cap and took a bracing swig. "News."

"You've got me worried, Finn. What is it?"

"We found Dawn's mother."

He watched Terry's face. Even though she

held her features still, he could see the emotional turmoil behind her eyes. He could feel the tension emanating from her. "You found her?"

"She turned herself in at a police station in Virginia. She'll be escorted back to Boston in a couple of days."

Terry leaned against the counter as if suddenly weak. He put down his beer and reached for her, but she found enough strength to evade him, ducking away from his arm and backing up a step. "She isn't going to get Dawn, though, is she?" Terry asked, her voice tight and thin. "I mean, she abandoned the baby, for God's sake. She left her baby to die. She isn't a fit mother. So we have nothing to worry about, right?"

"She said she was suffering from postpartum depression," he explained. "Temporary insanity."

"That's what she *said*."

"The DSS will have her examined by a psychologist. We'll see how it pans out."

"You mean—" Terry gulped in a frenzied breath "—there's a chance they'll give the baby back to her?"

"They prefer to have children stay with their birth parents. They like to keep families intact if possible."

"But it isn't possible in this case." Her eyes blazed with fear.

"I don't know, Terry. We just have to wait and let the system do its work."

Again he reached for her. Again she ducked, rearing back, her eyes now alive with as much anger as fear. "Why did you have to find her, Finn? Why did you have to track this woman down? Dawn won't be better off with her. Why couldn't you have just let it lie?"

"Terry." He'd guessed she would be upset, and he tried to stay low-key, his voice as soft and consoling as hers was shrill. "It's my job to solve cases. It's what I'm paid to do."

"So you did this to get paid?"

"I did it because I'm a police detective."

"And now you'll get—what's it called—a collar? A gold star next to your name? One more case solved by brilliant Detective Finn!"

"Terry, come on. You knew what my job was when I took your call on New Year's Eve. You knew I might solve this case."

"But—but Dawn is mine! She's ours, Finn! By doing your job, you've taken away our baby!"

"She was never ours, Terry. There was always just a slim chance we'd get custody."

Tears filled Terry's eyes. As her husband, he

longed to comfort her—but she'd already avoided his touch twice. How could he hug her when she blamed him for finding the baby's mother? In her view, he was the bad guy, the villain who could keep her from her baby simply by doing his job.

He could remind her that she still had a shot at adopting Dawn. But he knew the odds dropped precipitously once the mother surfaced. DSS liked to keep birth families together, and the mother's excuse—temporary insanity brought on by childbirth—was credible. Finn didn't want to string Terry along, trying to convince her that her chances were better than they actually were.

He held his hands at his sides even though it pained him to keep his distance when she was weeping. She spun away from him, and it took all his willpower not to grab her and turn her around, to haul her into his arms and let her sob against his chest. He stood silently while she walked out of the kitchen, then listened to her footsteps across the living room, down the hall to the bedroom and inside. He heard the door click quietly.

A heavy disappointment settled over him. He'd known going in that their marriage was about her getting the baby, not about her wanting to build a life with him. He'd also known from past experience that his being a cop made him less than ideal as a husband. His first wife had never been able to accept his work, its demands, its cost in time and emotion. Now Terry was learning what it meant to be married to a cop, and obviously, she didn't like the lesson.

If she couldn't get the baby, she could get rid of him. He knew why she'd married him, and when she'd reassured him that they could end the marriage whenever they were ready, she'd been reassuring herself, as well. Without Baby Jane Doe—her precious Dawn—she wouldn't need or want Finn.

So he would leave. If he couldn't give her the child she wanted, he could go away.

ONE WEEK LATER, Terry's bedroom closet was roomy in the absence of Finn's clothes. His favorite Boston Celtics coffee mug no longer sat in the drying rack beside the sink; his toothbrush was gone from the edge of the bathroom sink. "We can work out the rest later," he'd promised. "For now, I think it's best if I'm gone."

Yes, she assured herself, staring blankly at the bedroom sketches she'd done for her Louisburg Square client. She was seated at her drafting table in the study—the room that could have so easily been converted into a playroom for Dawn. Her jeans were torn at one knee, her sweatshirt too baggy, her bare toes curled around a rung on her chair. Everything her client wanted seemed trite to her—chintz, gilt, Louis XV. Why not contradict the proper Bostonian facade of the town house with a wild and crazy interior, something bright and colorful and fun?

As if Terry cared. Since Finn had departed from her life, *fun* was an inoperative term.

It wasn't losing Finn that bothered her, she reminded herself. It was losing the baby. The baby was what it had always been about.

And she'd definitely lost the baby. Janet Chou had phoned yesterday to tell her she was working with the birth mother, trying to locate housing for her so she'd have a home to bring her baby to. The mother had already seen the baby and claimed she was determined to learn how to raise it.

Terry had never had to be determined. She'd just picked up Dawn and *known*. It had been an organic thing, something as deep and transforming as—as making love with Finn.

Cursing, she tossed down her pencil and rubbed her bleary eyes. She was so damned tired of thinking about Finn, thinking about how quiet her apartment was without him, how lonely her mornings were without sharing a few precaffeine grunts and mumbles with him. She was tired of feeling a twinge of expectation every evening around six-thirty when she expected to hear his key in the lock as he arrived home from work. This wasn't his home anymore, though. He'd left the key behind when he departed.

Just because she missed him didn't mean she actually loved him. Just because her bed seemed as wide and empty as the Sahara didn't mean she needed him. Just because no man had ever made her feel the way he did with his sly caresses, his dangerous kisses, the almost incompatible strength and tenderness of his lovemaking—none of that meant she'd ever really thought of him as a true husband.

"Hell," she said, this time aloud. "He's my husband, and I let him walk out on me. What kind of idiot am I?"

Maybe she'd married him for the sake of a baby. But once he was her husband, that had changed. Once she'd lived with him and talked to him and gotten used to his wry laugh, his thoughtful smile, his devilish grin, his intelligence, his warmth, his moods, his clean, male smell, the wet shower towels he never hung up properly, the clatter of his coins when he emptied his trouser pockets and spilled their contents across the dresser, his fascination with meals that were actually cooked on a stove top or in an oven rather than in a microwave...

Now she had nothing. No baby and no husband. And the astonishing truth was, she was grieving more over the husband than the baby.

She shoved away from the drafting table, padded down the hall to her bedroom and donned socks and sneakers. She grabbed her purse and her key—and *his* key—and jogged out of the loft.

April's sunshine washed the street in a golden light. The trees lining the sidewalk were tipped in delicate green buds. The air was balmy, the sky that sharp, clear blue that seemed to exist only in New England. Terry fleetingly recalled a bitter cold walk through a falling snow last New Year's Eve. That walk had ended in a miracle. She prayed this walk would, too.

The precinct station house was less than a mile from her building. She walked inside and realized it was the first time she'd ever been in the building, even though her husband worked there. "Where can I find the detectives' squad room?'' she asked the desk sergeant posted near the front door.

''Up one flight and take a left,'' he directed her.

She bounded up the stairs, refusing to entertain the possibility that Finn might not be there, or that if he was he might not want to see her. He'd walked out because he didn't want to be married to her, because he'd accepted that without the baby there was no reason for them to stay together. She had to convince him that there *was* a reason.

Reaching the second-floor landing, she turned left. An open door at the end of the hallway beckoned. She marched through it and spotted Finn at his desk, his back to her and a phone pressed to his ear.

Before she could race across the room, the receptionist at a desk by the door halted her. ''Can I help you?'' she asked pointedly.

''I need to see Finn,'' Terry said.

''And who are you?''

''His wife.''

The woman blinked up at her, apparently perplexed. Had Finn kept his marriage a secret? Well, why shouldn't he? He'd never considered it real. Terry had never given him reason to.

The receptionist swiveled away and shouted, "Finn?"

He raised his hand to silence her, then continued on the phone for a moment. After he hung up, he turned and spotted Terry. A frown crossed his face, undermining her resolution. But he rose to his feet and circled around the desks to the entry.

"She says she's your wife," the receptionist noted skeptically.

"She is," Finn declared, giving Terry a tiny shred of hope.

He beckoned her into the room, past his desk and through an inner door to a small lounge area with a coffee machine, a refrigerator, a table and several chairs. The decor was less than inviting—Terry could have performed wonders in the room with a splash of yellow paint, some curtains and anything besides the Jackson Pollock–style linoleum covering the floor. But right now, her concern wasn't the room. It was the man in the room.

"Do you want a cup of coffee?" he asked.

She shook her head, searching for the courage to tell him what she really wanted: his love.

"I was talking to Pat this morning," he said. "She told me the baby's mother is going to have her first night soloing with the baby. Janet Chou will be monitoring things, but it doesn't look good. For you, I mean."

Terry swallowed a lump of tears. In terms of the baby, it hadn't looked good for her since the birth mother had returned to Boston. She thought she'd resigned herself to that fact, but it still hurt.

All she could do was heal the other hurt. "I didn't come here to talk about Dawn," she said.

"Oh?" As if they had nothing else to talk about.

"I want you to come home, Finn."

He stood perfectly still, watching her, saying nothing.

"I miss you. I wish you hadn't left."

"You didn't stop me," he reminded her.

"I should have."

He shook his head slowly. "You married me to get the baby. Now you're not getting the baby. There's no more reason for us to be married."

"Yes, there is." She drew in a deep breath, squared her shoulders and gazed into his eyes. "I love you."

He seemed taken aback. "How do you know that?"

"The same way I know lots of things. My heart tells me." She tapped her chest with her fingertips. "When I found Baby Jane Doe—" she'd never called the baby that before "—I named her Dawn because I felt a new life was dawning for me. It was. But she was just a part of it. You were there, too, Finn. Right from the start, just minutes into the new year. You were a part of it. The most important part."

"More important than the baby?"

She lowered her eyes so he wouldn't see how damp they were. "I can accept that I'm unable to adopt the baby even though it breaks my heart. I'm working on it and grieving over it, but I can accept it. I don't think—" she glanced up at him again, deciding she didn't care if he saw her weeping "—I can accept losing you. That hurts even worse."

He lifted his thumb to her cheek and wiped away a tear. "The last time you cried, I wanted to take you in my arms. But you wouldn't let me. When a man can't console his wife, it isn't a marriage. That was why I left."

"I didn't realize how much I needed you to take me in your arms," she murmured. "Console me now, Finn. Console your wife."

He opened his arms and she flew into them.

He held her tight and she sobbed into his chest, tears of sorrow for the baby and tears of joy for her husband. "All right," he whispered, pressing a kiss to the crown of her head. "I'll come home. I've missed you so much, Terry. If you really want me, I'll come home."

"I want you," she vowed through her tears. "More than anything else, I want you."

"You've got me," he vowed, then tilted her face up for a kiss.

EPILOGUE

TERRY WAS SPRAWLED OUT on her red leather sofa, several sections of the *Boston Sunday Globe* piled on her abdomen while she held one section—the comics—above her head to read. She heard the phone ring, but to answer it would mean moving the newspaper off her belly and then actually having to sit up, stand and walk all the way to the kitchen to answer it. And since Finn was already in the kitchen, refilling his Celtics mug and her Museum of Fine Arts mug with the gourmet coffee she'd gotten him hooked on, she let him answer the phone.

"Uh-huh," he said. She smiled simply because the sound of his voice coming from her kitchen made her happy. "Yeah, sure. Of course. Are you serious? Sure, no problem."

She heard the click as he hung up, and then he appeared in the doorway, empty-handed. "Where's my coffee?" she asked, deciding she'd much rather look at him than Dilbert.

''That was Janet Chou,'' he told her.

Terry ignored the twinge she felt at the mention of the caseworker's name. Janet had departed from their lives a month ago, when Baby Jane Doe's mother came back to town. Terry had struggled hard to overcome her sadness. She'd labored to persuade herself that becoming that little girl's mother hadn't been her destiny, that a truth she'd believed in her heart and her soul had proven untrue after all. She wasn't there yet, but she was trying. Thank heavens she had Finn with her, helping her to recover.

He was waiting for her to respond to his announcement, so she said, ''It's Sunday. Why would she call on her day off?''

''Dawn's mother vanished.''

''What?'' At that, Terry flung herself off the couch, scattering sections of the newspaper everywhere. ''She vanished? Where's the baby? *How's* the baby? Oh, my God! Is Dawn all right?''

''She will be, once we adopt her. If you still want to, that is.''

Terry's first impulse was to scream that of course she still wanted to. But the decision wasn't only hers to make. She and Finn were equal partners in this marriage. It was his decision as much as hers.

"What do you think?" she asked cautiously. "Should we adopt her?"

"Well, I already told Janet yes. I hope that's okay." He smiled tentatively.

Terry's heart felt ready to break free of her rib cage, it was beating so hard, swelling with so much love for Finn. She raced across the room and threw herself into his arms. "I love you," she murmured between greedy kisses.

"I love you, too."

"You are going to be the best dad in the whole world."

He laughed. "I'm not so sure of that."

"I am," she said, grinning and then kissing him again. "And when I'm sure of something, you'd better not mess with me."

"So I've learned," he said with a grin. He returned her kiss, a loving, passionate kiss, the kind of kiss only a husband and a wife caught up in the deepest, most encompassing joy could share.

Looking For More Romance?

Visit Romance.net

Check in daily for these and other exciting features:

Hot off the press

View all current titles, and purchase them on-line.

What do the stars have in store for you?

Horoscope

Hot deals

Exclusive offers available only at Romance.net

Plus, don't miss our interactive quizzes, contests and bonus gifts.

PWEB

Come escape with Harlequin's new

Series Sampler

**Four great full-length Harlequin novels
bound together in one fabulous volume
and at an unbelievable price.**

Be transported back
in time with a
Harlequin Historical®
novel, get caught up
in a mystery with Intrigue®,
be tempted by a hot, sizzling romance
with Harlequin Temptation®,
or just enjoy a down-home
all-American read with
American Romance®.

You won't be able to put this collection down!

On sale February 2000 at your favorite retail outlet.

HARLEQUIN®
Makes any time special ™

Visit us at www.romance.net

PHESC

HEART OF THE WEST

Every Man Has His Price!

Lost Springs Ranch was
famous for turning young
mavericks into good men.
So word that the ranch was
in financial trouble sent
a herd of loyal bachelors
stampeding back to
Wyoming to put themselves
on the auction block!

July 1999	*Husband for Hire* Susan Wiggs	January 2000	*The Rancher and* *the Rich Girl* Heather MacAllister
August	*Courting Callie* Lynn Erickson	February	*Shane's Last Stand* Ruth Jean Dale
September	*Bachelor Father* Vicki Lewis Thompson	March	*A Baby by Chance* Cathy Gillen Thacker
October	*His Bodyguard* Muriel Jensen	April	*The Perfect Solution* Day Leclaire
November	*It Takes a Cowboy* Gina Wilkins	May	*Rent-a-Dad* Judy Christenberry
December	*Hitched by Christmas* Jule McBride	June	*Best Man in Wyoming* Margot Dalton

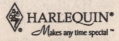

HARLEQUIN®
Makes any time special ™

Visit us at www.romance.net

PHHOWGEN